Lodovico Ariosto

Tales from Ariosto

Retold for children by a lady

Lodovico Ariosto

Tales from Ariosto
Retold for children by a lady

ISBN/EAN: 9783337088477

Printed in Europe, USA, Canada, Australia, Japan

Cover: Foto ©Andreas Hilbeck / pixelio.de

More available books at **www.hansebooks.com**

RETOLD FOR CHILDREN

By A LADY

'Of turneys and of trophies hung,
 Of forests and enchantments drear,
 Where more is meant than meets the ear'
                                    MILTON

𝔚𝔦𝔱𝔥 𝔗𝔥𝔯𝔢𝔢 𝔈𝔩𝔩𝔲𝔰𝔱𝔯𝔞𝔱𝔦𝔬𝔫𝔰

BOSTON
ROBERTS BROTHERS
1880

𝔘niversity 𝔓ress:

JOHN WILSON AND SON, CAMBRIDGE.

PREFACE.

THESE STORIES have afforded so much pleasure to
the little friends for whom they were written, that
they are published in the hope that they may be
found entertaining by other children. Whilst I
have, of course, left out all that was unsuited to
my purpose, and mercilessly curtailed what I have
translated, I have endeavored to alter no material
incident and to keep as close to the original as I
well could. And this must be my apology for re-
taining many of the allusions to heathen mythol-
ogy, and many of the fanciful similes, which are so
characteristic of the poet. It has been a question
with me whether I should discard these altogether;
but I hope an intelligent child may find some
amusement in puzzling out their meaning; and at
the same time, that they are neither so numerous
nor so lengthy as not to be easily skipped by
children too young to understand them.

My young readers ought to be told that the
poem of the 'Mad Orlando' is a continuation by
Ariosto of a poem by Boiardo, an earlier poet,
called 'Orlando in Love.' This helps to account

for the abruptness with which the characters appear on the scene, and for the allusions to adventures in which they have taken part in an earlier period of their history. I have been obliged to retain some few of these, which abound in Ariosto — such as the allusions to an earlier visit of Angelica to Europe with her brother Argalia, who was slain by Ferrau, and whose helmet was carried off by that knight; to the magic ring stolen from Angelica in Albracca by Brunello, who also on that occasion committed the thefts mentioned in the story of 'Ruggiero and Bradamante'; and others which refer to a time when Angelica loved Rinaldo and he disliked her, a state of things completely changed before the first story opens. This little explanation may, I hope, make all such allusions tolerably intelligible.

It only remains for me to thank most gratefully the kind friend who has so skilfully adapted the illustrations, from an old quarto edition of Ariosto, published in Venice, in the year 1583, and adorned with very quaint and spirited engravings by Giro-lamo Porro, an engraver of repute in his day.

CONTENTS.

THE STORY OF THE PRINCESS ANGELICA.

THE STORY OF GINEVRA.

THE STORY OF RUGGIERO AND BRADAMANTE.

ILLUSTRATIONS.

INTRODUCTION.

C/Count Orlando/, while in India paying his court
to the beautiful Princess Angelica, daughter of the
great Khan of Cathay, with whom he has long
been madly in love, hears of the invasion of France
by the Moors, under their King Agramante, and
hastens back to offer Charlemagne, Emperor of the
Franks, the help of his sword. Angelica, who on
her father's death has succeeded to his throne,
partly because she finds it an insecure possession
from the attacks of enemies within and without
her dominions, and partly to escape from the im-
portunities of her numerous suitors, all of whom
she has at various times made use of, in fighting
in defence of herself and her kingdom, resolves to
accept Orlando's escort and to accompany him to
Europe.

The poem opens with their arrival in the Christian
camp, on the eve of a great battle, in which Charlemagne is defeated and driven back into Paris, where
he is closely besieged by the Moors. Rinaldo, one
of his knights, goes to Britain, and, returning with
large reinforcements, raises the siege and enables
the Emperor to march out of Paris, and to inflict
a signal defeat upon Agramante, who, in his turn,
is surrounded and shut up within his entrenchments. Rinaldo greatly distinguishes himself in

this battle; and it is after this that the incident
of Medoro's midnight search for his master's dead
body, which is mentioned in the story of Angelica,
takes place.

Agramante, however, succeeds in breaking
through the Christian lines, and defeating Charlemagne, who is again forced to take refuge within
the walls of Paris; where Rinaldo comes once
more to his rescue. Another great battle takes
place, in which the Moors are defeated and driven
back with great slaughter to the south of France.
Orlando is absent all this time, wandering over the
world in search of Angelica, of whom he loses
sight after the first battle. The news he at last
hears of her so much distresses him that he goes
stark mad, throws away his armor, and abandons
his famous horse and as famous sword, which are
found and appropriated by Mandricardo. The
Count eventually turns up in Africa, where his wits
are restored to him in a very curious manner; soon
after which he pays the visit to the hermit mentioned in Ruggiero's story. Brandimarte, his great
friend, hears of his madness, goes in search of him,
and joins him in Africa, and his adventures are so
interesting and his story is so pathetic, that I much
regret not being able to include it in this volume.

In the absence of Orlando and Brandimarte,
Rinaldo occupies the principal place among the
Christian knights, his brothers and cousins, the
Scotch Prince Zerbino, Guidone, and Sansonetto all
being subordinate to him.

Agramante, in addition to his allies, King Sobrino,
and Marsilio, King of Spain, is supported by a
number of tributary princes; Rodomonte, King of
Algiers, Mandricardo, King of Tartary, Sacripante,

King of Circassia, Gradasso and Ferrau ; the three last are ardent lovers of Angelica, whom they follow in such hot haste from India that they arrive in France as soon as herself.

Ruggiero is also on the side of the Moors ; for though born of Christian parents, he was adopted and brought up from infancy by a Saracen magician, Atlante ; who introduces him to Agramante, with whom he becomes a great favorite, and whose affection he so gratefully returns, that he is found fighting under his banner until very nearly the end of the poem.

It may be as well to bear in mind that there appear in these stories four famous horses : Brigliadoro, belonging to Orlando ; Baiardo, to Rinaldo ; Frontino, to Ruggiero ; and Rabican, to Astolfo. And, also, four famous weapons : Orlando's sword Durindana, Rinaldo's sword Fusberta, Ruggiero's sword Balisarda, and Astolfo's golden lance.

These few words of introduction may, I hope, clear up some obscurities, which might otherwise be found perplexing, in the course of the narratives.

THE STORY

OF

THE PRINCESS ANGELICA.

CHAPTER I.

> Of Forests and Enchantments drear,
> Where more is meant than meets the ear.
> MILTON.

THE story I am going to tell you took place in the days of the great Emperor Charlemagne, when the Moors, under their young king Agramante, crossed the sea from Africa, in order to invade France and to revenge the slaughter of Trojano, their king's father.

The famous Paladin Orlando had long been enamoured of the beautiful Princess Angelica, and had, for her sake, encountered great perils and adventures in the distant countries of India, Media, and Tartary. He had just returned with her to Europe, in time to join the mighty army which Charlemagne had collected at the foot of the Pyrenees, and to take part in the battle, in which the Emperor hoped to punish Agramante and his ally Marsilio, king of Spain, for their audacity in bringing over the Moors and Spaniards to devastate the fair realm of France.

Here, however, Orlando met with a most unexpected misfortune. The beautiful lady whom he had in safety escorted through so many and various dangers, in the long journey from the far-distant isles of the Hesperides, was now taken from him, not by an enemy's sword, but by the decree of the Emperor, who, being displeased at a quarrel which had broken out between Orlando and his cousin Rinaldo, on account of their rival pretensions to the favor of this fair princess, had appointed the Duke of Bavaria her guardian, with the promise, that whichever knight should most distinguish himself in the approaching battle should obtain her hand as the reward of his valor. The expected victory, however, turned out a disastrous defeat. The Christians fled before the Moors, the Duke of Bavaria was taken prisoner, and his camp fell into the hands of the enemy.

Angelica foresaw early in the day that the fortune of war would turn against the Christians; so, mounting her horse, she left the field and entered a great forest, where she soon afterwards met a knight in complete armor, his sword by his side, and his buckler on his arm, coming in great haste towards her, along a very narrow path. No timid girl could have started from a venomous snake with greater horror than Angelica at the sight of Count Rinaldo, the lord of Montalbano, who, having by some strange mischance lost his famous horse Baiardo, was now in search of him. He also, lifting his eyes to her fair face, at once recognized the beautiful countenance which held him captive in the chains of love.

When Angelica saw him, she trembled and became deadly pale, and hastily turning her horse's head, she plunged into the very thickest of the forest, paying little attention in her headlong flight as to which of the many intricate and winding paths she took, until she reached the banks of a river, where stood the Saracen knight Ferrau. He had come here after the battle was over, wearied with fighting, and parched with thirst; and while bending over the brink of the stream to drink, his helmet had fallen into the water, and he was now occupied in trying to recover it. Startled by the damsel's loud cries for help, he rushed up the bank, and in spite of her agitation, and of the time which had gone by since he had last seen her, he knew her directly. He, no less than the two cousins, was filled with admiration for her wondrous beauty; he therefore courteously offered her his aid and, all unhelmeted as he was, drew his sword and hastened to attack Rinaldo, who had followed her, and whom he knew well by sight, having often fought with him before. Then began a fierce combat between these two well-matched warriors Thick and fast fell the mighty blows, but as swiftly and as skilfully were they parried, until Rinaldo, seeing that the princess had disappeared, said to the Pagan:

'If it is for the sake of the shining orbs of that new-risen planet you detain me here, will it much serve you to take me dead or alive, since, while we thus delay, the lady has escaped? Were it not better to go in search of her, and when we have captured her, then to allow the fortune of war to decide whose the fair prize shall be?'

This proposal pleased the Saracen so well that, forgetting their recent dispute, he invited Rinaldo to mount up behind him, and they galloped off in pursuit of Angelica. So loyal and gentle were the manners of those old times, that in the hearts of these rivals in love and enemies in religion there lurked not the slightest suspicion of each other's good faith.

They came at length to where two ways met, and as the prints of horses' hoofs were equally fresh upon both, it was decided that Rinaldo should take one road and Ferrau the other. That which the Saracen took, wound in and out of the wood until it brought him back to the place whence he had started, so, finding he had lost all traces of the beautiful lady, he set about trying to recover his helmet, which was deeply imbedded in the sand at the bottom of the river. While he was endeavoring to loosen it with a long pole, there suddenly rose from the midst of the waters the form of a knight of fierce aspect; his head was bare, but otherwise he was fully armed, and he held in his hand the very helmet which Ferrau was seeking to regain.

'Ah, faithless knave!' he wrathfully exclaimed: 'Have you forgotten Argalia, Angelica's brother, and that when you slew me, you promised to throw this helmet, with the rest of my armor, after me into the river? Lament not that the fates have restored it to me, but rather lament your own perfidy; and if you wish to replace it with one as precious, take the helmet of Almonte from Orlando, or that of Mambrino from Rinaldo, and leave me in peace with mine.'

When the Saracen saw the shade of Argalia appear, so unexpectedly, in the middle of the river, he grew pale with horror, and his hair stood on end. At the reproach of broken faith his heart sank with shame and remorse; and he solemnly vowed that henceforth no helmet should cover his head but that which Orlando had once taken in Aspromonte from the fierce Almonte — an oath which he kept better than his promise to Argalia.

Then, sorrowful and ill at ease, he set out in search of Orlando.

In the mean time Angelica rode fast and recklessly through the dark forest, fancying in the rustling of every oak or beech-leaf she heard the footsteps, in every shadow she saw the form, of Rinaldo. As some poor timid fawn which has seen its dam rent in pieces by the savage leopard, flies from copse to copse for shelter, and, brushing through the thick branches, imagines itself to be caught in the very jaws of the ravenous beast; so rode the lady all that day and night, little heeding whither her path led her, until, on the afternoon of the next day, she found herself in a beautiful little valley surrounded by lofty trees, whose leaves were softly fanned by the fresh air, and where two bright streams kept the rich grass ever green, and, gently breaking over pebbles and low rocks, maintained a constant harmony of sweet sounds. Here, thinking herself safe, and many miles away from Rinaldo, tired with her long ride, and exhausted by the heat, she determined to take some rest. She accordingly got off her palfrey, and unfastening its bridle, suffered it to feed at large on the abundant pasture which the banks of these clear rivers afforded. Close by she saw a thicket of flowering thorns and crimson roses, overhanging the water, in which they were reflected, and defended from the rays of the sun by high and spreading oak-trees. In a green glade of softest grass in the midst of this bower of roses, which was so thickly twined that neither the sun nor mortal eye could penetrate it, Angelica lay down and soon fell fast asleep.

It was not long, however, before the sound of

horses' hoofs awoke her, whereupon, rising quietly, she looked through the bushes, and saw a knight in armor, who had dismounted from his horse and was now lying beside the stream, resting his cheek on his hand, and so absorbed in thought, and so still that he might have been taken for a statue. She was uncertain whether this would prove to be a friend or an enemy, and her heart beating with alternate hope and fear, she awaited the end of the adventure, scarcely daring to breathe for fear her retreat should be discovered. For a long time the melancholy knight remained in the same posture; at last he began in plaintive tones to lament his hard fate as follows:

'Ah! why do I waste my affection on one who scarce bestows a thought on me; one who grudges me even a look or a smile, while upon others she lavishes tokens of her favor? Ah! unkind Fate, why must I languish in despair, while others rejoice in triumph? Yet when I try to banish the remembrance of this cruel beauty from my heart, I feel I would rather die than cease to love her!'

Sighs interrupted his complaint, and rivers of tears ran down his cheeks, a sight to have melted the hardest heart. He paused for a little, and then sang this sorrowful ditty:

> Ah! Lovely Rose, so proud and fair,
> 　Blooming upon thy thorny stem,
> So fresh and gay in morning air,
> 　Sparkling with many a dewdrop gem,
>
> Thou'rt formed some Beauty's brow to grace,
> 　Entwin'd amid her clustering hair,
> Or finding still a sweeter place
> 　To blush upon her bosom fair.

Alas ! when pluck'd how soon to fade,
  To wither and be cast aside,
Like some forlorn, forsaken maid,
  Who once was bright in virgin pride !

If any ask who thus wept by that river's bank,
you must know it was Sacripante, king of Circassia, and the cause of all his grief was love for
the beautiful lady who was now listening to him.
In India he had heard, to his great dismay, that
she had accompanied Orlando to Europe, and for
her sake he had now come from the far East to the
lands of the setting sun. When he arrived in
France he learned that the Emperor had taken her
from Orlando, and had promised her hand as a
prize to the knight who should best serve the cause
of the Golden Lilies in the great battle against the
Moors. Having joined the camp of Agramante,
he had witnessed the defeat of Charlemagne, and
was again pursuing his quest of Angelica. The
princess, who had soon recognized her old lover,
listened attentively to his lament, but with no intention of taking pity upon him ; for, colder and
harder than any stone, she treated all her ad-
mirers with equal disdain, and believed no one to
be worthy of her. Now, however, finding herself
alone and friendless in these wild woods, she determined to take him for her guide, knowing that
'He who is up to the chin in water had better cry
"Mercy !"' and that should she let this opportunity
slip, she might not again find so trustworthy a
champion ; for the king had long ago proved himself the most faithful of all her friends. She advanced from her concealment within the shady
thicket, a sudden and beautiful apparition, as Diana
or Venus of old might have appeared from some
dark grove, or gloomy cavern.

With what wonder and delight did Sacripante behold the angelic countenance, the fair and graceful form, standing so unexpectedly before him! He ran towards her with open arms, and the sight of him recalling to her mind her native country, and her father's palace, with some sudden vague hope of perhaps soon again seeing that beloved home, she embraced him with greater tenderness than she had ever shown to Orlando. She then related to him, at length, all that had happened to her since she had last seen him, and told him how often Orlando had saved her from death and defended her in danger. While thus conversing together, they were startled by a loud noise, which seemed to come from the neighboring wood, and the king, whose habit it was to go about fully armed, put on his helmet, and replacing the bridle, mounted his horse and held his lance in rest. Scarcely had he done so, when there rode towards them, out of the wood, a knight of proud and valiant bearing. He was habited entirely in white, and a snowy plume formed the crest of his helmet. Sacripante, angry at this unwelcome interruption to his pleasant discourse with Angelica, gave him furious and disdainful glances, and, when he came near enough, defied him to single combat, boasting that he would with ease hurl him from the saddle. But the stranger knight, who thought no whit less highly of himself, cut short these arrogant menaces by spurring on his charger and raising his lance. Sacripante attacked with like fury, and the two riding full tilt at each other, their shields were pierced through at the same moment. It was well for both that their stout breastplates stood them in good stead and resisted

the blow. So do two lions or two bulls hurl themselves at each other, making the very hills resound
with the thunder of their onslaught. The horses
met with such force that the one belonging to the
Pagan fell dead with his full weight upon his
prostrate rider. The other fell also, but at the
touch of the spur rose up again, and the stranger
knight, after gazing for a few moments upon his
vanquished foe, not caring apparently to renew
the contest, rode off at full gallop through the
forest, and was miles away before the Saracen had
disengaged himself from his dangerous position.

As the stunned and stupefied herdsman, when
the thunderbolt, which struck him down by his
slain oxen, has passed, rises and gazes in astonishment at the pine-tree, whose lofty summit he had so
often admired, now shorn of its great branches and
all its leaves, thus did the Pagan slowly and with
difficulty rise to his feet, and see Angelica standing
near him and looking down upon his discomfiture.
Silent and crestfallen, he stood before his fair
mistress, his cheeks crimsoning with mortification,
and groaning as much for shame as for the pain of
his bruised and shaken limbs, for not only had
Angelica seen his fall, but, with her own soft hands,
she had helped to free him from the weight of his
dying horse.

'Ah! my lord,' said she, 'let not your fall distress
you. It was caused, indeed, not by your fault, but
by that of your poor horse, who stood in need of
food and of repose, rather than of fresh combats.
Nor has yon knight much more cause to boast, if, as
I have always understood, he, who first abandons the
field, acknowledges himself vanquished.'

While the lady was thus consoling the Saracen,

there came galloping by, with horn and pouch slung at his side, a courier, who asked if they had seen the knight of the white shield and snowy plume pass by that way.

Sacripante replied: 'It is he, who, as you may perceive, has worsted me in battle, and even now ridden away. And that I may know who is my conqueror, I pray you tell me his name.'

'In that will I soon satisfy you,' said the courier. 'Bradamante is the famous name of the gentle damsel, who, valiant as she is beautiful, has dismounted you, and deprived you of your well-earned honors.'

So saying, he hurried on, leaving the poor Saracen more than ever burning with shame and vexation. For a while he stood thinking over his late misfortune, then silent and abashed, he mounted Angelica's horse, and signed to her to get up behind him, far too sad at heart to continue his former conversation with her. They had gone scarcely two miles, when the woods, through which they were riding, resounded with a strange and fearful noise, and there rushed out a mighty war-horse, magnificently caparisoned with rich gold-embroidered trappings. As he approached, vaulting over the streams and trampling down the bushes and shrubs that impeded his course, the Princess said, 'If the thick underwood and the deepening twilight do not deceive me, that charger, plunging through the forest with such uproar, is Baiardo. It is indeed Baiardo — I know him well, and he is come at the right moment to do us good service, for our horse will soon weary under his double burden.' The Circassian dismounted, but vain were all his attempts to catch hold of the charger's rein. Whenever he approached him, Baiardo turned round and round, quicker than lightning, and flung out his heels. Presently, however, he went up of his own accord to the princess, with the gentle fawning of a favorite spaniel, who joyfully greets his master on his return home. Baiardo, indeed, remembered her well, for she had often petted him in old days in Albracca, when she had much loved his master, the then obdurate and ungrateful Rinaldo. She caught hold of his bridle with her left hand, while with the other she stroked his glossy neck, and the horse under her familiar touch became as gentle as a lamb. Sacripante jumped quickly on his back and gathered up the reins, while Angelica seated herself again in her own saddle. She had scarcely done so when, lifting her eyes, she saw a tall knight fully armed coming towards her, and with terror and abhorrence she recognized Rinaldo, the Duke Amone's son. He now loved her more than life itself, but she hated and fled from him as the crane flies from the falcon. Once upon a time she had cared for him as much as he then disliked her, but a wonderful change had been wrought in their feelings towards each other by the waters of two fountains in the Ardennes, not far apart but very different in their effects, one causing the heart to overflow with love, the other turning all former love to bitter hatred. Rinaldo tasted of the first and was filled with admiration and affection for Angelica, while she drank of the waters of the other, and at once all her love for him changed to abhorrence.

Thus it happened that, when she saw him, she changed color, the light faded from her eyes, and with trembling lips and faltering accents, she begged Sacripante not to await his approach, but to escape with her as quickly as possible. 'Am I then,' said the Saracen, 'fallen so low in your estimation, that you think I am no longer able to defend you? In old days, in Albracca, you had more confidence in me; do you forget how often I there fought successfully in your behalf?'

The princess made no answer, and scarcely heard what he said, for Rinaldo had come near enough to recognize his war-horse, and also the angelic face whose beauty he so much admired, and now began to shout forth threats and imprecations against the Saracen.

CHAPTER II.

> Of most disastrous chances,
> Of moving accidents by flood and field,
> Of hair-breadth 'scapes.
> SHAKESPEARE.

AH! Perfidious Love. Why does it delight
thee to sow discord between loving hearts?
Why make Angelica so beautiful in the eyes of
Rinaldo, while he was so hateful in hers? Time
was when she thought him nobleness itself, but he
then despised her as she now despises him.

'Scoundrel, dismount!' Rinaldo haughtily called
out, 'give up my horse, as well as this fair princess. To allow so noble a charger, so perfect a
lady, to remain in the possession of so poor a
knave, were a disgrace to my chivalry.'

'Thou liest,' returned the Saracen no less
haughtily, 'no knave am I. He who should call
thee so, might, as I have heard, do it with some
justice. However, it shall soon be seen who best
deserves both horse and lady, for there I agree
with you, that so fair a princess is not to be found
all the world over.'

Without further parley the King of Circassia
and the Knight of Aspromonte drew their swords,
and advanced to the assault with shouts of fury

and defiance. It was of no advantage to the former that he was mounted, for Baiardo refused to attack his master, and neither with spur nor blow could he be induced to move a step. When urged to advance, he stood stock-still, when to stand firm, he trotted and cantered forward, or putting down his head between his fore-feet, plunged and kicked, until the Saracen, finding it was but lost time to try and master the restive animal, placed his hand on the saddlebow, and with a light bound jumped to the ground. Then indeed there began on foot a worthy trial of arms between this valiant pair. The blows of Vulcan in his dusky cave, when he forged the thunder-bolts of Jove, fell neither so fast nor so hard as those of these masters in the noble art. Now they bend low, then rise to their full height, now cover themselves with their shields, then uncover for a little space, now advance, then retreat, now redouble their strokes, and swing their swords swiftly round their heads. Where one yields, if but an inch, the other instantly places his foot. At last Rinaldo lifted high his good sword, Fusberta, and hurled it down with all his force on Sacripante, whose great shield it cut straight through. The forest groaned with the shock, and the fine ivory and well-tempered steel flew asunder like brittle ice.

When the princess saw the consequences of this tremendous stroke, her face grew white with fear, and not daring to linger, lest she should fall into the hands of the detested Rinaldo, she turned her horse's bridle and urged him up a steep and narrow path through the dense forest, often looking back to see whether he were following her. After riding for some time she entered a valley, where she met a venerable-looking hermit, riding upon an ass. His white beard fell low on his breast, and his gentle face, wasted with age and fasting, seemed to look with pity on the terrified and agitated lady. She asked him to show her the shortest road to some seaport, for her great wish was to leave France and to get away from the sound of Rinaldo's hated name. The pretended friar — for he was in reality an old necromancer — comforted her, and told her he would soon put her in the way of safety. He rode beside her for some time, finding great pleasure in her society, but she at length grew tired of his slow pace, and bidding him farewell, she rode on and left him.

After travelling for some days alone, she reached the coast of Gascony ; but she little knew that the wicked old necromancer, angry at her desertion, and determined to punish her for it, had summoned one of his malicious imps, and had ordered him to follow her, and to incite her horse to work her some mischief. So it happened that in spite of all her efforts to prevent him, the animal walked straight into the sea ; and it was of no use that she lifted up her dress and even her feet upon the saddle, so as not to get them wet through, for he soon got out of his depth and began to swim. Her golden hair floated loose upon her shoulders, and as if entranced at the sight of such great beauty, the winds and the waves lay perfectly still and calm before her. In vain she turned her weeping eyes towards the land ; farther and farther it receded from her, and fainter and fainter grew its outline.

At last, after swimming a long distance, the horse turned to the right, and landed just as night began, on a solitary part of the shore, surrounded by high rocks and gloomy caverns. When she found herself alone in this deserted place, the aspect of which caused her mortal terror, and saw Phœbus about to sink below the ocean and to leave the world to darkness; with dishevelled hair and clasped hands she stood for some moments so motionless that it might have been doubted whether she were a living and breathing woman, or some sculptured marble; then, raising her wearied eyes to heaven, she burst into tears and exclaimed:

'Ah! cruel Fortune, when wilt thou cease to persecute and torment me? It were far kinder to have allowed me to perish beneath these waves, than to have rescued me only to expose me to greater misery. Banished from my royal home, driven over the wide world a helpless and hopeless wanderer, I have nothing left me but my youth and this far-famed beauty, which, whether deserving of its renown or not, has been the cause of all my misfortunes. For its sake did my brother Argalia, in spite of his magic weapons, lose his life; for its sake also was my father, Galafrone, the great Khan of Cathay, slain in India by Agricane, the King of Tartary. Deprived of my dominions, my friends, and my home, for what greater evil dost thou preserve me? If the sea were too easy a grave, send, I beseech thee, some savage beast to devour me and so end my sufferings.'

Thus did Angelica pour forth her sorrows, until, worn out with weeping and fatigue, she sank down on the sands, and fell into a deep sleep.

And now I must leave Angelica for a while, and tell you about an island in the Northern Seas, to

the west of Ireland, called Ebuda ; which was but
very thinly inhabited, since Proteus had sent Orca
and all his sea-monsters to devastate it. There is
an old tradition — whether it be true or false I
cannot say — that once upon a time a powerful
king ruled there, who had an only daughter of
such rare beauty, that the sea-god Proteus seeing
her one day walking by the sea-shore, fell in love
with her, and persuaded her to marry him. After
a time the king, her father, found this out, and
was so furiously angry that he ordered her head to
be cut off on the spot. Proteus, when he heard of
the sad fate of his beautiful bride, determined to
avenge her, and therefore sent a large army of sea-
lions and bears, and the marine monsters which
Neptune had put under his rule, to destroy, not
only the flocks and herds in the island, but the
towns and villages with their inhabitants. After
they had done this, they surrounded and set siege
to the capital, in which all that were left of the
people had taken refuge. Within these walls the
natives defended themselves for many days and
nights with great courage, until, worn out with
privation and fatigue, they determined to go to the
temple and consult the oracle as to what they
should do in this dire necessity. The answer was,
that they must find out a maiden equal in beauty
to the princess they had beheaded, and expose her
on the sea-shore, as an offering to the angry sea-
deity in exchange for the wife he had lost. If she
should seem to Proteus sufficiently beautiful, he
would cease to molest them or their country, but
if not, they must go on offering him one victim
after another until he were satisfied.

Thus began the cruel custom by which so many

lovely damsels were sacrificed to Proteus; for as day by day he rejected them, a huge Orca or sea-monster, who remained behind in the harbor after the rest of the hideous tribe had departed, swallowed them up alive. Whether all this old story about Proteus be fable or not, I cannot tell, but certain it is that in this island the horrible custom existed of daily feeding this sea-monster with a young and beautiful maiden. Women in all countries are subject to hardship and trial, but here indeed was their lot deserving of pity. The unhappy maidens whom adverse winds or their unlucky star brought near the island, were captured and kept for these sacrifices, and this means not sufficing, expeditions were fitted out to seek for these poor victims in distant countries. Many fair damsels were thus captured enticed with deceitful promises, or bought with gold, and conveyed in barks and galleys to fill the dungeons of their castles and fortresses.

It came to pass that one of their galleys, happening to sail by the place where Angelica lay asleep, the sailors landed to take in wood and fresh water, and there discovered this pearl of perfect beauty. Alas! too precious, too exquisite a prey for so barbarous a people. Ah! cruel fate, can it be that you will deliver to that savage monster the rare beauty for whose sake Sacripante sacrificed his glory and his great kingdom, for whom the mighty Orlando tarnished his fame and wasted his noble gifts? Can it be that she, whose beauty turned the heads of half the East, is now so abandoned by all that there is not one to speak a single word in her behalf?

The sailors bound the beautiful princess while

she was still asleep, and carried her off to their ship, to join the wretched band of captives already there. As soon as they reached the island they placed her in the keep of the citadel, to await the fatal day when the lot should fall upon her. Perhaps her angelic face touched the hearts of these savages, for they kept her there many days. At last, however, her turn came, and followed by a pitying and weeping crowd, she was led forth to the monster. Who can describe her despair? Her cries and tears might have reached the ears of Heaven itself. Why did not the earth open and conceal her in its depths, and so save her from the terrible death which awaited her? The fierce tiger of the East, the ravening lion of the desert, might have wept with pity at the sight of this fair princess bound to the cold and naked rock.

What then would have been the feelings of Orlando, or of the two knights we left fighting for her in the forest, had they known her sorrowful plight! How willingly would they have dared a thousand deaths to rescue their beloved lady from such infinite peril!

CHAPTER III.

That snaky-headed Gorgon shield
That wise Minerva wore, unconquer'd virgin,
Wherewith she freezed her foes to congeal'd stone.
MILTON.

BY good chance it happened that the famous
knight Ruggiero, riding on his wonderful
winged horse Hippogriff, was passing through the
air on his way from Ireland to Brittany; and
when he came above the Island of Tears (for so
was the country inhabited by this barbarous and
inhuman people called) he chanced to look down,
and saw Angelica chained to the bare rock, waiting to be devoured by the Orca. Ruggiero at first
thought some beautiful statue, hewn in marble or
purest alabaster, had been placed on the shore, till
the tears which rained down her cheeks, and the
golden tresses of her hair which the breeze gently
lifted, undeceived him. As he looked into her
lovely eyes he was reminded of his own fair Bradamante, and was so overcome with pity that he
could scarcely refrain from weeping. Checking
his steed in his rapid flight, he thus addressed
her:

'O Lady! worthy of that chain alone with
which Love leads captive his servants, and most

undeserving of this or any other evil fate! who has been so barbarous as to bind and wound the pure ivory of those fair hands?'

Tears were at first the lady's only answer; and when she tried, in a voice broken with sobs, to speak, a fearful noise in the direction of the sea caused her to stop short. The huge monster, appearing half below and half above the waves, like some great vessel driven by favoring winds towards the wished-for port, was seen approaching and preparing to devour the fair morsel set forth for him. But a short space divided him from poor Angelica, and she had given up all hope of deliverance, when Ruggiero raised his lance and struck the huge shapeless mass between the eyes; for the creature could not be said to have any form, with the exception of his head, which, with prominent eyes and protruding tusks, somewhat resembled that of a hog. The blow fell as if on iron or steel, and as the Orca, leaving his sure prey on shore, furiously pursued the great moving shadow on the water, cast by the outspread wings of the Hippogriff, Ruggiero continued to aim blow after blow with sword and spear, but all in vain, for they only resounded back from the rough hard scales as if from jasper. So an eagle swoops down on a serpent gliding through the grass, or basking on the bare rock, its smooth and gilded skin glittering in the sun. And so also in hot July with its golden harvests, in dusty August, or in vintage-laden September, an impudent fly buzzes round and annoys some great mastiff, who with empty teeth snaps at it again and again, but all to no purpose.

The monster in his fury lashed the ocean with

his tail, till the very heavens were darkened with clouds of water, and the horse's wings were so drenched that Ruggiero scarcely knew whether he were flying or swimming, and longed for the help of a boat for fear they should become so heavy as to be useless. Casting over in his mind to what means he should have recourse, he all at once bethought him of his enchanted shield, and straightway flew to the rock and placed the magic ring on the little finger of the princess's right hand, partly that it might not hinder the effect of the shield upon the Orca, partly that it might defend her own eyes from its baneful influence, for its wondrous property was to render all enchantments vain. How Ruggiero became possessed of the famous winged horse, the enchanted shield, and the magic ring, I shall hope to tell you in the story of 'Ruggiero and Bradamante.'

When the monster, covering half the sea with its huge bulk, again approached the shore, Ruggiero stood ready, and raising the shield, he suddenly uncovered it, and it seemed as if a second sun had blazed forth in the heavens. The magic rays struck the eyes of the great beast, and dazzled and blinded by their exceeding brightness, he sank down in the foaming waves, even as a stone drops into the depths of some troubled mountain stream. Before Ruggiero could reach him with his lance he had disappeared, and the princess begged him to waste no more strength nor time on the scaly beast.

'For God's sake, my lord,' she cried, 'hasten to undo these chains before the Orca recovers from his trance. Carry me away, and rather drown me in the ocean than allow me to remain here a prey to this hideous monster.'

Ruggiero, moved by her distress, unbound the lady, and placing her behind him, took her away from that fatal shore on his flying steed, which after lightly pawing the ground with his feet, spread his wings and sped swiftly through the air to the nearest point on the coast of Brittany. There Ruggiero and the princess alighted on a green meadow, watered by a fountain in its midst, which lying between two high mountains and bordered by a grove of speading oak-trees, the haunt of innumerable nightingales, offered them a cool and pleasant retreat from the heat of the midday sun. Ruggiero could not help gazing with wonder and curiosity at the face whose exceeding beauty had filled the whole world with its fame, and when Angelica cast down her eyes from his admiring glance, she caught sight of her own precious ring — the magic ring which Brunello had stolen from her in Albracca, and which she had brought with her on her first journey into France with her brother Argalia, when he carried thither the golden lance, which afterwards fell to the lot of Astolfo the Paladin. Many dangers had she escaped with the help of this ring; and from the day she lost it, Fortune had never ceased to be unfriendly to her until it had driven her into banishment, an exile from her own kingdom. When she beheld it on her own finger again, she was so overcome with astonishment and delight that she could scarcely believe her senses. She took it off very gently, cautiously conveyed it to her mouth, and like a flash of lightning, or rather as the sun when hidden by a cloud, she disappeared from before the eyes of Ruggiero. He looked around him in utter astonishment, and stared as one in a trance, until he suddenly remembered the ring, when his surprise changed to anger — first, at his own carelessness in leaving it with Angelica, and then at her ingratitude and at the discourtesy with which she had repaid his kindness.

'Ungrateful lady!' he exclaimed, 'is this my reward? Will you rather carry off my ring than receive it from me as a gift? Why not accept it from me, and with it my shield, my steed, and all I have. Do what you will with it, but do not, I beseech you, hide from me your lovely countenance; for I know, O cruel one! that you hear though you will not answer me.'

Thus lamenting, he wandered around the fountain often, like some blind man, stretching out his arms to catch the fair damsel, and as often embracing an empty shadow.

The princess, in the mean while, went on her way, nor stopped until she came to a large cavern, in which, to her great joy, she found some food, of which she stood much in need. In this grotto there dwelt an old peasant, who had the charge of a herd of horses, which fed on the fresh green grass that grew on the low pasture-ground along the banks of the river. On each side of the cave were stalls, in which the herd took shelter during the sultry hours of noon; and in one of these Angelica rested all that day.

Towards evening, when she was sufficiently refreshed and the air had become pleasantly cool, she rose and put on some coarse garments she found lying about, very different from the gay vesture of many varied fashions and bright hues, green, yellow, gray, blue, and pink, to which she was accustomed; yet this humble raiment could not so disguise her as to make her appear aught but a most noble and lovely lady, to whom none of those so famed by the ancients, neither Phyllis, nor Amaryllis, nor Galatea could compare in beauty. She chose from among the herd the palfrey which appeared best fitted for her use, and mounting it, started on her journey. She thought her best plan would be to try and make her way back to her own beautiful kingdom in the East, only she somewhat wished that either Orlando or Sacripante could accompany her; not that she cared for one more than the other — indeed, all her many lovers were equally indifferent to her — but foreseeing that on her way to India she must pass by many cities and castles, she felt she had need of a companion and guide, and knew she could find none more trustworthy.

She travelled far without finding any trace of them, until after having sought for them fruitlessly in cities and villages, through great forests, and on many different roads, fortune at last led her to the castle where Orlando, Sacripante, and Ferrau were held bound in strange enchantments by the famous magician Atlante, and with them Ruggiero and Gradasso and many others, as you shall hear more particularly when I come to the history of these knights. She entered the Enchanted Castle, and making herself, by virtue of her ring, invisible even to the magician himself, she searched it in all directions until she found Orlando and Sacripante together, both pursuing an empty shadow in her likeness, by which Atlante had allured them into the castle, and by which he still kept them there.

Between these two knights she was puzzled which to choose, whether would the Count or the Circassian king serve her best? Orlando might with greater valor defend her in perils and dangers by the way; but she knew that if she accepted him as her guide, she must also take him for her lord: he could not be got rid of and sent back to France when she grew tired of him. Whereas, for the Circassian, however highly she might favor him at first, she thought she would find no great difficulty in dismissing him afterwards; and for this reason she decided upon trusting herself to his zeal and affection, and making him her companion for as long as she had need of him. She therefore took the ring out of her mouth and raised her veil, thinking to show herself only to Sacripante; but it chanced that Orlando and Ferrau saw her also; and as now that Angelica had put the ring on her finger, all the magic arts of Atlante were dispelled, the three knights mounted their horses and rode in pursuit of the golden hair, the dark eyes, and blooming cheeks of the beautiful princess, who, not caring to be accompanied by three such devoted lovers, had urged her palfrey to flight. As soon as she had led them sufficiently far from the castle to render them safe from the machinations of the sorcerer, she again placed the ring between her rosy lips, and vanished from their sight. At the same time she abandoned her intention of asking either Orlando or Sacripante to return with her to her kingdom of Galafema, in the far-off East, for she suddenly took a dislike to both and determined to trust herself alone, to the all-sufficient protection of her magic ring.

The forsaken knights, like blind and dizzy fools, turned their amazed eyes now to one side of the wood, now to the other. So do hounds when the wolf or the hare they are following in the chase suddenly burrows into some hole or furrow, and the scent is lost. The haughty Angelica, meanwhile, laughed to herself as, unseen, she watched their movements. There lay but one path before them through the forest, and they saw no outlet by which she could have escaped them : therefore, supposing that after all she must be in front, Orlando galloped on, with Ferrau at his heels, and Sacripante spurring on behind; while Angelica followed at a more moderate pace. When they came to where several paths diverged and lost themselves in the thicket, they began to look for the prints of her horse's hoofs on the grass ; and Ferrau, who among the proudest might well be said to hold his head highest, turned defiantly to the other two and cried : 'Wherefore do you follow me ? Retrace your steps, or choose some other road ; unless, indeed, you are prepared to lose your lives by my hand. Think not I brook rivals either in the pursuit or in the favor of this fair lady.'

Orlando replied, no less haughtily : 'Villain ! saw I not that thy helmet was lacking, I would soon make thee learn whether such words were well or ill-spoken.'

'Why shouldst thou concern thyself with that which troubles not me ?' answered the Spaniard. 'All helmetless as I am, I fear not to hold my words good against ye both.'

'I pray thee,' said Orlando, turning to Sacripante, 'lend the fellow thy helmet, that I may cure him of this folly, the like of which I have never seen.'

'Who would then be the greater fool ?' replied the king, 'but if it seem a fair request, I pray thee lend him thine, for I, forsooth, am no less apt at the punishing of a fool than thou.'

'Fools are ye both,' cried Ferrau. 'Think ye, had it pleased me to wear a helmet, that one of you would not, ere this, have been bareheaded? But to let you somewhat into my confidence, know, I go, and shall go thus, until I get possession of that noble and famous helmet which the Paladin Orlando now wears.'

'Then,' said the Count, with a smile, 'wilt thou, bareheaded, pretend to do to Orlando that which he did in Aspromonte to Almonte? I believe, dids' thou but see him face to face, thou wouldst tremble from head to foot, and rather than try to deprive him of his helmet, wouldst gladly agree to give him up every bit of armor thou hast upon thee.'

The vaunting Spaniard thereupon answered:

'Often and often have I this same Orlando so hardly pressed that I could, with ease, have taken from him his arms as well as his helmet, and if I refrained, it was because, at that time, I cared but little for them. Now, however, I desire his helmet, and I hope soon to succeed in obtaining it.'

At this the Count could no longer keep patience, and exclaimed: 'O liar! O foul Moor! In what land? where and when canst thou boast of having overcome me in battle? Know I am that Paladin Orlando of whom thou pratest, thinking him far enough away. Come! try and win my helmet, and think not I will take thee at disadvantage.'

So saying, he unfastened his helmet and hung it up on the branch of a beech-tree close by, at the same moment drawing his good sword, Durindana. Ferrau, however, did not lose heart, but drew his sword also, and with it and his raised shield guarded his uncovered head. Wheeling round their horses, they advanced to the fierce encounter, endeavoring to strike each other between the joints of the harness, or on the weaker parts of their armor. In all the world, no two warriors could have been found so equally matched in skill, in strength, and in valor. Fast and furiously did the battle rage. Ferrau aimed not a blow in vain, and each stroke that Orlando let fall broke the plated steel, or burst asunder the linked mail.

Angelica looked on unseen, the sole spectator of this fearful fight; for the King of Circassia, thinking she was still in advance, when he saw Orlando and Ferrau fairly engaged in combat, had ridden on, following the path which he supposed the princess to have taken. She stood for some time watching the encounter, which seemed to her fraught with equal peril to both; at last, from mere curiosity to see what the knights would do when they missed the helmet, she determined to carry it off, intending to return it to the Count as soon as she had sufficiently amused herself with playing him this trick. She took it down very gently, and after watching them a little longer she quietly went on her way, and had gone some distance before the theft was discovered by either of the two angry knights. Ferrau was the first to find it out, and starting back, he cried: 'Ah! See! how has that knight our companion befooled and betrayed us! What prize can now reward the victor, since he has stolen the precious helmet?'

Orlando turned and looked, and when he saw the helmet was no longer hanging on the bough, he was almost beside himself with rage. He also supposed that the knight, who had gone on in front, had carried it off; and turning his rein, he put spurs to Brigliadoro, and galloped off in pursuit of him; Ferrau followed close at his heels, until they came to a place where they saw fresh foot-prints on the grass, made by the horses of the Circassian and the princess. Orlando took the path to the left, down the valley, whither Sacripante had gone, while Ferrau went up the mountain by the ascent which Angelica had followed.

She in the mean while had arrived at a pleasantly situated fountain, which invited all who passed by to taste of its sweet waters, and to rest near its cool and shady brink. Angelica thought she would take some repose by this clear brook, not dreaming that any one could overtake her, and feeling, moreover, safe from all unforeseen peril under the protection of her magic ring. She hung the helmet on a bush, near the grassy bank of the shining stream, and was just about to fasten up her horse's bridle, so that he might feed on the rich pasture, when the Spanish knight, having followed her horse's tracks, reached the fountain. Angelica no sooner saw him than she put the ring into her mouth and disappeared, and forgetting in her haste to pick up the helmet, which had fallen on the grass, she urged her horse to flight. When the Spaniard caught sight of her, he rushed towards her with great delight, but as I have said before, she vanished like some phantom at the awakening from a dream; and search as he would among the trees, his sorrowful eyes beheld her no more. Cursing all magicians, sorcerers, and their magic arts, Ferrau turned back towards the brook, and there, behold! on the grass before him, lay the helmet of Orlando. He recognized it at once, even before he read the words inscribed upon it, which told how Orlando had obtained it, and when, and where, and from whom, he had taken it.

However much disappointed at the disappearance of Angelica, who had vanished as a shade of the night, the Pagan did not neglect to pick up the helmet, and to put it on his head, and when he had securely buckled it, seeing that nothing was now wanting to complete his happiness but to find this lady, so continually vanishing from and reappearing before his eyes, like flashes of lightning, he set out to seek for her in every direction, up and down the wide forest. At last he was obliged to give up all hopes of finding her; and he started to return to the camp of the Spanish king before Paris, his grief at the loss of the princess being lessened by the satisfaction he felt in having fulfilled his vow, and in wearing the helmet of Orlando.

8

CHAPTER IV.

HOW CUPID TAKES HIS REVENGE UPON THE HAUGHTY ANGELICA.

> Come live with me and be my Love,
> And we will all the pleasures prove,
> That hills and valleys, dale and field,
> And all the craggy mountains yield.
> There will we sit upon the rocks,
> And see the shepherds feed their flocks
> By shallow rivers, to whose falls
> Melodious birds sing Madrigals.
>   C. MARLOWE.

ANGELICA, invisible and alone, continued her journey with a troubled brow; for she was vexed at having, in her needless haste, left the helmet by the fountain: 'Owing to my foolish whim and to my meddling with that which was no concern of mine,' she said to herself, 'I have lost the Count his helmet, and have made him but a sorry return for his many and great services to me. With only good intentions (and Heaven knows I speak truth, though the event has turned out so disastrously), I took it, thinking that so perhaps a truce might be put to their battle; not indeed that through my help that hateful Spaniard should obtain his wish.'

Thus regretting that she had carried off Orlando's helmet, sorrowful and ill at ease, she took what she supposed to be the most direct road to the

East. She generally travelled invisible, but sometimes, and on fitting occasions, she allowed herself
to be seen. She had gone through many provinces
of France, when one day she entered a wood, and
came upon a youth wounded and pierced through
the breast by a lance, lying beside two companions
who were already dead. He was a young Moor,
named Medoro, whose story was a very touching
one, and as an example of faithful and disinterested
affection, worthy of being related.

Medoro, and his friend Cloridano, had come into
France in the train of their beloved lord and más-
ter, Dardinello, whom they had followed in good
and evil fortune, until he had met his death in a
battle recently fought near Paris, in which the Saracens had been defeated by the Christians under
Charlemagne, and driven back in confusion to their
camp, leaving their dead unburied on the field.
The night after the battle, the two friends kept
guard together on the entrenchments, discoursing,
sadly enough, upon the events of the day, and
Medoro, more especially, thinking about his beloved master, and lamenting that his body should
be left, unhonored and uncared for, out on the
plain. He was a youth of a most charming and
beautiful countenance, admired by all for his fine
dark eyes and curly golden hair, and of a disposition as sweet and engaging as his face. Turning
to Cloridano he said:

‘I cannot tell thee how it grieves me to think
that the precious body of my lord lies out there, a
prey to the wolves and to the ravens. Remembering how kind and good he always was, it seems to
me that even if I lost my life in doing honor to
his memory, I should but pay back a very small

part of the debt of gratitude I owe him. I will therefore if possible make my way, unobserved, through the camp of Charlemagne, and seek for my lord's body, that it may no longer lie there without honorable sepulture. Do thou remain here, and should death be my fate, tell in what cause I found it.'

Cloridano was surprised to find such love and devotion in the heart of this young boy, and at first tried to dissuade him from so perilous an adventure; but Medoro would not listen to him; he said he was determined to give his lord honorable burial, or to die in the attempt. Cloridano, who had been a hunter, and was a strong and active man, said that he could not suffer a friend he loved so dearly to go alone upon this glorious enterprise, and that rather than be left alone in the world without him, he would go and die with him. They therefore sallied forth together, and after many dangers and many hairbreadth escapes, they made their way in safety through the Christian camp, and reached the plain on the other side. Here a scene of horrible carnage met their eyes. The bodies of men and horses, kings, nobles, squires, and footmen, lay bathed in blood, heaped up in dire confusion, among broken lances, swords, shields, and bows and arrows.

The two friends might have wandered about in their vain search over the battle-field until the day dawned, had not the kind moon suddenly burst forth from behind a dark cloud, clear and lovely as when she once shone upon the adoring Endymion, and lighted up the scene. The city of Paris and the two hostile camps lay outspread in her bright rays, with the undulating plain beyond, and the hills of Montmartre and Valerien in the distance; while at their feet they saw distinctly, in the clear pale light, the lifeless body of Dardinello. Medoro recognized him at once by his white and crimson shield, and kneeling down beside him, he bathed his dear face with bitter tears. Then sadly and very quietly, lest they should be disturbed by the enemy, the two took up the corpse of their king, and bore him away between them as quickly as the weight of their precious burden would allow.

By this time the lord of light, who chases darkness from the earth and blots out the stars in heaven, began to appear, and betrayed the two friends to Zerbino, a Christian captain, who after chasing the flying Moors all night, was returning with his troop to Charlemagne's camp.

No man knows how he is really loved when borne aloft on the prosperous wheel of fortune. True and feigned friends then keep together at his side with equal show of outward devotion; but when evil days come, the flattering crowd turn upon their heel, and only true and faithful hearts, who, like Medoro, love in life, in death, and even after death, remain. When Cloridano saw the horsemen he said quickly: 'Brother, we must put down our burden and take to our heels. It would scarcely be acting like prudent men to risk losing our two lives for this one lifeless body.'

So saying, he let go his hold and fled, thinking Medoro was following him. But he, poor boy, loved his lord too well to abandon him; so taking the whole weight upon his shoulders, he made for a wood hard by, hoping to conceal himself in its thickets. It was, however, so overgrown with tangled underwood, and was such a labyrinth of narrow, intricate paths, that only wild animals could have made their way through it; and impeded by his heavy burden and unable to find a road, he could make little progress, and was soon overtaken by his pursuers. In the mean while Cloridano, hearing no footsteps behind him, looked round, and not seeing Medoro, he immediately repented of having left him, for what would life be worth without his friend ? He, therefore, retraced his steps, and taking one of the narrow winding paths into the wood, he was soon led by the sound of arms, horses, and threatening voices to where Medoro, alone and on foot, was defending himself against a whole troop of horsemen. He had placed his sacred charge upon the ground, and stood over it with his back against a beech-tree, making the best stand he could against such fearful odds. So the bear, whom the Alpine hunter has tracked to her rocky lair, stands before her cubs roaring with mingled rage and fear. Anger and native ferocity urge her to put forth her claws and quench her thirst for blood ; but in the midst of her fury, love softens and draws her back, to keep guard over her young.

Cloridano, not seeing what help he could give in joining his friend against so many, drew his bow and sent an arrow among the assailants, which killed a young Scotch squire, and when they all turned round to see whence the unexpected attack came, he let fly another with as fatal effect. Zerbino, the Christian captain, upon seeing this, lost all patience, and seized Medoro by his golden hair ; but when he looked into his soft eyes and fair young face, he was touched with pity and could not find it in his heart to slay him. Medoro thereupon besought his compassion, in the following words :

' Sir, I pray you be not so cruel as to deny me leave to bury the body of my king. I ask no other boon, for I care not for life, and when I have paid the last honors to my beloved master, you are welcome to throw this poor carcass to the ravening beasts and to the carrion birds.'

He spoke with such moving accents that Zerbino was filled with pity ; but one of his troopers coming up at that moment, plunged his spear into the poor youth's breast, and he fell apparently lifeless to the earth. Cloridano, when he saw him fall, rushed out upon the Christians with his sword drawn, but he also was soon overpowered and stretched dead beside his friend. Medoro lay for some time unconscious, his life's blood ebbing fast away through his open wound, when, just in time to save him, unlooked-for help appeared. A damsel approached him in the humble attire of a shepherdess, but of most noble appearance and exceeding beauty, with manners as courteous as they were dignified. I need say no more, for you must have guessed that this was Angelica, the royal daughter of the great Khan of Cathay ; who, since she had regained possession of her ring, had grown so proud and so haughty that she held the whole world in scorn.

She journeyed quite alone, and disdaining the company of even the most renowned knight among her former friends, scarcely deigned to remember that she had once called Orlando and Sacripante by that title, and despised herself for having ever cast her eyes with favor on Rinaldo. But lo ! Cupid, angry at having been so long set at defiance, now fixed the arrow in his bow and placed himself in ambush, near the spot where Medoro lay.

When Angelica saw the youth, who, lying at the point of death, sorrowed more for his unburied king than for his own evil case, unwonted pity touched her heart, which softened with emotion such as she had never before felt, when in broken accents he related to her his sorrowful story. Recalling to mind her knowledge of the art of surgery, which she had learnt in the Indies (for in those countries this is looked upon as a great and noble science, handed down by father to son, without much study of parchments), she set about preparing a balsam from the juice of certain herbs, with which to heal his wound. She remembered having seen on her way a plant growing in the meadows — I know not if it were dittamus, or wound-wort — which was of singular virtue in stanching wounds and in relieving acute and deadly pain. She went back and gathered it, and meeting, on her return to the wood, a shepherd riding in search of a heifer which, two days before, had strayed from his herd, she took him with her to where Medoro lay, so bathed in blood that but a faint spark of life remained.

Angelica alighted from her palfrey, and having bruised the herb between two stones, she collected the juice in her white hands and poured it into the wound, at the same time applying the balsam to his breast and limbs. The remedy was of such sovereign power, that it not only stopped the flow of blood, but so restored his failing strength that he was soon able to sit up and to be placed upon the shepherd's horse. Not however before he had seen the body of his king laid under the earth, and Cloridano placed in the same grave, did he permit himself to be led to the humble abode of the friendly shepherd, who dwelt with his wife and children in a clean and pretty cottage he had but lately built, sheltered by low-lying hills and pleasantly situated at the edge of the wood.

Angelica determined not to leave the wounded youth until he was quite restored to health, and tenderly she nursed him, until by degrees his handsome features and his gentle manners transformed the pity she had felt for him, from the moment she had first seen him lying wounded on the ground, into a still softer passion. The wound of Medoro soon healed under the skilful tending of the lady, but the wound made in her heart by the arrow of the winged and unseen archer, only grew deeper and more poignant. As he regained health and spirits, she became gentler and sadder; till at length, overcome by the dread of having to part from him, she laid aside all her native pride and confessed to him her love.

O Count Orlando! O King Sacripante! of what avail were all your high achievements, your noble birth, your great renown? What reward did all your faithful services obtain? Could you point to one act of favor shown to you at any time by this fair princess, in gratitude for all you encountered for her sake? How would it have enraged you and Ferrau and many others, whom I do not name, who dared a thousand deaths in this ungrateful lady's service, could you have seen her love bestowed, unsolicited, upon this unknown youth!

Under the auspices of the shepherd's good wife the wedding of Angelica and Medoro took place with all holy and fitting ceremonies, and with as much festivity as the simple household could afford. They stayed on with their kind hosts for some weeks; Angelica never tiring of the society of her dear Medoro, and he as devoted a lover as the most exacting princess could desire. Hand in hand they wandered through the green meadows and pleasant valleys; or rested in some cool grot, where Medoro would carve verses on the smooth rock to celebrate his lady's beauty and his own happiness; or spent the sultry noontide hours in shady groves, where they would amuse themselves by cutting their names and initials, interlaced in many curious and intricate devices, on the trees.

Of all her rich and costly ornaments, Angelica had only preserved one, a massive gold bracelet studded with gems, which Orlando had once given her, and which she valued so much for its great beauty, that she never suffered it to quit her arm, and had managed to keep it, even when exposed to the Orca, by the barbarous people on the Isle of Tears. This she now unclasped, and when bidding farewell to the kind shepherd and his wife, she begged them to accept it, and to keep it for her sake, as a token of her gratitude for all their goodness to her.

She then continued her journey with Medoro. Crossing the Pyrenees into Spain, they went to Barcelona, where they found a vessel about to sail for the Levant, in which they took their passage and had a prosperous voyage to the East.

Soon afterwards Angelica had the happiness of

being received with joy by her people, and of presenting to them the amiable and beloved Medoro, as the chosen partner of her throne.

And thus ended in peace and happiness the many adventures of the beautiful Princess Angelica.

THE STORY

OF

GINEVRA.

CHAPTER I.

O Caledonia! stern and wild,
Meet nurse for a poetic child!
Land of brown heath and shaggy wood,
Land of the mountain and the flood.

SCOTT.

YOU remember that when Angelica met the pretended hermit in the forest, she told him that she wished to leave France in order to get beyond the reach of the hated Rinaldo, whom she had just left fighting with Sacripante. The hermit assured her that she might set her mind at ease on that score; and taking a book out of his pocket, he repeated from it an incantation which summoned up one of his attendant sprites, whom he commanded to go, straightway, in the form of a squire, to where the knights were still engaged in combat. He, obeying this command, placed himself boldly between them, and said: 'Sirs! I pray you consider what will it avail either of you to kill the other? and what gain do you propose to yourselves from this desperate encounter, seeing that Count Orlando, without even breaking a lance, has carried off towards Paris the lady who is the cause of your deadly fray? I met him with the Princess Angelica, not a mile from here, on the road to Paris, laughing and jesting over your fruitless dispute. Were it not wiser to try and overtake them? For if the Count has her once safe within the walls of that city, you run small chance of seeing her again.'

Both the knights were much troubled at this news, and cursed their own folly in having allowed the lady to escape them. Rinaldo swore in great anger that if he came up with Orlando, he would tear the very heart out of his body, and without bidding adieu to the dismounted Circassian, he vaulted on Baiardo's back, and with a hasty shake of the rein, he and his fiery steed were soon out of sight. So eager was he to overtake the Count, that he rode on all through that night and the next day, until he reached the great city in which, with the remains of his beaten and routed army, Charlemagne had taken refuge.

The Emperor expected the African king to pursue him and lay siege to the town; he was therefore making all diligence to procure reinforcements, to collect provisions, and by deepening the trenches and repairing the walls, to strengthen the fortifications. He was determined, as soon as he could get together a fresh army, to march out against the enemy and again try the fortune of war; and on Rinaldo's arrival he at once despatched him to England to ask for aid and for permission to levy soldiers. This errand was any thing but welcome to Rinaldo, who would far rather have continued his vain pursuit after the fair face which had made conquest of his heart; however, he knew his knightly duty too well to hesitate for a moment in obeying the Emperor's commands.

He started for Calais, which he reached in a few hours, and embarked the same day for England, much against the advice of all the sailors in the port, who foresaw, from the rough and angry sea, that a great storm was coming on. But Rinaldo could brook no delay, so impatient was he to conclude his mission and to return to France. The wind soon increased to a tremendous gale, and when the waves rose so high that even the masts were often under water, the frightened sailors proceeded to furl the sails and tried to tack the ship in order to return to the haven from whence, in an unlucky moment, they had put out. But the wind blew so furiously off shore that, to save themselves from shipwreck, they were obliged to continue their course, and for two whole days and nights their bark, carrying but one small studding-sail, was driven before the south-west gale. On the third day they approached the coast, and the dark woods of Caledonia, which have so often re-echoed to the din of arms, came in sight. Some of the most renowned knights-errant of Britain as well as of more distant countries, such as France, Germany, and Norway, have traversed those forests in search of glory. None but the brave ventured into their wild recesses, where death was more easily and more surely found than fame ; and many great deeds were performed there by Tristan, Lancelot, Galasso, Gawaine, Arthur, and other knights of the famous Round Table ; trophies and monuments of whose prowess are even yet to be found there.

Rinaldo donned his armor, and with his gallant Baiardo landed on this wooded shore, telling the captain to put to sea again, and make for Berwick, there to await his arrival. Alone and unattended, he pursued his way in search of new adventures, and that evening alighted at a beautiful abbey, which spent great part of its large revenues in hospitably entertaining, within its walls, the knights and ladies who journeyed in those parts. The abbot and his monks gave a cordial welcome to Rinaldo, who, after heartily partaking of their good cheer, asked them how a knight, in quest of glory, might best set about finding some opportunity of distinguishing himself and of gaining deserved renown, in that country. They replied, that wandering in those woods, he would indeed find no lack of strange adventures, but that as to fame, what happened in those obscure regions was for the most part as little known as the place itself.

'Go rather,' they added, 'where well-earned renown may reward your labors and the danger you incur. No more fitting or worthy occasion for the display of chivalry could be found than now awaits you at our court. The daughter of our king stands in sore need of help and defence against a baron named Lurcanio, who threatens her with the loss of life and fair fame, for having broken her plighted faith to his brother; he has accused her to the king, most unjustly as we all believe, with having favored the suit of another nobleman, with whom, he declares, he saw her conversing in secret from the balcony of her room. By the stern law of Scotland she is condemned to perish by fire for this breach of faith, unless within the space of one month, now nearly expired, some valiant knight appears as her champion to defy and overcome her wicked accuser. The king, sorrowing greatly over his fair Ginevra, has proclaimed throughout the land that to any one who takes up her cause and disposes of this foul calumny, provided he be of

gentle blood, she shall be given for wife with such lands and estates as shall be a fitting dowry for so noble a lady. This is an enterprise far more befitting you than roaming those wild woods in search of chance adventures. For, besides honor and glory, you would win the hand of as lovely a lady as can be found in all Christendom, with abundant riches, fine estates, and the favor of our king; and moreover, you would fulfil the law of chivalry, which bids you vindicate the honor of this paragon of gentle virtue from so base a slander.'

Rinaldo, indignant at the cruel law which had condemned the innocent Ginevra to death, burned with ardor to appear in the lists on her behalf. He set off on Baiardo the next morning as soon as the first rosy streaks of dawn appeared in the east. He was attended by a squire, whom the abbot sent to guide him over the many leagues of moor and forest which he must pass on his way to the town where the combat in defence of Ginevra was to be fought.

He had left the high road and was taking a short cut by a path through a coppice, when he heard a sound of loud weeping, which seemed to come from no great distance. He spurred Baiardo fast down a green dell from whence the crying came, and found a damsel, who appeared to be young and fair, but who was in such an agony of tears and mortal terror that the like was never seen. Two ruffians stood over her with drawn swords, threatening to kill her, while she, with sobs and screams, was imploring them to have pity and to spare her life. When Rinaldo, with loud shouts of anger and horror, hurried towards them, the villains turned and fled, concealing themselves in the depths of the dark glen. He did not take the trouble to follow them, but went up to the lady, and asked her whether it was through fault or misfortune that she had been brought into so terrible a strait?

However, not having then time to wait and hear her answer, he ordered his squire to take her up behind him, and continued his route. As he rode beside her and saw that she was of gentle breeding and great beauty, though still much agitated and discomposed with the peril from which she had just escaped, he again asked wherefore, and by whose order, she had met with such evil treatment?

The beasts of the field, whether they rest secure in their dens, or ravage the woods and fields for food, and even when they attack their natural enemies, everywhere and at all times treat their mates with kindness and gentleness. The she-bear and the bear roam the wilds in peace; the lioness dwells in safety with the lion; even the savage wolf is tender to his mate; and the raging bull inspires the heifer with no dread. Man is the only exception to this beneficent law. How often do loud voices and angry gestures mar the peace of home! How often do blows and tears prevail where all should be love and happiness! What an outrage against the laws of God and of nature, that a man should raise his hand against a defenceless woman, the very hairs of whose head should be precious in his sight! Such were the reflections of Rinaldo upon the two murderers, whose uplifted swords had been so near slaying the poor lady, who now, in a low voice, related the story which you shall hear in the next chapter.

CHAPTER II.

> To think how she through guyleful handeling,
> Though true as touch, though daughter of a King,
> Though faire as ever living wight was fayre,
> • Though nor in word nor deede ill meriting,
> Is from her Knight divorced in despayre.
>
> SPENSER.

'I HAVE to tell you a story of greater and
more malign cruelty than any of which the
annals of Argos, Thebes, or Mycene have told ; and
if the sun in his daily rounds sheds less of his dear
rays on these regions than elsewhere, I believe it is
because he cares not to look down on so barbarous
a nation. I must begin by informing you that my
name is Dalinda, and that, as a child, I was taken
into the service of the king's daughter, and growing up with her, was placed in an honorable position in her household. There I should have
remained had not cruel Cupid, envying my innocent happiness, caused me to fall in love with the
Duke of Albany, and to distinguish him above all
the other nobles of the court. Pleased with his
courtly manners and handsome person, I listened
with favor to the declaration of his regard ; and
from a balcony, upon which the window of my
lady's favorite apartment opened, I often conversed

with him in the evening when all was still; and
as this part of the palace looked upon some ruins
where no one was in the habit of passing either by
day or night, there was little risk of our interviews
being discovered.

'This intercourse was carried on between us for
many months, and so blinded was I by my affection, that I never discovered, or at any rate never
acknowledged to myself, that while my love only
increased, that of the duke became gradually cooler.
At last, he one day confessed to me that he intended presenting himself as a suitor for the hand
of the king's daughter.　He protested, indeed, that
only ambition, and care for the grandeur of his
house, drove him to this step; and assured me that
however ardently he might, to all outward appearance, pay court to the princess, his heart would
ever remain true to me.　Such entire empire had
he gained over me that, in time, he even persuaded
me to promise to help him in his suit; and to
please him, I took occasion to speak to the princess in his favor.　I praised his courtly bearing,
and hinted at his devotion for herself, but she
listened coldly, and plainly showed that she took
little interest in my discourse.　Indeed, she had
already bestowed her affections upon a handsome
young knight, who with his brother had lately
come from Italy, on a visit to the Scottish court.
Gentle in manner and renowned in arms, Britain
could boast of no so perfect a nobleman, and so
highly did our king esteem him that he gave him
castles and domains, and such dignities as made
him equal in rank with the chief of our barons.
The amiable Ariodante was beloved by the king,
but still more beloved by his daughter, who soon

discovered that the heart of this noble knight beat with as pure and faithful a passion for her as hers for him; and therefore had she listened with cold disdain to all I said in praise of the duke, towards whom she was at no pains to conceal her dislike.

'I often counselled Polinesso to desist from his vain suit, telling him that the princess's heart was so entirely given to Ariodante that there could never be the faintest hope of success for him. In time he saw this himself, and angry at the preference shown to his rival, his baffled love changed to hatred, and he devised a most base and cruel means to satisfy his longing for revenge.

'He one day accosted Ariodante, with whom, before their rivalry for the good graces of Ginevra, he had been intimate, and said:

'"Much do I wonder that you should pay me so poor a return for the friendship and affection I have always shown you. I am sure that you must be acquainted with the love that has so long existed between Ginevra and myself, and must know that I am on the point of suing to her father for her hand. Why, then, do you come between us, interfering with my just claims, and wasting your time in so hopeless a pursuit? Were I in your place, Heaven knows that I would treat you with more regard."

'"And I," answered the other, "marvel at you with much greater reason; you know that I was in love with her when you had barely even spoken to her, and that my love, great as it is, is returned with equal fervor. I feel sure also that you are aware she does not care for you. Why, therefore, have you not that consideration for me which is due to our old friendship, and which, were you pre-

ferred by her, I should certainly show you? Not
less than you do I aspire to her hand, and though
my possessions may not equal yours, I flatter myself I rank as high in the favor of the king, and
much higher in that of his daughter."

'"Oh!" said the duke, "great indeed is the error
into which your vanity has led you. If you can
show me any token of the princess's affection for
you, I engage to give you much greater proof of
her regard for me; and I pledge myself to reveal
to none the secret you may confide to me, if you
will promise to do the same by me."

'To this Ariodante agreed, and then told him
that Ginevra, both by word of mouth and by letter,
had promised, not only never to marry any one but
himself, but if the king refused his consent to their
union, to retire from the world and remain un-
wedded to the end of her days. He had, however,
every reason to hope that the king would, for the
sake of his daughter's happiness, accept him for her
husband. "To win her hand," he continued, "is
now the sole object of my existence; and with this
hope before me, I am content to wait in patience,
until it may be the king's good pleasure to give
her to me."

'The duke replied, with a scornful laugh, that
he could boast of much more distinguished proofs
of the princess's regard; for that she would grant
him secret interviews, and converse with him from
the balcony of her apartments, and had indeed
often jested with him over Ariodante's mad passion,
and his presumption in aspiring to her hand.

'Ariodante grew deadly pale when he heard
these words, but he answered firmly that, after all,
these were mere assertions on the duke's part,

which he not only did not believe, but which he should call upon him to make good with his life.

'"Then," said the duke, "if nothing else will serve you, your own eyes shall satisfy you of the truth of what I have told you."

'He thereupon arranged that Ariodante should the very next evening conceal himself in the ruined buildings, exactly opposite the window of one of the princess's favorite rooms. Ariodante agreed, but, having a suspicion that under all this manœuvre there might be some plotting of a jealous rival against his life, he determined to take with him his young brother Lurcanio, in whose prudence and valor he had entire confidence. He stationed him in another part of the ruins, a stone's throw from his own hiding-place, saying:

'"Brother, if you hear me call out, fly to my succor; otherwise, at all hazards, do not leave this spot until I tell you to do so."

'Lurcanio readily promised to obey his instructions, and accordingly he also concealed himself in the ruins.

'The duke had often piqued my foolish vanity by telling me I so much resembled Ginevra that, were I but dressed like her, we could scarcely be known apart; and that he, for one, thought me the more beautiful of the two. With such flatteries and cajoleries he had persuaded me (for, as I have said, I was so bent on pleasing him, that I could refuse no request he made me) to promise that I would, some time or other, dress myself up in the princess's clothes. That evening, therefore (little dreaming that I was to be an innocent accomplice in so atrocious a plot), when I knew that the princess was occupied in another wing of the palace, I stealthily took away one of her court robes, and having put it on, I stepped out upon the balcony from the window of her room, just as by the light of the newly risen moon I saw the duke approaching. I leant over the balustrade to greet him, and suffered him to take my hand, which he held in his, and caressed with more than usual tenderness. He told me I might easily be mistaken for the princess, and this I could well believe, for her long white satin robe, with its rich fringe and embroidery of gold, fitted me exactly. My hair was of the same hue as hers, and I had gathered it up in a gold net, fastened with rose-colored ribbons, which she alone, among all the ladies of the court, was privileged to wear. Quite unconscious of the misery I was helping to bring upon my mistress, I stood and listened with childish pleasure to the duke's expressions of love and admiration.

'The unhappy Ariodante looked on, and satisfied by what he saw of the truth of all the duke had said, he was plunged into such despair that he drew his sword with the intention of then and there ending his miserable existence, but Lurcanio rushed forward in time to prevent him from committing the desperate deed.

'"Ah! my brother," he said, "is it possible that you have so far taken leave of your senses as to think of dying for the sake of a woman? Are they not all as changeable as clouds driven before the wind? Rather take the life of the lady who has shown herself so unworthy of your devotion, and keep this good sword to prove her faithlessness in the face of the king and all his court."

'Ariodante offered no resistance to his brother,

but, cut to the heart by sorrow for what he supposed himself to have seen, he suffered him to
lead him to his house. Early next morning, giving himself up to despair, he, without saying a
word to any one, left the court, and for some days
nothing was heard of him. With the exception
of the duke and Lurcanio, no one knew of any
cause for his departure, and there was much
wonder and conjecture about it in the palace and
among the people, by whom he was greatly beloved.

'At the end of eight or ten days there came a
pilgrim to the palace, bearing evil tidings. He
asked to be brought before Ginevra, and told her
that, with his own eyes, he had seen Ariodante
cast himself from the top of a high rock, headlong
into the sea. "He had," added the pilgrim,
"shortly before met me on the road, and said,
'Come with me, that you may see what is about to
befall me, and that you may carry an account
thereof to the Princess Ginevra, with this message
to her from me: tell her the cause of all was
my having seen too much. Happy for me had I
been blind!'"

'On hearing the pilgrim's story, Ginevra turned
as pale as death, and shutting herself up in her
room, gave way to an agony of grief. She often
and often repeated Ariodante's last words, but tried
in vain to understand what he could have meant
by such a message.

'The king and his courtiers, with whom Ariodante was a great favorite, mourned for him sincerely, and Lurcanio was in the deepest distress.
Thinking that Ginevra was the sole cause of this
misfortune, he was so blinded by the desire to re-

venge his brother's death, that, heedless of incurring the wrath of the king and the hatred of the nation, he appeared in the audience chamber, and in the presence of the assembled court, accused the princess of having driven Ariodante to this act of despair; declaring that, after having pledged her troth to him as his future wife, she had broken her vow, and that they had but too sure proof of her perfidy, having together witnessed her interview from the balcony of her apartment with some unknown nobleman. He could not indeed tell the name of the favored lover, for he had not recognized the Duke of Albany, whose back was turned to him, and who was partly concealed under the shadow of the balcony.

'I leave you to imagine the distress of the unhappy king; not indeed that he believed the accusation, but he could not disprove it, and he knew that by the stern laws of the land his daughter would be sentenced to death, unless within thirty days some champion appeared to give the lie to Lurcanio, and to maintain her innocence against him in arms. He has caused proclamation to be made that her hand, with a rich dowry, shall be the reward of the knight who undertakes her defence, but the strength and skill of Lurcanio are so well known that as yet no one has ventured to defy him; for cruel Fate has willed that her brother Zerbino, her natural and most efficient champion, should be now absent, distinguishing himself by feats of arms in other countries. Had he been here, Lurcanio would not have wanted a worthy opponent.

'As for me, I dared not confess my share in the deception, for fear of bringing about the ruin of the

Duke of Albany, whom I still loved, and lest I should be tempted to betray his guilty secret, he prevailed upon me to retire to one of his castles. I was on my way thither, escorted by two of his servants, when you, my lord, came up with me. You have heard how many proofs I gave to my perfidious lover of my unbounded devotion ; and may judge of the ingratitude and cruelty of his nature when I tell you that it was by his command I was to be put to death, in order that he might run no risk of my repenting and revealing to the king this wicked plot against the happiness and life of his daughter ! Lo ! how Love rewards those who too blindly follow him !'

This was the story told by Dalinda, as she rode beside the Paladin, who was overjoyed at having fallen in with the lady in time to hear this full account of the Princess Ginevra's innocence. If he had before hoped to defend her in the lists, with how much greater confidence did he now look forward to the issue of the combat ! He therefore hastened on with all possible speed to St. Andrews, where the king and his court were then residing. Within a few miles of that city he met a yeoman, able to give him the latest information, who told him that an unknown knight had arrived and offered himself as champion for the princess. His arms and device were strange to all, and he kept his visor so carefully closed that no one as yet had seen his face ; indeed, the very squire who waited upon him persisted in saying that he did not know who he was.

When they arrived before the walls of the town, they found the gates closed, and on Rinaldo asking the reason, the warder told him it was because the people had all gone out to witness the combat now taking place in a wide meadow on the other side of the city, between Lurcanio and an unknown knight. The gates, however, were thrown open to the great Baron of Montalbano, and closed behind him as he passed in. As Rinaldo went through the deserted streets, he stopped before the first inn, and left the lady there, telling her to await his return. He then hurried to the field, where he saw the Unknown Knight pressing hard upon Lurcanio.

Six knights, armed *cap-à-pie*, were posted within the boundaries, with the Duke of Albany at their head as grand constable, charged with keeping the lists. Seated upon a powerful and high-mettled charger, the duke was looking on with proud and cruel satisfaction at the hoped-for humiliation of Ginevra.

The iron tramp of Baiardo's hoof made the people give way quickly before Rinaldo, and they looked with admiration after the tall and stately knight who rode through the throng, until he stopped opposite the place where the king was seated, and thus addressed him, while all crowded round, eager to know his errand :

'Great king ! do not, I beseech you, allow this combat to proceed any further. The death of either of these knights would do violence to all the laws of right. One, though assured of the justice of his cause, is wrong ; he thinks to speak truth, and knows not that he lies. The other cannot know whether he has right or wrong on his side, and from pure compassion and mere chivalry risks his life in defence of this fair lady. I bring truth in place of falsehood, assured innocence instead of doubt and danger. First, for the sake of Heaven, put a stop to this battle, and then give audience to my tale.'

Rinaldo spoke with so much dignity and authority that the king could not but give heed to him, and he made a signal to stay the combat. Thereupon, Rinaldo exposed the deception which had imposed on Ariodante, offering to make good his words with his sword. The duke was summoned, and though he changed countenance on hearing the charge against him, he began with great audacity to deny its truth. Rinaldo, however, cut him short, saying, 'Let us put it to the proof.' As they were both fully armed, and the lists were ready marked out, the combat took place without delay.

Ah! how did the king and his people rejoice that the truth and goodness of their dear Ginevra was made clear beyond a doubt! How did they hope that God would punish the cruel and wicked nobleman, whose character was too well known, to cause the story of his treachery to be received with much surprise! At the third call of the trumpet, the duke, pale and downcast, with a trembling heart, put his lance in rest, but at the first assault he was run through the body by the spear of his antagonist, and fell to the ground. Rinaldo dismounted and unfastened the helmet of the dying man, who, with his last breath, confessed his guilt.

The king, who rejoiced more over the safety of his daughter than if he had recovered a lost crown, thanked Rinaldo over and over again. He had known him in former days, and recognized him as soon as he raised his visor. The Unknown Knight meanwhile stood apart and looked on in silence; until the king turned to him also, and begged that he would reveal his name and make himself known to them. At first he refused, but after much entreaty, he consented to take off his helmet, and disclosed the features of Ariodante, the man whom they had all so much loved and mourned, and for whom the king and Ginevra and Lurcanio had shed so many tears.

And yet the pilgrim's story was true; he had, indeed, seen him leap from the rock into the sea; but as a man in despair often calls upon death, and when death comes flies from it, even so Ariodante when he found himself about to sink, repented of his intention, and being a strong and practised swimmer, he succeeded in reaching the shore. Not far from the spot was the cell of a good hermit, who gave him kind and hospitable entertainment; and with whom he remained until he heard with surprise of the great grief of the Princess Ginevra at his supposed death, and of Lurcanio's accusation against her, which distressed him exceedingly. He could not banish the memory of his love; and when he found that no champion had taken up her cause, he determined to do so. She had been the mistress of his heart, the light of his eyes, and he could not stand aside and allow her to be put to death for her broken vows to himself. Rather would he risk all, and if need be, die for her sake, were she innocent or guilty; then let her judge whether his love were not truer than that of the duke, who had not stirred a finger in her behalf.

With this determination he forthwith procured a charger and suit of armor, choosing coat of mail and shield of black inlaid with gold. He was fortunate enough to secure the services of a squire who was a stranger, but just arrived in that country, and assuming the title of the Unknown Knight, he offered himself as champion for the Princess Ginevra.

The king was almost as much delighted at the recovery of his favorite knight as at that of his daughter, and knowing how much she loved him, and feeling sure that he could never find for her a more faithful or a more devoted bridegroom, he, nothing loath, listened to the request of Rinaldo, and gave the hand of the beautiful Ginevra to the noble Ariodante, at the same time bestowing upon him the dukedom of Albany, with all the forfeited estates of the wicked Polinesso.

Rinaldo did not forget Dalinda, but obtained her pardon; and she, wearied of the world and penitent for all her follies, left Scotland for ever and retired to a convent in Dacia, where she spent the rest of her days in the service of Heaven.

Rinaldo remained for some little time at the Court of Scotland, where he was treated with the greatest distinction. He laid before the king the object of his voyage, and asked, in the Emperor's name, for aid in prosecuting the war against the Moors. The king replied that as far as lay in his power, he would gladly place his forces at the disposal of Charlemagne and the Empire. Were he not, he added, too old, he would put himself at their head, but for this there was no necessity, as before they could be assembled, he hoped his son Zerbino would have returned, than whom they could have no more brave or skilful commander. He sent his marshals through the land to levy soldiers and collect horses, munitions of war, and supplies of all kinds; while he himself accom-

5

panied Rinaldo to Berwick, and there took affectionate leave of him.

Rinaldo embarked on board his galley for England with a favorable breeze, which soon brought him to the mouth of the beautiful Thames. Taking the flood-tide, his sailors rowed him up the river, and landed him in safety in the fine port of London. There he delivered to the Prince of Wales the letters and despatches with which Charlemagne had intrusted him, and requested that as large a force of cavalry and infantry as the kingdom could spare might be sent to Calais, to the assistance of France and the Emperor. The Prince of Wales received the Paladin with much honor, and graciously acceding to his demands, proceeded to assemble an army from all parts of Britain and the neighboring islands, and appointed an early day for their embarkation for Calais.

THE STORY

OF

RUGGIERO AND BRADAMANTE.

CHAPTER I.

There is a lady sweet and kind,
Was never face so pleased my mind,
I did but see her passing by,
And yet I love her till I die.
OLD SONG.

I HOPE you have not forgotten the white-plumed
knight who overthrew Sacripante, and who
turned out to be the noble Lady Bradamante, the
daughter of Duke Amone of Montalbano and of
his wife Beatrice, and the sister of Rinaldo. This
lady had often done good service to Charlemagne
by her prowess, and was not less esteemed by him
than the brave Rinaldo himself. She was beloved
by a knight called Ruggiero, who had come over
from Africa in the train of King Agramante; and
though they had only once seen and spoken to
each other, she returned his regard.

Bradamante, when she came upon Angelica and
Sacripante, was in search of Ruggiero, and though
journeying quite alone, she felt herself as safe as
if guarded by whole squadrons of lances. After
giving one glance at the prostrate Saracen, she
rode on through the wood, till she came to a
meadow traversed by a running rivulet, which invited all who passed by to rest, to taste its sweet

waters, and to listen to its pleasant murmur. On the bank of this sparkling stream, where wild flowers of every hue grew in rich profusion, sat a solitary knight under a tree, to which he had fastened the rein of his horse, while his shield and helmet hung from one of its branches. Seeing that he looked weary and sad, with that curiosity to know the affairs of others which is so common to our nature, Bradamante asked the reason of his dejection, whereupon, moved by her courteous speech and stately bearing, he told her his story, in the following words:

'I was coming, gentle sir, in command of a troop of soldiers to assist Charlemagne in defending the passage of these mountains against the Spaniards, and I was accompanied by a fair lady, whom I tenderly loved. We were approaching Rodonna, when I looked up suddenly and saw a man in armor seated upon a great winged horse, who swooped down like some falcon on its prey, and at the same moment mounted up again, bearing aloft as his prize the dear lady, of whose absence from my side I was not aware until I heard her terrified shrieks in the air, high above me. I gazed in despair at the aerial robber, knowing that, with my poor wearied horse, pursuit must be in vain. Nevertheless, allowing my men to pursue their route without me, I started to follow him, and for six long days I rode through these mountain fastnesses, along giddy precipices where there was scarcely footing for my horse's steps, and over rough and stony wastes where no road nor sign of human habitation was to be seen. At last I entered a wild glen, sunk low between high mountains, in the midst of which there rose a magnifi-

cent castle on the top of a high rock, shining in
the distance like flame. The nearer I approached
the glittering walls, the more strange and beautiful
they appeared. Neither brick nor marble could
have shone so bright; and I afterwards learnt that
they were the work of demons, who, by the aid of
sorcery and magic, had surrounded the stately
edifice with steel, tempered in the flame and in the
waters of Styx, so that neither rust nor stain can
dim them. I was also told that that cruel and
wicked brigand, who had robbed me of my dear
lady, after scouring the country far and wide in
search of such booty, was accustomed to find sure
refuge within them, for none can defend themselves from his attacks, nor, though they follow
him with cries and curses, can they ever hope to
overtake him.

'In that impregnable fortress had he imprisoned
my fair lady, while I could only gaze at it from
afar in helpless despair. Long did I wander below
the steep rock with its shining castle, which seemed
to be inaccessible to all but the birds of the air;
until some hope was given me by the arrival of two
knights, guided by a dwarf, who told me that they
were two bold warriors of great repute, Gradasso,
King of Sericania, and Ruggiero, a brave youth,
held in high esteem at the Moorish Court; and that
their purpose was to defy to battle the lord of the
castle, who, thus armed, rode in such a strange
and unheard-of fashion on this four-footed bird.

'"Ah! my lords!" said I to them, "take pity, I
beseech you, upon my hard case, and when you
are victorious, as I pray you may be, restore to me
my dear lady," and then I told them how she had
been taken from me. They made me kind promises,

for which I thanked them, as they began to mount the steep precipice; while I stood and looked on from a distance at the impending strife, and prayed to Heaven for their success. On the top of the rock before the castle there was a narrow level space, not more than two bow-shots wide. When the knights had ascended to it, there seemed to be a dispute between them as to which should first do battle; the lot fell apparently to Gradasso, for he raised his horn, and blew a blast so long and so loud that it made the fortress and its rock resound from top to bottom.

' Thereupon, I saw the armed warrior issue forth from the gateway on his winged courser, and slowly rise in the air, till he was almost lost in the clouds, far above the eagle's flight. So do southward-flying cranes flutter along the ground for a little space, then rise a foot or two above it, and as the whole flock unite, suddenly soar away on swiftly moving pinions and disappear. All at once the creature closed its wings, and plunged down to earth again, as the managed falcon swoops upon the dove, and with couched lance the warrior came whizzing through the air so swiftly that Gradasso was struck before he had time to defend himself, and his gallant war-horse fell to the ground. The flying steed again mounted even to the stars and next descended, like a shot, upon Ruggiero, while he was occupied in helping Gradasso. For a moment he staggered under the blow, and by the time he had recovered himself and was preparing to wield his weapon in return, his adversary was again high in the air above his head. Whirling round in wide and rapid circles, he aimed now at Gradasso, now at Ruggiero, while they, confused by his swift

movements, did but strike the air in vain. This un-
equal strife between the two knights on the earth
and the warrior in the air, lasted until night began
to draw its dark veil over the world. And now
happened a marvel, which I, who saw it, can hardly
credit, so much more is it like fiction than truth, and
which, therefore, I can scarcely expect you to believe.

'The aerial warrior bore on his arm a shield
covered with a veil of rich silk. This shield, on his
suddenly removing the covering, (why he did not
do so before, I cannot tell,) blazed forth like some
bright carbuncle, and so dazzled the eyes of all
beholders that they fell to the ground blinded and
senseless. Even as a dead body falls, so did I fall,
and when after a time I recovered consciousness, I
could see neither knight nor dwarf, the field was deserted, and mountain and plain were sunk in darkness. I thereupon turned my back upon that shining castle, with what despair I leave you to imagine.'

He who related this doleful story was Count
Pinabello, of the house of Manganza, who in vice
and knavery surpassed the worst among that
wicked race. The fair damsel listened to him in
silence, with a varying countenance. At the first
mention of Ruggiero joy lit up her eyes, but glad-
ness gave place to sorrow and agitation when she
heard of his disappearance. She begged the knight
to repeat to her the particulars of this strange occur-
rence, and then said: 'Sir, I pray you, be of good
cheer. Haply my arrival may be of great service,
and make this a happy day for you. Let us without delay proceed to the shining castle, and if
fortune favors me, our journey shall not be in vain.'

'Is it indeed your will,' said the Count, 'that I
should guide you over these wild mountains? For

me, indeed, having lost all I most loved, it little matters what more I risk, but I must warn you that certain captivity will be the only result that can await you. However, if it be your pleasure, I am ready to accompany you.'

So saying, he mounted his charger and led the way, followed by the brave damsel, who, in Ruggiero's service, was willing to encounter captivity and even death itself. They soon afterwards heard loud cries of ' Halt! tarry!' and the courier, who had passed Angelica and Sacripante, galloped up behind them, and informed Bradamante that Narbonne and Montpellier had raised the standard of Castile along the whole coast of the Mediterranean, and that Marseilles, finding itself without captain or governor, sent her an urgent request for help and counsel. The Emperor had given this city, with all the coast between the Var and the Rhone, to the daughter of Duke Amone, in whose valor he had perfect confidence, having often witnessed with surprise the feats of arms performed by her, when fighting under his command. Therefore the courier's errand was to ask for her instructions. The damsel was in doubt what answer to send. Duty and honor were on one side, love and inclination on the other ; but it ended in her making up her mind to continue her route, and either to release Ruggiero from the magician's castle, or to remain there a prisoner with him.

She dismissed the courier with some plausible excuse, and rode on after Pinabello, who was greatly dismayed when he found out who was his companion, and foresaw danger to himself should she discover him to be a Manganzese. Great enmity had long existed between the houses of Man-

ganza and Chiaramonte. Many battles had been
fought between them, and much blood shed on
both sides. The wicked Count began to contrive
some scheme for betraying, or, at any rate, for de-
serting the all-unsuspecting damsel, and so entirely
was he occupied with these base designs and with
his own hatred and fear of her, that he lost his way
in the dark forest. Seeing the sharp peak of a
high mountain rising above the trees before them,
he turned round and said to Bradamante :

'Were it not well, before darkness comes on, to
make our way to some hostelry where to pass the
night? If I mistake not, there lies a castle low
down in the valley on the other side of this mountain. If you will await my return, I will mount
that bare rock and ascertain if I am right in my
conjecture.'

He spurred his horse up the lonely peak, in
hopes of being able to turn aside down some by-
path and make his escape from her; instead of
which he found himself before a deep hollow or
cavern hewn out of the rock. A wide doorway at
the bottom of this hollow gave admittance into a
larger cavern, from whence issued a bright light,
as from torches burning within the mountain
grotto. While he stood looking down into the
cave, the lady came up, and he bethought himself
of a strange device for getting rid of her. Leading
her to the mouth of the cavern, he told her that
on looking down into it he had seen a fair young
maiden, whose appearance and rich vesture betok-
ened noble descent, but who seemed to be in such
sore distress that he supposed her to be detained
there against her will; and that when he was
about to enter the passage, some one had come out

from the inner chamber, and dragged her back with great violence and show of anger.

The generous Bradamante, who was as rash as she was bold, believed this story, and desired to help the maiden. Considering how to get down into the cavern, she caught sight of a long straight branch of an elm-tree above her head, and straightway cutting it off with her sword, she gave one end to the Count, while she took hold of the other, intending to let herself gently down by it. But when Pinabello felt her swinging on the pole, he gave a cruel laugh, and letting go his hold, called down after her:

'Would that all thy hated race might thus perish with thee!'

The cowardly traitor, thinking Bradamante had found her death and her grave in one, at the bottom of the pit, turned away with a pale face from the fatal spot. He mounted his horse, and adding crime to crime, he also took Bradamante's charger, and rode off quickly, soon, we trust, to meet with the punishment due to his misdeeds.

CHAPTER II.

Merlin, who knew the range of all their arts,
Was also Bard, and knew the starry heavens ;
The people called him Wizard.
                                    TENNYSON.

FORTUNATELY for Bradamante, her fate was
very different from .that intended for her by
Pinabello. The stout pole came first to the ground,
and so much lessened the shock of her fall that,
after lying for a few minutes stunned on the stone
floor of the cave, she was able to get up, and
though somewhat giddy and shaken, to pass
through the entrance into the larger hall within.
This spacious chamber was square, and seemed to
be some sacred chapel. The beautifully ornamented roof was supported by pillars of finest alabaster, and an altar stood in the centre, before
which swung a lamp, whose clear bright flame
gave light to every part of the hall. The pious
damsel finding herself in so holy a place, knelt
down and began to pray aloud, when a small door
opposite slowly creaked on its hinges, and a woman
with bare feet and long flowing hair appeared, and
saluting her by name, said :

'O noble Bradamante! by the permission of
Heaven, the shade of Merlin revealed to me that

through some strange adventure you should be led hither to visit his holy relics. Many days have gone by since I came to this sepulchre to ask Merlin to help me to unravel some mysteries which I had come upon in my studies; and because I had a great desire to see you, I have remained until now, a month longer than I intended, this being the day predicted to me for your arrival. The wizard Merlin, in his lifetime, caused this ancient and famous grotto to be hewn for his own tomb, and here his body has lain since the day he first placed himself in it; the body is indeed dead, but his spirit is permitted to hover around it, until the angels' trump summon him to bliss or woe. You shall soon hear how clearly his voice issues from the tomb, and how truly it tells of past and future events to those who consult the shade of the seer.'

The astonished Bradamante listened in attentive silence, so full of wonder that she could scarce tell whether she were awake or asleep.' Being naturally of a lowly and modest disposition, she looked up when the lady had ended, and said respectfully :

'Of what merit am I, that prophets should foretell my coming ?'

Then, pleased with the strange adventure, she followed the fairy to the spot where the spirit and body of Merlin reposed. The tomb was formed of transparent marble, the color of red flame, and whether from the natural brightness of the porphyry, or from magic and sulphurous fire, as is most likely, the rays reflected from it lit up the whole chamber, so that the beautiful and many-colored sculptures with which it was richly adorned

could be plainly distinguished. Scarcely had Bradamante crossed the threshold of the inner hall,
when a voice from the tomb thus addressed her,
and in clear tones said:

'Pure and noble maiden, fortune shall favor
thy wishes! Thy descendants who shall not be
unworthy of their ancient lineage, sprung from
Troy itself, are destined to do honor to Italy.
Dukes and emperors of great renown shall be
numbered among them. Valiant captains and wise
rulers, who shall recall the early glories of their
country, and give it cause to boast of thy sons.
Heaven has decreed that Ruggiero should be thy
chosen husband, therefore pursue thy way with
steadfast courage, and allow nothing to hinder thee
in thy purpose of releasing him from the power of
that brigand who now holds him captive.'

The damsel spent great part of the night in
conversing with Merlin about Ruggiero, and in
listening to all he foretold to her of the future
greatness of the house of Este. When the wizard
was at length silent, the fairy said to Bradamante:

'As soon as the first rays of dawn appear in the
sky, you shall take with me the most direct road
to that castle of shining steel, in which Ruggiero
is now a prisoner. I will be your guide through
the dark forest, and when we reach the sea-shore,
I will point out your path so clearly that it will not
be possible for you to go astray.'

Accordingly at early dawn she left the grotto,
and the fairy guided her along a narrow path
through the wood, which brought them out upon
the edge of a precipitous and overhanging cliff.
All that day they toiled on, up and down steep
rocks, crossing and recrossing streams and torrents

among the mountains. Pleasant discourse upon the subject nearest to Bradamante's heart beguiled the rough and weary way, while the wise fairy impressed upon her the devices through which she was to procure the release of Ruggiero.

'Were you,' said she, 'Pallas or Mars, or had you the armies of Charlemagne and Agramante in your pay, they would be of no avail against the necromancer; since, besides the steel ramparts of his lofty castle, and the winged steed, he possesses the magic shield, which he no sooner uncovers than, dazzled by its splendor, all who behold it fall petrified and dismayed to the ground. Hope not to resist it by keeping your eyes shut, for then you could neither defend yourself nor attack your adversary; but listen, and I will make known to you the only sure means of setting at nought that and other such enchantments. King Agramante possesses a ring, stolen some time ago from an Eastern princess, which renders any person who wears it on his finger proof against charms and enchantments of all kinds. He has lately intrusted it to Brunello, one of his courtiers, whose cunning and dexterity are well known to him, in order that he may, with its help, release his favorite knight Ruggiero from the magician's fortress. But do you carefully follow my instructions, that Ruggiero may have to thank you, and not the king, for his escape from that prison. For three days keep along the sands by the sea, which we shall soon discover below us, until you come to an inn: the bearer of the ring will arrive at it about the same time as yourself — a man of low stature and dark complexion, with short, black, curly hair, with dim prominent eyes and bushy eyebrows, a broad flat nose and a pale and bearded face. He wears a short and close-fitting doublet like that of a courier. You must so contrive that the conversation shall fall upon the castle, and while proclaiming your intention of trying the fortune of arms with the magician, you must take heed not to betray any knowledge of the ring. He will offer to guide you, and do you consent to accompany him, but as soon as the castle comes in sight, you must set upon him and slay him, and that so suddenly that he may have no time to put the ring into his mouth, for should he do so he would disappear, and vanish from before you in an instant.'

Thus discoursing they reached the sea-shore near Bordeaux, not far from the mouth of the Garonne, and here, not without tears, the two ladies took leave of each other. Bradamante, to lose no time in putting an end to Ruggiero's captivity, hastened on her way, and reached the hostelry; and found that Brunello had arrived there that same evening. She recognized him at once from the fairy's description, and asked him whence he came, and whither he was going. His replies were so full of falsehood and deceit that she deemed it but prudent to conceal from him her name and her family. They were engaged in a conversation, during which her eyes often glanced towards the ring on his finger, when their ears were assailed by a loud noise, the cause of which you shall hear in the next chapter.

CHAPTER III.

Saw
Fired from the West, far on a hill, the towers.
TENNYSON.

WHEN Bradamante heard this strange sound,
she cried out, 'O Holy Mother in heaven,
what may this be ?' for she saw the host and all
his servants rush, some to the windows, and some
out into the road, and look up to the sky, as if
expecting to see an eclipse or a comet. Then she
beheld a great wonder so great that if it had been
told her she could scarcely have believed it.

There came passing over head a great flying
horse, with wings wide-outspread of many varying
colors, and a man seated between them, clad in a
complete suit of armor of shining steel. He took
a straight course through the air, towards the east,
and was soon lost to sight among the mountains.
Then the host turned towards her and told her that
this was a necromancer, who often made such expeditions, scouring the country far and near, sometimes mounting up to the very stars, at others
skimming along close to the earth, carrying off any
unlucky maiden he came across, so that, for fear of
him, all the fair women in the neighborhood shut
themselves up, and scarcely ventured to cross their
door-steps.

'He possesses,' continued the host, 'a castle in the Pyrenees, built by enchantment, all of polished steel, so bright and so beautiful that I do not believe there is anything of the kind so admirable to be seen in the whole world. Many knights have gone thither, but I have never heard of one who returned from thence; therefore, sir, I much fear that they are kept there as prisoners, or that they have met with some violent end.'

As the lady listened, it rejoiced her to think that, with the help of the ring, she might be able to destroy the necromancer, and to make his castle a ruin. She told the host she would go and defy this wicked magician to battle, and begged him to procure for her a horse and a guide, and that speedily, as she could brook no delay. On hearing this, Brunello called out: 'You need no guide, for I will conduct you to this castle. I have the directions for the road carefully noted down, and I can also in other ways be of use to you in your project.'

She thought of the ring, as she replied :

'Sir, I thank you ; and your escort will be most grateful to me.'

She bought a good serviceable charger from the host to replace the one carried off by Pinabello, and the following morning, at the early dawn of a beautiful day, set out with Brunello, who sometimes led the way, and sometimes followed her along the road which lay for some distance through a narrow valley until it turned off up the mountain. They climbed by a long and steep ascent through a dense forest to a high point in the Pyrenees, from whence, on a clear day, France and Spain and the sea on either side can be plainly seen — even as from a height, on the crest of the Apennines, near Camaldoli, you can look down at the same time upon the Gulfs of Tuscany and Venice. From this point a steep and stony lane descended into a deep valley far below them, in the midst of which rose a glittering castle on a lofty and apparently inaccessible eminence ; for the rock was quite perpendicular on all sides, and no vestige of path or ladder, by which to scale it, was to be seen. Truly it was an eyry fit only for the abode of some winged creature. When Brunello caught sight of the shining towers, he exclaimed :

'Lo ! see where the magician holds captive those brave knights and fair ladies !'

Bradamante remembered the instructions of the fairy, but it seemed to her so vile and so ignoble a deed to shed the blood of a defenceless and un-suspecting man that she determined to get posses-sion of the ring without taking Brunello's life. All unawares, she attacked and soon overpowered him, and then bound him, with a stout cord, to a fir-tree. She drew the ring from his finger, and paying no heed to his cries and entreaties, she left him and slowly rode down the lane and along the valley, until she reached the foot of the precipice, when she blew a note of defiance on her horn, and sum-moned the necromancer to combat. As soon as he heard the blast and her loud menaces, he came forth from the gate of the castle mounted on his Hippogriff, ready to do battle with the young warrior.

Bradamante saw that he would not be able to do her much harm, for he had neither spear nor club, only, on his left arm, the shield veiled with crimson silk, and in his right hand a book, from which he read the spell that worked this great marvel. The horse, however, was no creature of magic, but a real animal, named Hippogriff, having the wings, beak, head, and hind feet of a griffon ; all the rest of his body being like that of a horse. A very few of these strange animals exist in the Rifean mountains beyond the frozen seas, and the magician had, by enchantments, procured him from thence; with much trouble and patience he had broken him in to the use of saddle and bridle, and had brought him so completely under control that he could direct his course through the air, or on land, whither-soever he would.

At first, according to the instructions of the fairy, Bradamante made as if about to do battle with him, wheeling round her horse and spurring him on to repeated assaults ; but, after a time, she dismounted, and the magician, thinking the moment come for his final resource, uncovered his shield, fully expecting to see her fall senseless to the ground, and become his easy prey. So did he ever dally with his victims, as the cat plays with the mouse, before she gives the final pat, and proceeds to devour it. But the lady was no timid mouse, and was well prepared for the bold part she meant to play. No sooner did the shield blaze forth than she shut her eyes, and fell prone on the ground, when, as she expected, the Hippogriff descended with rapid flight, and the magician, having re-covered the shield and hung it to his saddle-bow, dismounted, and came on foot towards her. She awaited his approach ; then she jumped up and seized him, and with the very chain which he held ready for his captives, laid him fast bound at her feet. She was on the point of lifting her sword to strike off his head, when looking down and seeing the pale wrinkled face and snow-white hair of a feeble old man, she hesitated, disdaining so poor a triumph ; whereupon he said :

'Ah, good youth ! I pray you, for Heaven's sake, put an end to this poor life.'

This, however, she refused to do, but asked him rather to tell her who he was, and to what end he had built his fortress in so wild a place, and from thence had preyed upon all the neighboring country ?

'Alas !' replied the old necromancer, 'with no evil design did I erect the beautiful castle on the summit of this rock, nor from any desire of gain have I been a robber in these lands ; but solely from my care for the safety of a gentle knight, who is very dear to me. Between this and the South Pole, the sun shines upon no youth so beautiful or so accomplished. Ruggiero is his name, and I, who am Atlante, have brought him up and educated him from infancy, cherishing him as a father does his son. The love of glory and his evil fate have brought him to France in the train of King Agramante ; and I, taught by my magic art that he is there to become a Christian and to die by treachery, have sought to withdraw him from that fatal country, and save him from the threatened danger. Therefore did I build this castle and take him captive, hoping to keep him secure within its walls ; and for his pleasure and amusement have I filled it with noble cavaliers and fair ladies, that he might pass his time so pleasantly in their company, as not to weary nor to feel the tedium of imprisonment ; for, with the exception of freedom, they have there every joy that the heart can desire — music and dancing, rich vesture and costly food, all that the world affords delightful to the eye, or pleasant to the taste; and success had crowned my efforts had you not come to destroy my work. Ah! if your gentle aspect does not belie your heart, you will surely not interfere with my innocent purpose. Take the shield, take my winged steed, but leave me in undisturbed possession of my castle; or take away one or two of your friends, or, indeed, if you will, take all, I care not for them; only leave me my Ruggiero. But, if you will not grant me this one request, then, before you take him back to France, I beseech you to pierce this weary heart, and so to end this worn and worthless life.'

The damsel replied as follows:

'Your entreaties and protestations are all in vain, for it is my firm resolve to set Ruggiero free. Little does it beseem you to offer to bestow upon me the horse and shield which are already mine; nor, were they yours to give, think that I would stoop to receive them from you. You boast to have placed Ruggiero in safety beyond the reach of fate; ah! how dimly can you divine the decrees of Heaven, or, divining them, how much less is it in your power to change them! Unable to provide against your own misfortunes, how can you pretend to change the destiny of another? Ask me not to put an end to your days (a man can do that for himself, if he so will), but understand it is my pleasure that you should yourself throw open the gates of your prison.'

The lady drove the magician before her, following close behind him, for though he appeared submissive enough, she did not much trust him. They had not gone far when they came to a cleft

.up which a narrow winding stair led
.ry gate of the castle. When they had
..ed the top, Atlante raised a stone, graven
with strange signs and unknown characters, which
lay across the threshold, and underneath it were
seen large earthen jars, whence issued thick smoke,
as if from some hidden fire. The magician broke
these to pieces, and in one second the hill was bare,
and no vestige of wall or tower was left to show that
a castle had ever stood there. At the same moment
the necromancer freed himself from his chain, as a
thrush frees himself from the net of the fowler; and
as he and the castle vanished, all his captives,
gallant cavaliers and fair ladies, found themselves
free, transferred from their magnificent apartments
to the bare hill-side — rather to the regret indeed
of some, to whom liberty was a poor, exchange for
the pleasures of luxury.

Ruggiero was among the company, and when
he recognized Bradamante, he ran towards her with
joyous welcome, as to one whom he had loved,
since the day he had first seen her, better than life
itself. It would take long to relate how perse-
veringly he had sought her, through how many wild
woods and deserts he had passed, without gaining
any tidings of her; now, when he at last saw her,
and learnt that he owed his release from captivity
to her efforts alone, his heart so overflowed with
joy and gratitude, that he deemed himself the
happiest and most fortunate of men.

When they reached the bottom of the rock,
they found the Hippogriff in the valley below, with
the shield, which was now covered, hanging to his
saddle. The lady went up to him in order to
take hold of his bridle, and he let her come quite

close, but then spread his wings, and after hovering for a little in the clear air, alighted on the ground a few paces off. The lady followed him, but again he rose a little above the earth, and again descended at a short distance from her; so the plover often leads the fowler's dog a fruitless and tantalizing chase over the dry sands. Ruggiero, Gradasso, Sacripante, and all the knights who had come down the hill together, joined in pursuit of the flying creature. After having led some to the highest points of the rock, and others into the low swampy ground below, he at last stood perfectly still by Ruggiero, and allowed him to seize his rein. The old magician was the cause of this, for still intent upon withdrawing his favorite from the dangers which threatened him, he sent the Hippogriff to carry him away safe out of Europe. Ruggiero tried to lead him on, but finding that he refused to move, the brave knight leapt down from his own horse, Frontino, and vaulted upon the flying steed. The fiery animal, excited by the touch of the spur, galloped on for some distance, and then, leaping up into the air, soared away to the skies, more swiftly than the managed falcon, when the keeper removes its hood, and it catches sight of its prey.

The beautiful lady, when she saw Ruggiero in such great peril so high above her, stood motionless with amazement. The story of Ganymede came into her mind, and how he had been carried off from his father's home to be made cup-bearer to the gods, and much she feared lest some like fate should befall her beloved knight. Her uplifted eyes followed him until he was quite lost to sight, and then for a time she gave way to grief with sighs and many tears. Determined, however, not to abandon herself to despair, she turned to the good charger Frontino, and taking hold of his bridle, led him away, in the hope of some day being able to restore him to his master.

CHAPTER IV.

Oh follow her not, Oh follow her not,
Though she lure thee with smile and song,
Fair is her cheek, but her heart is black,
And the poison of Death's on her tongue.
OLD SONG.

THE bird-like creature continued to ascend, and vain were all Ruggiero's endeavors to restrain him. One peak after another disappeared beneath him, until he could no longer distinguish where the plains ended, and the mountains began. When he had mounted so high that he appeared but as a tiny speck to those watching him from below, he found himself taking a straight course towards the setting sun, gliding swiftly through the air like a bark before the favoring breeze. In spite of the stout courage, to which his unchanging cheek bore witness, I cannot believe but that his heart trembled as a leaf within him.

Europe had been left behind, and they had long passed the Pillars which the great Hercules placed as the utmost limit of navigation, when the huge four-footed bird, whose flight was fleeter than an arrow, more rapid than the thunderbolts of Jupiter, began gradually to descend, and at length alighted on an island, which reminded Ruggiero of the de-

scriptions of that far-famed spot where the nymph
Arethusa disappeared under the earth, to take her
unseen and secret course below the sea.

In all the wide world, no more sweet and lovely
scene could have been found. Clear streams flowed
between shady banks and soft pastures, through a
richly cultivated plain bounded by low hills, where
groves of laurels and palms, fragrant myrtles and
lofty cedars, and of orange-trees covered with snowy
blossom and golden fruit, offered shelter under
their deep shade, from the sultry heat of summer.
Nightingales fluttered among their branches, and
sang in joyous flight. Hares and rabbits scam-
pered fearlessly among the red roses and white
lilies, and antlered stags, with no dread of the hunter's pursuit, roamed at will in the green glades.
As soon as the Hippogriff was within reach of the
ground, Ruggiero leapt hastily down from the saddle, taking care, however, to keep firm hold of the
rein, for fear the creature should mount up again.
He fastened him securely to a myrtle-bush on the
sea-shore ; and then, laying down his buckler by
the side of a fountain, which gushed forth close by,
and taking off his helmet and gauntlets, he turned
his face, now to the sea, and now to the hills to
enjoy the sweet fresh air which murmured softly
among the high branches of the pines and beeches
by which he was surrounded. He refreshed his
parched lips and bathed his hot hands in the clear
cold water, for he was tired and heated with the
weight of his armor, and not without cause, for
this had been no holiday parade, but a journey of
more than three thousand miles, at lightning speed,
and in complete harness.

Whilst he was standing thus, the Hippogriff,

alarmed by some moving shadow in the thicket, suddenly tried to break loose, shaking the myrtle to which he was fastened so violently that its leaves fell thickly down about his feet.

As when a log of hollow wood is put on the fire, the air within, expanded by the heat, hisses and whizzes, until it forces for itself an outlet, so the myrtle shrilly piped and whistled, until a high and doleful voice burst, as it were, the riven bark, and clearly and distinctly uttered the following sentences:

'If thou be as pitiful and courteous as thy fair countenance would lead me to suppose, I implore thee to let loose this animal from my boughs. The sufferings I endure from my own griefs may surely suffice me without additional injury and indignity from without.'

At the first sound of this voice, Ruggiero turned quickly round, and perceiving that it came from the shrub, he stood, for a moment, petrified with amazement, and then ran hastily to unfasten the steed, while, his cheek crimsoning with remorse, he exclaimed:

'Whoever thou mayest be, mortal spirit or some goddess of the wood, I pray thee, pardon me, and to my ignorance that a human spirit could be concealed within this rough bark alone ascribe it, that I have dared to harm thy fair leaves, or to molest thy fragrant branches. Hasten to tell me who it is thus speaking with the voice of a reasonable soul, from beneath so rude a covering. So may the hail from heaven ever spare thee; and if now, or at any time, I can offer thee amends for this all unintentional indignity, I promise, by the fair lady to whom my heart is devoted, that by word and deed I will so act as to give thee reason to be grateful.'

The myrtle trembled all over, and then began : 'Your courtesy constrains me to tell you my name, and who it was that turned me into a myrtle on this pleasant shore. I was Astolfo, a Paladin of France, well accounted of in war, and cousin to Rinaldo and to Orlando of world-wide renown. Heir, after my father Ottone, to the kingdom of England, I lived with the nobles and ladies of the court, and was a favorite among them. Returning with Rinaldo and other knights from those far-off Eastern Isles watered by the Indian Ocean, where we had been kept in captivity until released by the valor of Orlando, we had crossed the sandy deserts which are swept by the north winds, when one morning our road brought us out on that beautiful part of the coast where the castle of the great fairy Alcina, overlooking the ocean, is situated. There, on the sands below the castle, stood the fairy. No net had she in her hands, nor any bait, but simply by the charm of the spell she uttered was she calling up to her feet all the fishes of the sea. The dolphins, with the great tunny open-mouthed, came bounding swiftly in ; the John Dory, and other ancient sea-tribes, roused from their tardy sleep, with shoals of stockfish and salmon hurried along ; while further out the dark fins of great whales, orcas, sea-lions, and such marine monsters were seen moving through the waters. One huge whale, at least a furlong in length, lay along the surface of the sea close to the shore, so still and motionless that we all fell into the self-same error, and supposed it to be some small islet moored there. As we approached, Alcina looked up, and I imagine something about me must have struck her fancy, for she at once prepared with cunning artifice to allure me from my companions; and succeeded, alas! but too well in her design. Coming towards us smiling, with gracious and kindly greeting, she said :

' " My lords, if it please you to take up your abode with me for this day, I will show you a great variety of strange and curious fishes — some covered with scales, others with fur, and some quite smooth ; and if you will with me pass over to those sands opposite," and she pointed to the monstrous whale, which we supposed to be an island, "you shall see a siren, whose custom it is to resort thither at this hour; and who can, with her sweet song, calm the stormy waves."

' I, who have always been too venturesome (much do I now repent me thereof), in spite of warning signs from Rinaldo and Dudone, stepped over upon those seeming sands, and Alcina, with a gay laugh, jumping after me, the whale, obedient to her signal, swam away over the salt billows. Too late I saw my folly, for in one second we were far out of reach of land. Rinaldo, indeed, plunged into the sea to swim off to my help, but I fear me with much peril to himself, for a sudden squall covered sky and ocean with a thick black cloud, and to this hour I know not what became of him. The fairy kept me all that day and night floating over the sea on the back of the monster, and then brought me to this beautiful island, the greater part of which she possesses. She has indeed usurped it from her sister Logistilla, who is as virtuous as she is wicked, and who was her father's rightful heir, but Alcina rebelled against her, and after having fought and won many battles, she took from her these rich plains with more than a hundred castles. She would have driven Logistilla out of the island altogether, had not her territory been defended by a gulf and a high mountain, just as a river and a mountain chain divide England from Scotland.

'For a long time I was in great favor with this fairy queen ; she made me one of her most trusted councillors of state, and put me at the head of all her armies. No office was too high, no favor too great for me ; and I lived in such splendor and luxury that I thought no more of my country, and regretted neither France nor my family and friends. But alas ! why do I recall past enjoyment in the midst of present misery ? After I had spent about two months at her court, Alcina suddenly chose a new favorite, and I fell into as great disgrace as I had before been held in high esteem. She dismissed me with contempt, a fate which I found out had befallen many before me. In order that her discarded favorites should not go through the world relating her misdeeds, it was her custom to transform some into pines, cedars, olive-trees, or (as myself) into myrtles, scattered over this fair island ; while others are turned into fountains or animals, according to the humor of that proud and capricious fairy.

'And, now, sir, since you have alighted upon this fatal shore after so strange a fashion, haply for your sake some poor wretch may be changed into stone, fountain, or tree. Alcina for a time will bestow upon you power and riches, and will place you above all others at her court, but, believe me, your turn will surely come, and you will be changed into tree or stream, beast or rock. I am glad to give you this warning, though I fear it be of little use; yet it is well that you should know what you are about to encounter. All are not alike, and perhaps you may resist successfully where so many have ingloriously fallen.'

Ruggiero, who knew that Astolfo was cousin to his lady-love, grieved much over his fate, and had he known how would, for her sake, have gladly helped him. As it was, he could only try to comfort him with consoling words. Having done his best in this way, he asked him to direct him to Logistilla's kingdom, either by the plain or over the mountain, but so as not to pass through Alcina's dominions.

There was a path, the myrtle said, but a terribly rough one; it turned off to the right up a steep ascent, which would lead him over the highest pass in the mountains. Even up that road he must not expect to climb unmolested. Alcina kept upon it, instead of walls and ramparts, a great troop of bold and savage people who drove back all who tried to escape from her wiles. Ruggiero thanked the myrtle for all these instructions and kind advice, and then said farewell. He unloosed his steed and led him by the bridle, not caring to mount him, for fear of being again carried up into the air against his will. He walked on, meditating how he should best manage to take refuge with Logistilla, and quite determined to dare everything rather than fall under the empire of Alcina. 'At all events,' said he to himself, 'I will force my way through, or perish in the attempt.' Alas! this good resolve was all in vain.

He had gone for about two miles along the coast when the beautiful city of Alcina came in

7

sight. It was surrounded by a wall, which enclosed a great space of country, and was so high
that it seemed almost to touch the skies. To
Ruggiero it appeared to be of shining gold, but
some say that it was only made to imitate gold by
the art of the alchemist. When he drew near
those resplendent walls, he left the wide straight
road which led across the plain to their gates, and
turned aside up the narrow but safer mountain
path and soon after came upon the monstrous
rabble stationed there to dispute his further progress. Never was seen so strange a crowd of mis-
shapen beings. Some had cats' or apes' heads on
human bodies, some goats' feet, others were like
centaurs. Bold youths and imbecile old men were
among them. Many were half naked, while others
were wrapped in furs and skins of strange animals.
Some galloped on bridleless horses, others paced
slowly on asses, or oxen, or were mounted on centaurs, or rode astride on eagles or cranes. Some
were blowing horns, some were drinking; others
carried hooks or scaling ladders, iron shovels or
files. The leader of this wild horde was a great
fat man, seated on a slow-moving tortoise. He
was so unwieldy that, incapable of holding himself upright, he was supported by an attendant on
either side, while two others wiped his brow and
fanned his heated face.

As Ruggiero appeared, a creature, in the form
of a man with a dog's head, sprang forward howling and yelling, to make him turn back to the
beautiful city which he had left behind him. 'But
that,' said the bold warrior, 'will I not do, while I
have strength to wield this weapon,' and pointing
his sword at the monster, he ran him through the

body, and holding up his buckler, attacked the
rest of the rabble-rout with great fury. He cut
down a great many, for they were defended by
no armor; neither helmet nor shield, coat of
mail, nor cuirass. Yet as fast as he destroyed one,
another came on in his place, and he had needed
as many arms as Briareus to make his way through
them. If it had only occurred to him to uncover
the necromancer's shield which hung at his saddle-
bow, he might quickly have rid himself of the
hideous crew; but, maybe, he despised such means,
preferring to conquer by his own valor rather than
by charm and artifice, and fully resolved to die
rather than give in to so vile a rabble.

Just then there came forth from the gates of the
city two young ladies, apparently of high rank, for
they were dressed with great magnificence, and
were seated on a unicorn as white as any ermine;
they were of such rare grace and loveliness that
they might have been called Beauty and Delight.
As soon as they appeared, the hideous crowd made
way for them, and they took the knight by the
hand, who colored as he thanked them for their
kindly aid, and readily consented to return with
them to the golden gate. The gate was studded
with Indian gems and precious stones, and the
portal, which covered it, was supported on four
columns of purest crystal. When Ruggiero passed
through this magnificent gateway, it seemed to him
that he had entered an earthly Paradise, where no
anxious thoughts, no weary cares, could ever find
a place; where sweet April with smooth and
joyous brow ever smiled; where all were young,
and all were happy.

In whatever direction he turned his eyes, he

saw gay groups of people dancing under the shade of forest trees, or sitting around sparkling fountains listening to soft strains of music, or strolling through bright gardens engaged in lively conversation, or joining in some merry pastime. A noble charger, richly caparisoned with housings embroidered in gold and precious stones, was brought out to him, and mounting it, he gave the old magician's winged steed to the care of a groom, to be led after him.

Then the two ladies addressed him, saying:

'Noble knight! the fame of your gallant deeds, which has reached us, emboldens us to ask your aid against a giantess, called Erifilla. We shall soon come to a ravine, which divides the plain into two parts, and this witch, with her long teeth and poisonous breath and sharp talons, defends the bridge, robbing and wounding all who try to pass over to the other side. Besides disputing this passage, which would otherwise be free to us, she often makes incursions into our gardens, and disturbs and molests us in our games and pastimes. Many of those brigands who attacked you outside the golden gate are her sons, as rapacious and impious as herself.'

'Gladly will I fight for you in one or a hundred battles,' replied Ruggiero. 'Believe me, I do not wear this mail or wield these weapons for my own advantage, or to gain lands or riches, but to defend the oppressed, to redress the wrongs of the unfortunate, and more especially to serve such fair ladies as yourselves.'

Thus conversing they reached the bridge, over which they found the haughty Erifilla keeping guard.

CHAPTER V.

HOW RUGGIERO ESCAPES FROM ALCINA'S WICKED CITY OF PLEASURE.

> Some call her Pleasure, and some call her Sin,
>   Some call her a lady gay,
> For her step is light, and her eye is bright,
>   And she carols this blithesome lay :
> 'Oh come to the bower where care is forgot.'
> But follow her not.   Oh follow her not !
> OLD SONG.

THOSE who travel in foreign parts see many things new and strange, and when they return home and tell of them, it is with difficulty they persuade people to believe them ; for the silly multitude only credit that which they can themselves touch and see.   I foresee, therefore, that I shall find few to lend faith to the wonders I am about to relate.   Some however among my readers will, I hope, be wise and learned enough to understand me.

The witch was clad in armor of fine steel, inlaid with gold, in which were set many glittering gems — crimson rubies, green emeralds, yellow chrysolites, and amber jacinths.   Her saddle was as richly ornamented as her armor, and she rode upon an enormous wolf, which stood as high as an ox ; in all Apulia none could have been found so large. As she had neither bit nor bridle, I cannot tell how she guided it.   A mantle, such as bishops wear at court, of a dull gray color, hung from her shoulders, and for crest, on shield and helmet, she bore a venomous toad.

On seeing Ruggiero, she called out to him to turn back, and putting her lance in rest, she spurred her wolf upon him, making the ground tremble beneath her. The bold knight grasped his spear, and uttering his loud war-cry, ran full-tilt at her, striking her helmet with such force that he hurled her six cubits' length from her saddle. He drew his sword, and as she lay senseless on the flower-spangled grass he was about to cut off her head, when the ladies cried out:

'Stay, gentle knight! be content with having overcome her. Take no base vengeance, but sheathe your sword, and let us go on our way.'

A narrow path led through the wood up a steep ascent, at the top of which they came out upon a wide park, and saw before them the finest and most beautiful palace in the whole world. The fairy Alcina, surrounded by all her court, stood before the great entrance, and advanced some few paces to welcome Ruggiero, who, had he fallen from the skies, could not have been received with greater deference and respect by the assembled courtiers — gallant lords and fair ladies — all, however, surpassed in beauty by their queen, who shone among them as the sun among the stars. Her golden hair fell in long thick curls around her lovely face; her dark eyes sparkled like stars beneath their black and delicately-arched eyebrows; and two rows of small teeth, white as pearls, were disclosed by the sweet smiles, which parted her rosy lips.

When Ruggiero saw her, and marked the gentle courtesy of her greeting, he only remembered the

warning of Astolfo to set it at naught; he refused
to believe that this noble-looking queen could have
done wrong, and felt sure that base ingratitude and
dishonorable conduct on the knight's own part
had brought down its just punishment upon him.
Let us not judge too harshly the folly of brave
Ruggiero, for the spells of the fairy Alcina had
blotted out all earlier impressions from his heart,
and now occupied it entirely with the present moment, and with herself.

The queen invited him to a great banquet in
the palace for that evening. Soft strains of music
from cither and harp, alternating with song and
chorus, accompanied the feast. At night the great
saloons were brilliantly illuminated with innumerable tapers, and various games and amusements
were provided for the diversion of the company.
On the next and following days, jousts and tournaments were held in Ruggiero's honor. These were
succeeded by large hawking and hunting parties,
when they drove out the pheasants from the coverts
and stubble-fields, or chased the timid hare over
hill and dale with fleet hounds. The evenings
were spent in feasting and dancing, the acting of
light comedies, and festivities of every description,
and week succeeded week in ever new diversions.

While Ruggiero gave himself up to this inglorious life in the City of Pleasure, Charlemagne and
Agramante were living 'laborious days,' and Bradamante was toiling through the world in search of
her absent knight. Many long weary days she
passed in wandering over mountains and valleys,
through dense forests and wide plains, in cities and
villages, but nowhere could she hear tidings of him.
As she still possessed the ring she had taken from

Brunello, which, when held in her mouth, rendered her invisible, she was able to pass unimpeded from one hostelry to another, and from camp to camp, pursuing her search through the pavilions of the captains and the tents of the soldiers; but all without success. Sometimes the poor damsel would give herself up to despair, and weep and lament for him as dead; then she would comfort herself with the assurance that the death of so renowned a knight could not have remained hid, but must have been made known throughout the world, from the Hydaspian wave to the isle nearest the setting sun.

At last, she bethought herself of returning to the cave where Merlin lay in the marble tomb, and of entreating the spirit of the great wizard to take pity upon her, and to tell her where Ruggiero was, if alive, and if not, where and how he had met with death; at the same time asking his advice as to what she should do. With this intention, she took the road to Poictiers, in a wild forest near which place the tomb lay.

However, the good fairy Melissa, who had given her such wise counsel, and who had been so kind to her in the wizard's cave, had not forgotten or lost sight of her all this time; but had watched over her and knew how she had released Ruggiero, and had so soon lost him again; and how he had been carried off to India in that long and perilous flight through the air by his ungovernable steed. She also knew that he was now in the City of Pleasure, giving himself wholly up to amusement, and forgetting his duty to his king, his lady, and his good name. And there that gallant knight might have wasted the best years of his life in idleness, and have at last lost both body and soul, and that

fair fame which keeps the memory of a good man
bright long after his body has mouldered in the
dust; had not the wise and beneficent fairy taken
more care for him than he did for himself, and had
she not been determined in his own despite to recall
him to the path of virtue, however rude and rough
that path might be — like the good physician, who,
with his hot iron sears, or with his sharp knife
probes, the ugly wound, and is, after the momentary
agony, thanked by the grateful patient.

The kind fairy, knowing that Bradamante was
seeking her, went straight to meet her; and as
soon as the damsel saw her, sorrow turned to hope.
But when Melissa told her that Ruggiero was at
the court of Alcina, and she heard that her lover
was so far away and so forgetful of her, her heart
sank within her, and she turned as pale as death;
the fairy, however, comforted her, quickly healing
the wound she had made by promising that ere
long her knight should be restored to her.

'Since, fair lady,' said she, 'you have with you
the ring which is of such sovereign power against
enchantments, I have no doubt but that with its
help I shall be able to break all Alcina's spells, and
bring you back your beloved knight. I will set
off this same evening, and shall be in India before
the day dawns.'

Bradamante drew the ring from her finger, and
gave it to the fairy; gladly would her heart and
her life have gone with it could they have helped
Ruggiero; but she sent him many messages, and
after recommending him to Melissa's kind care,
she left her and took the road to Provence. The
fairy went in the other direction, summoning up
for her use a palfrey, which, with the exception of

one chestnut foot, was all jet-black. I believe it to have been some dusky night-flying moth, that she thus transformed by her art. Mounted on this, with bare feet, and unbound girdle, her loose hair streaming in the wind, she rode all night with such speed that early next morning she found herself in Alcina's isle.

Here she took the form of a tall old man, with white hair and flowing beard, at the same time imitating so exactly the voice and manner of Atlante, that any one would have taken her for the old magician. She came upon Ruggiero, fortunately quite alone, as enjoying the fresh morning air, he reclined by the side of a beautiful stream, which flowing down from the hills, formed a calm and limpid lake at their feet. He was clad in loose flowing silk garments, embroidered by the fair hands of the fairy queen. A splendid collar with a pendant of precious stones hung from his neck, and round each muscular arm was wound a golden bracelet. His ears were pierced with gold rings, from which depended large Arabian pearls, and his curled and perfumed hair fell low upon his shoulders.

Melissa, in the venerable likeness of Atlante, came towards him with the grave and severe aspect which from a child he had been accustomed to revere, and said :

'O degenerate youth ! is this the fruit of all my toil ? Was it for this that I accustomed you from infancy to strangle serpents, to track the panther and the tiger to their lair, to spear the wild boar, and to hunt the savage bear and the African lion ? That you should become the effeminate courtier of an Alcina ? Was it for this that I nightly watched

the constellations in the heavens ? Did the au-
guries, the dreams, all the forbidden arts I have
studied but too persistently, point to this, when
they foretold that your youth should be passed in
deeds of arms so glorious that the wide world should
ring with their fame ? I dreamed you were to
rival an Alexander, a Julius, a Scipio, and little
thought to see you the minion of an Alcina ; displaying on your breast and arms the badges of your
slavery. But that you may learn the real nature
of this fairy queen, take this ring, look at her, and
judge for yourself.'

Silent and abashed, with eyes cast upon the
ground, Ruggiero suffered Melissa to place the ring
upon his little finger ; then in one moment he saw
what he had become, and was so filled with scorn
of himself that he would have been glad to hide
from the sight of all men, a thousand feet below
the earth. The fairy, who had now reassumed her
own shape, told him why she had come, and whose
tender love had bidden her give him the ring, that
it might free him from the chains of enchantment,
which bound him so fast. She gave him Bradamante's affectionate messages, and much praised
her virtue and constancy, doing her errand so dis-
creetly that Ruggiero was now prepared to hate
Alcina as much as he had before admired her.

When he next beheld her, and by virtue of the
ring saw through all her artifices, instead of a
youthful and beautiful queen, she seemed to him a
veritable old hag, with false hair and teeth, and
painted face. He looked upon her with abhorrence, and was only too anxious to leave her court ;
but for fear of being found out and detained he
set about doing so with great caution and secrecy.

He first brought out his long disused and neglected armor; having put it on he girt his good sword Balisarda by his side, and hung the magic shield, in its silken cover, to his neck. Then he went to the stables and chose, by the advice of Melissa, a coal-black charger of great swiftness, called Rabican, which had formerly belonged to that knight, who now the sport of the winds on the sea-shore, had been brought to the island on the great whale. He might have taken the Hippogriff, who was in the next stall, but Melissa advised him not to do so, promising that he should be sent after him in a day or two, when he might have leisure and an opportunity of learning how to guide and restrain him in his aerial flights: she added that, by leaving him, less suspicion would arise of the escape which he meditated.

Ruggiero obeyed the directions of his prudent counsellor, and bidding her farewell, took his departure with great secrecy from the luxurious city of the wicked fairy queen by the gate which opened upon the road leading to Logistilla's dominions. Sword in hand, he attacked the warders so suddenly that unharmed he made his way through them, leaving one dead and the others wounded, and was far on his way before his departure was suspected by Alcina. What happened to him on his journey you shall hear in the next chapter.

CHAPTER VI.

Soon sobered, when slunk from the flames
That enveloped her navies — one ship.
BULWER'S HORACE.

FORTUNATE Ruggiero! to be in possession of
Angelica's ring, which enabled him to discover and escape from all the wiles of the wicked
Alcina : still more fortunate are those who carry
about with them the shining lamp of Truth, with
which they can dispel the mists of falsehood and
error surrounding them in this naughty world,
and escape into the serene daylight beyond.

Ruggiero, having crossed the drawbridge and
burst open the portcullis, took the path through
the wood, but had not gone far before he met a
falconer, one of the queen's servants, who held a
hawk on his wrist, which he had been flying near
a pool in the plain outside the town. He was
mounted on a sorry-looking nag, and his dog ran
beside him. As soon as he saw Ruggiero riding
away from the gates at such full speed, he guessed
that he was making his escape ; so he went up to
him and boldly asked the cause of such great
haste. Ruggiero made no answer, which, convincing the falconer that he was flying from the city,
he determined to arrest his progress. Stretching
out his left hand, he cried :

'I charge thee, halt! and know that against this bird thou canst not defend thyself.'

Thereupon, letting go the hawk, which flew in front of Rabican, and throwing down his rein, he leapt from his horse, which bounded forth as an arrow shot from the bow, and ran after Ruggiero, his dog joining in the pursuit, as a leopard in chase of a hare. The knight turned upon them, and seeing only a slight cane in the man's hand, he at first scorned to use his sword. But the falconer struck him, the dog bit his foot, the nag kicked him, and the hawk flew in circles round him, wounding him, and so terrifying his charger with its cries that he refused to obey either spur or rein. At last Ruggiero drew his sword, but he could neither reach them, nor induce Rabican to face them; so foreseeing danger and disgrace if he allowed them to delay him any longer, for he knew that Alcina and all her people would soon be upon him, and, indeed, already heard behind him the sound of drums and trumpets and the ringing of alarm-bells in all directions, he thought best to make short work of it, and to uncover Atlante's shield. No sooner did he draw aside the crimson silk, than the well-known scene took place. The falconer and his dog, the nag and the hawk, all lay motionless on the ground : and Ruggiero, leaving them to their slumbers, joyfully hurried on.

By this time, Alcina had discovered his flight. At first she was absorbed with grief and lamentations over her own heedlessness in not having kept better watch ; but she soon roused herself, and with great fury gave orders to collect all her people. She divided them into two armies, and sending one by land in pursuit of Ruggiero, she

led the other down to the port, and embarked it on
board her ships.   As they sailed out of the harbor
the whole strait appeared to be covered with their
wide-spread sails.   With these went the distracted
queen, so intent upon recapturing her favorite, that
she left the city utterly defenceless.   Not even a
guard remained at the palace, which enabled the
good fairy Melissa to go at her leisure through the
city, and release all the poor wretches whom she
found confined there, under various spells and
charms ; as well as to burn the images, and break
open the locks and seals, and to destroy the wands,
and circles, and other instruments of magic she
met with.

From thence she went out into the country,
restoring to their proper shapes the poor discarded
courtiers, who had been transformed into fountains,
trees, or beasts.   These all followed Ruggiero and
took refuge with Logistilla, returning after a time
to their native countries — such as Scythia, India,
Persia, or Greece.   Chief among them was the
English Duke Astolfo, whom Ruggiero had urgently recommended to Melissa's good offices, telling her of his relationship to Bradamante.   When
the fairy had restored him to his own form, she
sought to recover his armor, more especially the
famous golden lance that overthrew all it touched,
which had formerly belonged to Argalia before it
came into Astolfo's hands, and had done to both
these knights glorious service in France.   She
found it and the armor, hidden away in the palace,
and gave them to Astolfo ; then, taking him up
behind her, on the necromancer's winged steed, she
brought him in safety to Logistilla's court, just an
hour before Ruggiero arrived there.

He, meanwhile, was making his way over rough stones, through thorny briers, along giddy precipices, and by paths, one more wild, and steep, and solitary than another. At last, after great labor, he came out at burning noonday upon a parched and sterile plain, lying between the mountains and the sea, and open to the south. The blazing sun beat full upon the bare rocks, and the heat reflected from them might almost have melted glass. The birds cowered in silence in the patches of scanty shade, while the cicada, among the withered reeds and grass, deafened the hills and the plain, the sky and the sea, with its weary chirp.

When Ruggiero had journeyed for some distance along this barren plain, with heat, thirst, and fatigue for his wearisome companions, exposed to the fierce rays of the sun, which seemed to make the fine white sand to boil beneath his feet, and his very armor to glow like fire, he came upon three ladies, reposing under the shadow of a ruined tower close by the edge of the sea, whom, by their dress and appearance, he at once recognized as belonging to Alcina's court. Seated on rich Alexandrian carpets, they were enjoying the refreshing shade, and goblets of various kinds of wine, with dishes of sweet confections and delicious fruits were spread before them. Their little skiff was moored close by, gently rocking on the waves; not a breath of air was stirring, and they were waiting for the breeze to spring up. When they saw Ruggiero coming towards them on the straight road along the arid sands, thirst and fatigue depicted in his parched lips and streaming face, they called out to him to give up for a time his arduous journey, to

come and rest with them in the cool, sweet shade,
and to restore his wearied frame by partaking of
their refreshments. One stepped forward to hold
his stirrup that he might dismount, while another
handed him a crystal cup full of foaming wine, the
sight of which served only to increase his thirst.
He however paid no heed to their invitation, for
he knew that any delay would give Alcina, who
was not far behind, time to overtake him. Salt-
petre and sulphur do not blaze up more fiercely at
touch of fire, nor does the ocean, when the dark
tempest descends upon it, rage more furiously, than
did the third lady, when she saw Ruggiero dis-
regard their attractions and hold on his straight
way.

'Churlish knave!' she screamed after him.
'You are not worthy to be called either knight or
noble; your charger is stolen, and your arms are
none of yours. Would that I could see you pun-
ished as you deserve; burned, quartered, or impaled
alive! Vile thief! proud, ungrateful villain!'

He made no answer to the abuse the indignant
lady hurled at him, deeming such contention beneath him, whereupon she got into the boat with
the other two ladies, and rowing along the shore,
continued to scream out curses and imprecations
after him as long as she kept him in sight.

After a time Ruggiero came to a narrow inlet of
the sea, and saw a pilot put off his boat from the
opposite side, as if he had been stationed there on
purpose to look out for his arrival. When he was
come across, he, with a smiling and kindly countenance, invited the knight into his boat, and offered
to carry him over to that safe and joyful shore.
Ruggiero, devoutly thanking God, stepped on board,

and as they glided over the smooth waves, he entered into profitable conversation with the venerable pilot, who praised him for having withdrawn himself in time from Alcina's court, before she had given him the magic potion which had proved so fatal to all her former favorites; and also for having betaken himself to the city of Logistilla, where he would find virtue, true courtesy, eternal beauty, and infinite grace to nourish and support the soul in the path of duty.

'This wise queen,' said he, 'will at once inspire you with wonder and veneration, and the longer you contemplate her divine beauty, the more will you learn to esteem it above all other. While earthly love consumes the heart with as much fear as hope, that which she inspires will give you the fulness of perfect content. She will bestow upon you more profitable pleasures than songs and dancing, feasting or fine clothing: she will teach your thoughts to soar aloft as on the wings of an eagle, and make you taste on earth some of the joys of the blessed.'

While thus discoursing, the old mariner was steering straight towards that happy shore, when happening to look back he saw the sea covered with galleys, in evident pursuit of him. At their head was the infuriated Alcina, so determined to recapture the fugitive, that she had put her kingdom in jeopardy rather than tamely submit to be set at defiance by him. She urged her fleet to such speed that the flashing oars covered the banks on either side with foam, and made the hills re-echo with their measured beat.

'Uncover the shield, O Ruggiero!' exclaimed the boatman hastily; 'you risk death or capture.'

Without waiting for reply, he himself drew aside
the silk, and the dazzling light shone forth. Blinded
by the magic blaze, their enemies fell from poop
and prow, helpless and prone, upon the decks of
their ship; meanwhile, the watchman from the
tower on the top of the rock had seen the approach
of the hostile fleet and had rung the alarm-bell,
which soon brought help to Ruggiero. Logistilla
sent four of her ladies, the brave Andronica, the
prudent Fronesia, the just Dicilla, and the modest
Sofronesia, at the head of a great army, which descending from the citadel, spread along the shore,
and directed the thunder of its artillery on the enemy. In the tranquil harbor below the castle a
fleet of large vessels was always kept ready to put
to sea at the first stroke of the bell; it now sailed
out, and a fierce battle took place, in which Alcina
was completely routed, and was deprived of the
kingdom that she had usurped. How often is the
issue of a battle other than that looked for! So far
from Alcina succeeding in recapturing the fugitive
knight, she alone with one small bark, escaped
from the flames which destroyed her ships, while
her unfortunate army was burnt or taken captive,
drowned or cut to pieces. The wretched Alcina
wandered over the earth, lamenting her miserable
fate, and envying the sword of Dido or the poison
of the Egyptian queen; but alas! a fairy can never
hope to end her sorrows by death.

As soon as Ruggiero set foot upon the hard sand,
he thanked God for having brought his enterprise
to a successful termination; and turning his back
on the sea, he hastened along the path which led
up to the citadel. Mortal eyes have never beheld
anything more beautiful than those shining and

enduring ramparts. The stones of which they are built are far more precious than diamond or carbuncle. Unknown in other lands, those who would see them must go thither, for, except in Heaven, nowhere else are they to be found. More pure and transparent than all earthly gems, a man can see his inmost soul therein reflected, his virtues and his vices so plainly mirrored that henceforth he is indifferent alike to flattery or to blame. Beholding himself in those shining mirrors, self-knowledge teaches him wisdom; and their bright light sheds such splendor that he who has it needs thine, O Phœbus! no more, but makes day unto himself. The structure of those walls is as rare and excellent as the stones of which they are built. Upon the top of the high ramparts are broad and beautiful gardens. Sweet-scented trees and shrubs, covered all the year round with lovely flowers and delicious fruits, bloom among the glittering battlements. Plants like unto these are not seen out of these exquisite gardens; no such roses or lilies, no such violets, jasmines, or amaranths. Elsewhere flowers bloom, and fade, and die, drooping from their widowed stems; but here, the verdure never fades, the blossom never withers; under Logistilla's fostering care spring immortal reigns.

The good queen expressed pleasure at the arrival of the noble knight, and commanded every honor and attention to be shown him. Astolfo was already there to welcome him, and the other knights, whom Melissa had freed, soon joined them. After two or three days' repose, Ruggiero and Astolfo came before the queen, Melissa at the same time interceding in their behalf, and humbly besought her to allow, and also to help them, to make their way back to Europe. The queen replied that she would take two days to think over the matter, and would then send them away. She determined to despatch Ruggiero upon the flying steed, but first ordered a proper bit to be made, and taught the knight so to manage him that he was able to guide him in the air, to make him go gently, to stop, ascend or descend, just as easily as he could ride a horse upon the ground. When he found himself thus at home upon his winged courser, he took a grateful farewell of the fairy queen, for whom he ever afterwards retained the highest esteem, and departed.

CHAPTER VII

RUGGIERO PASSES OVER MANY COUNTRIES AND VISITS ENGLAND.

> My genius spreads her wing,
> And flies where Britain courts the western spring.
> . . . . . .
> Pride in their port, defiance in their eye,
> I see the lords of human kind pass by.
> GOLDSMITH.

RUGGIERO, like the Magi when they wished to avoid Herod, took a different course from that by which the Hippogriff had brought him over the Indian ocean. He now passed over Cathay, China and Margiana, above the mountain chain of Ismaus. Leaving Sericania to the right, he turned away southwards from the Hyperborean Scythians and the Hyrcanian ocean, and reached the parts of Sarmatia, and coming to the boundary between Asia and Europe, he flew over Russia, Pruth, and Pomerania. Though he often longed to see Bradamante, still he found so great pleasure in thus voyaging over the world, that he went on to visit the Poles and the Hungarians, the Germans also, with other savage northern tribes, and, at last, reached the far distant England. Many days and months he spent in this way, so much delight did he take in seeing new and strange countries. Nor need you suppose that in this long journey he was always flying through the air; for every evening he

came down and looked about for a comfortable
inn, where he rested and spent the night.

So it came to pass that one morning his steed
flew down upon London, and he saw near the city,
in the meadows along the banks of the Thames, a
great army defiling in battle-array, to the sound of
drums and trumpets, before the bold Paladin Rinaldo, whom, as you may remember, Charlemagne
had sent to Britain to ask for aid against the
Moors.

Ruggiero asked a knight standing by the reason
of this great gathering; who courteously replied
that these troops had been collected from Scotland,
Ireland, England, and all the neighboring islands,
and were now about to march down to the coast,
where vessels were ready waiting to transport
them across the Channel; and that the French
were anxiously looking for their arrival, hoping
that they would help them to raise the siege of
Paris. The knight then pointed out to him the
most distinguished among the nobles and leaders
of this great host.

'That large banner, displaying the leopard and
fleur de lys, is the standard of Leonetto, Duke of
Lancaster, nephew to our king, a captain as renowned in council as in war, who has the com-
mand-in-chief. Next to him come the banners
of the Duke of Gloucester with a stag's head, and
of the Duke of Clarence with a torch; then those of
the Duke of Norfolk with the broken lance, the
Earl of Pembroke with the griffin, the Duke of
Suffolk with the scales. The wreath on a ground
azure belongs to Northumberland. The Earl of
Arundel has a sinking bark, the Earl of Rich-
mond a fir-tree, the Earl of Dorset a chariot.'

He named many more noble captains with their titles and devices, but it would only weary you were I to repeat them all.

'Forty-two thousand English troopers and archers,' he continued, 'and eighty thousand foot soldiers follow these leaders. There they stand, to the east. Farther west come thirty thousand Scotch under Zerbino, their king's son. There flies his standard, showing a lion between two unicorns holding a sword in his paw. Among all these nobles none can compare with him in virtue, dignity, and grace : when Nature had made him, she broke the mould. He takes his title from the Duchy of Ross, and with him are the Dukes of Mar and Albany. The Irish are in two bands, commanded by the Earls of Childers and Desmond. That forest of lances, you see them yonder, rising round the snow-white banner, which Moratto, who commands them, hopes soon to tinge with Moorish blood, are borne by sixteen thousand of that wild and hairy people who have come from the caves and woods of Norway, Sweden, and even from far-off Iceland, to lend help to the Emperor.'

Whilst Ruggiero was admiring this great host, and learning the names and devices of the nobles of Britain, they one after another came up to admire the rare and strange creature upon which he rode. He was soon surrounded by a curious crowd, and in order still more to excite and to amuse himself with their wonder, he shook his rein, touched the Hippogriff with his spur, and soaring high above the surprised multitude, directed his course towards Ireland, where he visited the famous cave of the old saint of that island.

It was on his flight from thence to Brittany

that he met with the adventure on the Isle of
Tears, of which you have heard in the story of the
Princess Angelica. He was greatly mortified at
her vanishing from his sight, and carrying away
with her the precious ring, which he did not know
had originally belonged to her. This loss was
quickly followed by another, for when, after wandering about for some time, calling upon Angelica
to reappear and to restore to him his ring, he returned to the spot where he had left his steed, he
found the Hippogriff had slipped his head out of
the bridle, and had flown away out of sight. This
was a great addition to his misfortunes; for he had
been hurt at the disappearance of the ungrateful
princess; but more than all did the loss of the
ring distress him, not so much on account of its
wonderful virtues as because it had been the gift
of his dear lady.

Vexed and disappointed, he took up his sword
and shield, and leaving the sea-shore, wended his
way across the grassy plain towards a wide valley.
He had not gone far down this valley, by a broad
and well-beaten track which led through a wood,
when he heard on the right hand, where the underwood was thickest, a great and terrible noise as
of the clashing of arms. He pushed through the
bushes and came to a small open space, where he
found two men engaged in deadly strife. One
was of gigantic stature and savage aspect, the other
a frank and bold cavalier, who on foot, for his
horse lay dead beside him, was defending himself
with sword and shield, and trying by swift parrying
to avoid the blows which the giant aimed at him
with his huge mace. Ruggiero stepped aside and
looked on; but soon found himself wishing that

the cavalier might be the victor, though he could not interfere in his favor unless called upon for help.

At last the giant, wielding his club with both hands, dealt the other such a blow on his helmet that he fell to the ground. Thereupon the giant unbuckled his vizor, and Ruggiero saw beneath it the sweet face of his beautiful and loved Bradamante, and found that it was even she who was on the point of receiving her death-blow. He drew his sword, and rushed on the giant, defying him to battle; the latter did not await his attack, but took up the unconscious form in his arms, and carried it off, as the wolf carries off the tender lamb, or as the eagle seizes the dove in its talons. Ruggiero, seeing how great was the need of help, ran after him; but the giant went with such speed and took such long strides, that it was all he could do to keep him in sight. Thus, one running in front and the other following along the dusky and gradually widening path, they came out upon a meadow, in the midst of which stood a large and handsome palace, built entirely of variously-colored and richly inlaid marbles.

The giant carried the damsel through the gilded gates, and Ruggiero quickly followed. No sooner had he crossed the threshold than he looked round the court and up the galleries, from side to side, but neither giant nor lady were to be seen. He searched the palace up and down in every direction, leaving no hole or corner unvisited, even looking below the stairs, but he never saw either again, and was lost in wonder as to what could have become of them. At last he was turning to leave the palace, to seek for them in the woods without, when he heard a voice calling him, which made him quickly return, to begin again his fruitless search. I dare say you have guessed that this was the same castle in which Angelica found Orlando and Sacripante pursuing a shadow in her likeness; the same phantom which now assumed the shape and voice of Bradamante, to attract Ruggiero.

This new enchantment was invented by Atlante, in order to keep Ruggiero endlessly employed in this vain pursuit, and thus to save him from the doom which foretold his early death; since his castle of shining steel and Alcina's City of Pleasure had failed in that object. He enticed into his palace not only Ruggiero, but many other famous knights and Paladins, that his favorite might not meet with death at their hands; each was attracted by the appearance of whatsoever he most loved or desired in the world, and once in, all were provided by Atlante with rare wines, costly food, and every possible luxury.

It is now time to return to Bradamante. Hoping every day for the arrival of her dear Ruggiero, she was in her own city of Marseilles, acting the part of a prudent governor and brave warrior, and engaged in constant warfare with the predatory bands of Moors who made daily raids among the hills and valleys of Languedoc and Provence. When weeks and months had passed by without tidings of her knight, she began to imagine innumerable accidents and misfortunes which might have happened to him.

One day she was sitting alone, tormenting herself with fears of this kind, when the fairy, by whom she had sent him the ring, stood before her. When Bradamante saw her, after so long an absence, return alone, she became very pale, and trembled so violently that she could scarcely stand. The kind Melissa, seeing her terror, smiled, and approaching with the joyful countenance of a bringer of good tidings, said:

'Fear not, dear lady! thy Ruggiero is safe and well, and loves thee as truly as ever; although he has again lost his liberty through the arts of thine old enemy. If thou wouldest have him restored to thee, mount thy horse and follow me without delay, and I will show thee how to set him free.'

She then told her how Ruggiero and other knights had been enticed into the enchanted palace, and how they remained there, for ever pursuing a phantom, which for ever eluded their grasp.

'When,' she added, 'thou comest within his magic circle, the magician will appear to thee under the form of Ruggiero, in such strait, that thou wilt be induced to go to his help and wilt thereby be enticed into the same durance as those others of whom I have told thee. To escape the trap into which so many have fallen, pay heed to my warning, and however close may be the resemblance, advance boldly, and take the life not of Ruggiero, but of his and of thine enemy. Promise to obey my instructions, for if through timid distrust, thou sparest the life of the magician, there is no hope that Ruggiero will regain his liberty.'

The valiant damsel at once donned her armor, and promised to do all that Melissa told her, knowing how true a friend she was to both Ruggiero and herself. The fairy guided her by rapid journeys over fertile plains and through dense forests, giving her repeated instructions as to how she was to defeat the machinations of the necromancer, until

they approached the palace, when, that she might
not be seen by Atlante, she took leave of her.

After going on alone for about two miles along
a narrow path, Bradamante came upon Ruggiero
(as she imagined), struggling in the hands of two
ferocious giants. When she saw him in such imminent peril, she at once forgot all Melissa's warn-
ings, all her own good resolves, and even fancied
that the fairy had purposely deceived her.

'Can I believe that this is not Ruggiero?' she
said to herself, 'he who is always before my heart,
as he is now before my eyes. Why should I trust
another, when I can see so clearly for myself?
Even did I doubt the evidence of mine own eyes,
does not my heart tell me but too plainly that he
is near?'

While thus reasoning with herself, she heard the
voice of Ruggiero calling upon her to help him,
and hesitating no longer, she spurred her horse to
his rescue, and was drawn into the fatal palace.
No sooner had she stepped through the gate than,
sharing the general delusion, she sought him day
and night, up and down, in and out, through long
passage and on winding stair, and was so fast
bound in the magician's chain, that though she
saw Ruggiero and spoke to him, she neither recognized him nor he her.

CHAPTER VIII.

Blew his war-note loud and long,

The blast alarmed the festal hall,
And startled forth the warriors all.

SCOTT.

MANY weeks had passed by, when one day
there came to the gate a knight who had a
wonderful horn that had been given him in the
East, a single blast from which was able to destroy
all the enchantments in the world.   The history
of this knight deserves a story to itself : suffice it
now to say, that he blew his horn, and the palace
vanished in an instant like light smoke.   Ruggiero
and Bradamante found themselves together.   He
looked at her and she at him, and then to their
great astonishment and intense delight they recognized each other ; and Ruggiero kissed her, and
told her how overjoyed he was to see her again,
and how he hoped never more to part from her, for
that he would forthwith go and ask her hand from
her father, Duke Amone.   She blushed and consented ; only she begged him first to be baptized ;
to which he agreed, all the more willingly for that
his father and all his ancestors had been Christians ;
he added, that to give her pleasure he would gladly
if need be sacrifice his life.   To receive baptism,

and then to gain the lady for his wife, Ruggiero, guided by Bradamante, took the road to Vallombrosa, a rich and beautiful abbey, which was noted for its sanctity and hospitality.

As they left the forest they met a lady, who seemed to be in the greatest distress. Ruggiero, always kind and courteous, more especially to ladies, took pity upon her, and with a respectful salutation asked her why her face was so bedewed with tears. She, raising her streaming and beautiful eyes, replied in a low voice :

' Gentle sir, you must know that the cause of my weeping is the pity I feel for a youth, who lies condemned to die this very day in a castle hard by. He ventured to raise his eyes to the daughter of Marsilio king of Spain, and gained her affections in return. A report of this reached the ears of the king, who, on discovering its truth, was so incensed that he confined them both in separate fortresses, and has even now sentenced the young man to a cruel and painful death. I have fled that I may not be a witness of such torture, for he is to be burnt alive; and were I to behold the sight I should be so haunted by it, that in my happiest moments a shuddering horror would come over me at the bare recollection.'

Bradamante was so moved by this tale that had it been one of her own brothers, she could scarcely have felt greater sorrow, and as you will learn, such feeling was not without cause. She said to Ruggiero :

' Surely for such a case as this do we carry arms.'

And then turning to the lady, she added :

' If you can but bring us to this fortress, I promise you, that unless he be dead already, you may take comfort, for they shall not kill him.'

Ruggiero, glad to see such tokens of his lady's kind and tender heart, desired as ardently as herself to save the youth, and said to the lady, who was still weeping bitterly :

'Why this delay ? Surely help is here needed, and not tears. Only lead us to the spot, and I promise you to rescue him, were it from a thousand lances or a thousand swords. Use your utmost speed, that we may be in time to snatch him from the flames.'

The confident speech and gallant bearing of the noble pair might have restored to the lady's despairing heart the hope which had fled; but she must have known of other difficulties than mere distance, for she still sadly answered :

'Taking the plain and straight road, I believe we might yet be in time; but we must go round by so crooked and so rough a way, that one day will scarcely suffice for the journey, and ere we arrive he will be already dead.'

'And why not go by the shortest road ?' exclaimed Ruggiero.

'Because,' she replied, 'a castle of the counts of Ponthier lies half-way, and Pinabello, the most wicked man alive, son of Count Anselm of Altariva, has, within the last few days, declared that neither knight nor lady shall pass by it without being robbed and maltreated, and that their horses shall be taken from them, with all their armor, mantles, and ornaments. Four of the best cavaliers of France are in that castle, and have sworn to uphold this practice, the origin of which I will tell you. Pinabello has a wife as wicked and discourteous as himself. Riding together one day, they met a knight with an old lady on a pillion behind him. The unmannerly pair jeered at her, and the knight attacked Pinabello, unhorsed him, took away his charger, and made his wife give up her rich mantle to the old lady. Infuriated at this insult, she gave Pinabello no peace day or night, until he promised her that a thousand knights and ladies should pay for it by being unhorsed and deprived of their armor and mantles. It happened that the same day there alighted at the castle, travelling from distant lands, four noble cavaliers, Aquilante, Grifone, Sansonetto, and young Guido Selvaggio, among the most famous warriors of this age. Pinabello entertained them, but when they were asleep in their beds he made them all prisoners, and would not release them until they swore to remain with him for a year and a day, and to plunder all the knights and ladies passing below the castle. It seems that none can withstand them, for the compact is, that one, chosen by lot, should go out first, but should he be overcome, the other three are forced to set upon the travellers all together, and many have already left horse, armor, and mantle behind them; and now, if we go that way, even supposing that you were able to vanquish these four knights, it would not be done in an hour, and such delay would be fatal.'

' Let us not think too much of this,' said Ruggiero ; ' it is our duty to do the best we can, and to leave the result in God's hands. We will try a tilt with these knights, and you shall thereby judge of our power to help your friend.'

Thereupon, the lady in silence led the way, and after riding for three miles, they came to a gateway leading to a bridge ; above it was a fortress, from which two strokes of a bell announced their

9

approach. Almost at the same moment, a knight in a scarlet cloak embroidered with white flowers crossed the drawbridge. Bradamante besought Ruggiero to leave it to her to hurl this knight from the saddle, but he would not listen to her, and obliged to do as he desired, she could only sit still and look on. Sansonetto, for he it was, and Ruggiero, put their lances in rest and rode full tilt at each other, with such fury that their bucklers resounded with the shock. The magic shield of Ruggiero, however, was too curiously wrought to sustain any damage. Not so Sansonetto's; it shivered to pieces, and Ruggiero's lance pierced through his arm and hurled him to the ground. In the mean while Pinabello had issued forth, and had accosted Bradamante, anxious to know who it was that with such skill and force had discomfited his champion. It chanced, or rather a just Providence ordered, that he was mounted on the very horse he had basely stolen from Bradamante; for it was just eight months since, as you may remember, he had thrown her into Merlin's cave. She recognized her charger and the villain count, and steadfastly looking at him, she said:

'Surely you are the traitor who tried to compass my death. Your own sins have brought you here that you may receive the punishment which is their due.'

To put herself between him and the fortress, to draw her sword, defy, and assault him, were all the work of the same moment. Pinabello, pale and terrified, fled howling like a wolf cut off from his den, into the forest; but the brave damsel pursued him so closely that her weapon almost touched him; nothing, however, of all this was observed from the

castle, so intent were they upon Ruggiero. The
other knights had come out accompanied by
the wicked countess, who, reminding them of their
oath, held them bound to attack him all three together. So unknightly a proceeding caused them
much shame; they all protested against it, and
begged her to allow them to assault him one by
one, but she refused, and kept them to the letter
of their oath; as they lingered Ruggiero shouted,
'Come on! behold my armor, my charger but
newly saddled and bridled, and this lady's mantle,
all at your service. If ye would have them, why
this delay?'

Boldly, and with as light a heart as if they had
been little children, he advanced against the three
knights with the spear which had overthrown Sansonetto, and with Atlante's shield, to which only
as a last resource had he ever had recourse: as yet
but thrice since it had been in his possession, and
each time had he been in imminent peril. Indeed
he always kept it carefully hidden, yet in such
wise that he could easily, if there were need, uncover it. He now struck Grifone in the centre of
his shield with such force, that reeling in his
saddle, he fell from his horse; but his lance had
also touched Ruggiero's shield on the edge instead
of in front, and becoming entangled in the silk,
had torn it right across. The terrible light at
once blazed forth, and not only Grifone but also
Aquilante and Guido fell back dazzled and senseless. Ruggiero, knowing nothing of the sudden
end thus put to the combat, wheeled his horse
round and grasped his sword, but lo! no one stood
against him; knights, ladies, and even the poor
panting horses all lay motionless on the ground.

At first he gazed at them with astonishment, until seeing the silken veil hanging loose at his side, he understood what had happened.

He cast his eyes quickly around, looking for his dear lady where she had stood when the fight began ; but not seeing her, he supposed she had hurried on to stop the execution of the young man. The lady who had guided them thither lay near the others, so he took off her mantle and wrapped it round the magic shield. Then gently lifting her up, and placing her before him on his horse, for he knew that the blinding light once hidden, she would soon recover her senses, he rode away saddened and crestfallen, and not daring to lift up his face, which was crimson with shame, for he thought every eye would look reproach at him for his inglorious victory. He said to himself, 'What penance can atone for such disgrace ? They will say of me that by enchantments, and not by valor, I have gained all my victories.' Riding along, a prey to these mortifying reflections, he came to a well by the road-side, placed there for the use of herds and flocks during the summer droughts.

'Now,' said he, 'oh shield ! I will take care that thou shalt not again disgrace me. This is the last time that I shall reproach myself with thy use.' So saying, he dismounted, and fastening a large and heavy stone to the shield, he threw it into the well which was very deep and full of water. With a heavy plunge it sank to the bottom, and the clear still water closed over it for ever. Fame did not allow this glorious deed to remain concealed, but carried the report of it throughout France and Spain and to other countries. Many a brave warrior started in quest of the wondrous shield, but none ever found it, or ever lighted upon the well or the forest, for the lady, his companion, who first told the story, never divulged the name of either.

Some little time after Ruggiero had left the fortress, the four champions came to their senses, and for the rest of the day they could talk of nothing but the terrible shining light which had so dismayed them. They were still conversing about it when news was brought them of the death of Pinabello. The brave Bradamante had overtaken him in a narrow pass, and had plunged her sword up to the very hilt in his breast. Having freed the world of this miscreant, she turned her back upon the wood, leading away with her the horse which the villain had formerly stolen from her. She intended to return to where she had left Ruggiero, but she missed the way, and it was her ill luck to wander long in those parts before she found him again.

CHAPTER IX.

BRADAMANTE RETURNS TO HER FATHER'S CASTLE.

Their three gay suits of armor, each on each,
And bound them on their horses, each on each,
And tied the bridle-rein of all the three
Together, and said to her ' Drive them on.'
TENNYSON.

BRADAMANTE wandered about among the intricate and narrow paths in the wood, until the sun left the world to darkness, when, not knowing where to find shelter for the night, she lay down upon the soft green turf, and spent it partly in sleeping and partly in watching the course of the bright planets above her head, Saturn and Jupiter, Mars and Venus ; but whether waking or sleeping, Ruggiero was never long absent from her thoughts. When at length the wished-for dawn appeared, she remounted her horse and turning his head towards the east, she soon got out of the forest, and found herself near the spot where the enchanted palace had stood, and there saw before her her cousin Astolfo, holding the Hippogriff by the bridle, and much puzzled what to do with his horse Rabican, which stood beside him. It chanced that the knight had just taken off his helmet, so she at once recognized him, and calling him by name she joyfully hastened towards him, and lifting her vizor that he might also know her, affectionately embraced him. Astolfo would at any time have been pleased to see her, but was now doubly so, as he could not have found any one with whom he would so willingly leave Rabican, knowing that she would take good care of him, and restore him as soon as he returned to claim him. How he had come into possession of the Hippogriff belongs to his own story.

He told Bradamante, after kind inquiries as to her welfare, that he wished to hasten to his native land on the flying steed, which he had learned to manage at the same time as Ruggiero from Logistilla; and he begged her to take charge of Rabican, who was much prized by him for his exceeding swiftness ('fleeter than the wind' he called him), as also of his arms, which would be of no use to him in his aerial ride, and which he asked her to lay by safely for him in Montalbano, her father's castle, until he returned. Intending to take so long a flight through the air, he thought it best to make himself as light as possible, and therefore, keeping only his sword, he gave into her care all his armor, and the far-famed golden lance, whose slightest touch could, at the very first onset, unhorse the stoutest adversary.

Astolfo, on the flying steed, mounted slowly into the air, and then soared straight away so swiftly that in one moment Bradamante lost all sight of him. So does the prudent pilot at first steer slowly through the rocks and shoals, then port and coast left behind, with full-spread sails fly before the wind.

The lady, when the duke had left her, found herself in a great difficulty; for her heart being so ardently set upon rejoining Ruggiero, whom she hoped to find, at all events at Vallombrosa, if not sooner, she did not see how at the same time to convey her cousin's horse and armor to Montalbano. While debating what to do, she chanced to see a peasant coming towards her; so she fastened all the armor as best she could upon Rabican, and bade the rustic lead him, as also her own horse just recaptured from Pinabello, after her. She took the road which seemed most likely to lead in the direction of Vallombrosa, for the peasant could give her no help, being as ignorant of the country as herself. She rode on all that morning without meeting any one, until about noon on coming out of a wood she saw a castle crowning the top of a hill at some little distance. She looked, and it seemed to her like Montalbano; she looked again, and felt sure it was her home, where her mother and her brothers were living. Her heart grew dull and heavy as she recognized the place, for she knew that if she went there she would not be allowed to depart from it again, nor to see Ruggiero, nor to go to Vallombrosa, and there accomplish what they had determined upon. She stood for a moment in suspense, and then resolved to turn her back upon Montalbano and to take the direct road, with which from here she was quite familiar, to the abbey. But, as her good or ill luck would have it, before she left the valley she met Alardo, one of her brothers, without having time to conceal herself from him or to close her vizor. He was returning from distributing and billeting in the neighborhood some troops, which Charlemagne had asked him to collect in his province. When he saw his sister, he embraced her with great joy, and they turned back together to Montalbano, discoursing affectionately about their family and relations.

Her mother Beatrice received her with delight and bestowed many sweet kisses upon her; for after having caused her to be sought for throughout France in vain, she had long given her up and wept for her as lost. In spite, however, of all these tender caresses, Bradamante was sore at heart; until at last she bethought herself of sending some one to Vallombrosa to tell Ruggiero why she could not meet him there, and to beseech him, if there were need of such entreaty, to be at once baptized, and to come as he had promised, and demand her in marriage from her father.

By the same messenger she designed to send him Frontino, who used to be so great a favorite with him, and not without reason, for with the exception perhaps of Baiardo and Brigliadoro, neither among the Saracens, nor in Gaul, could so gallant or so handsome a steed have been found. Bradamante had taken charge of him the day Ruggiero was carried away by the Hippogriff, and she had sent him to Montalbano, where great care was taken of him, and where no one was allowed to mount him, except for gentle exercise; so that he was now in excellent condition, sleek and glossy.

She set all her maidens to help her in embroidering a rich pattern of finest gold, upon white and purple silk, and with this she ornamented the bridle, saddle, and housings of the noble charger. Then she chose the daughter of her nurse, her favorite attendant Ippalca, to whom she had often confided the story of her love, and had told her of Ruggiero's valor and good looks, and of all that made him so worthy of her regard. Calling the maiden, she said to her:

'Dear Ippalca! I know I could not choose a better

messenger, none more faithful or more prudent;
now therefore go!'

She told her whither, and fully instructed her as
to what she had to say to her knight; that she was
to tell him why she could not go to the abbey,
and to assure him, that this was no idle excuse, but
that it was forced upon her by an adverse fortune,
which she could not resist. She mounted her upon
a palfrey, and placing Frontino's richly ornamented
bridle in her hand, told her that if she met any
foolish or base enough to attempt to deprive her of
him, she had need only to mention his master's
name to make them quickly come to their senses
and desist, for she felt confident that she could
meet none so bold as not to tremble at the name
of Ruggiero.

Ippalca set off and rode for more than ten miles
without meeting any one to annoy her, or to ask
her errand.　About noon she was going down a
steep hill by a narrow path, when there met her a
knight on foot, clad in armor and followed by
a dwarf. This was the Moor Rodomonte, who, lifting upon her his bold eyes, cursed aloud his unlucky fate at finding so gallant and so richly
caparisoned a charger in the hands of a woman.
For he had shortly before sworn to take, if need be
by force of arms, the first horse he should meet
with on his way.　Frontino was the first, and he
could never hope to find one handsomer or better
suited to him ; and yet it were a cowardly action to
take him from a defenceless maiden.　Longing to
possess him, he stood in suspense, looking, admiring, and often exclaiming :

　'Would that his master were here!'

　'Would he were!' cried Ippalca, 'for then perhaps you might change your mind. His owner is far more worthy to mount him than you. Indeed, in the wide world no warrior equal to him can be found.'

'And who may this be,' asked the Moor, 'who can so trample under foot the glory of all other men ?'

'Ruggiero !' was the reply.

'Then,' returned the other, 'the horse shall be mine, since I take him from so renowned a knight. If he be as valiant as you pretend, let him some day try to recover his charger, with the hire thereof as well, if he choose. He shall himself fix the ransom. Say that I am Rodomonte, ready to do him battle, whenever and wherever he will. He can soon find me, for the brightness of my glory suffers me not to remain concealed. Like the thunderbolt of Heaven, my path leaves its trace.'

He threw the golden rein over the horse's head, vaulted upon him, and followed by the weeping Ippalca, rode up the hill, paying no attention to her threats, or to the curses of Heaven, which she called down upon him.

CHAPTER X.

> The rushing of a host in rout ;
> With groans of trampled men, with smarting wounds,
> And all that noise, as of a rushing crowd.
>   COLERIDGE.

RUGGIERO had left the well about a mile behind, when he saw a courier riding towards him with great speed. This was one of those sent by King Agramante to all such knights as were friendly to him, to entreat them to hasten to his succor; and to tell them that the Saracens were so straitly hemmed in by the forces of Charlemagne, that unless help speedily reached them, they must forfeit honor or life. Ruggiero was assailed by many conflicting emotions at the news, and doubted what he ought to do. But as this was neither the place nor the time for deliberation, he allowed the courier to go on his way; whilst he himself continued in the direction of the fortress, towards which the lady persistently urged him, often repeating that there was no time to spare for delay.

The sun was setting as he reached the town. Although situated in the centre of France, it belonged to King Marsilio, who had captured it in the course of this war. Ruggiero was detained neither at drawbridge nor gateway; for although the port-

cullis and the moat were lined with men-at-arms,
they allowed him to pass without challenge or
question as to whence he came, the lady who accompanied him being well known to them.

When he reached the market-place, he found it
lighted up with the blaze of a great fire, and full
of people gazing with cruel eyes on the pale face
of a youth who stood in their midst, condemned to
perish by the flames. When Ruggiero looked at
his sad and weeping countenance, he thought he
saw Bradamante, so exactly did the young man
resemble her. The more he considered his form
and features, the more certain he felt that it was
she, and he said to himself:

'As sure as I am Ruggiero, that stand here, so
surely is that Bradamante. Too rashly, she must
have undertaken alone, to rescue the condemned
youth, and not succeeding, she must herself have
been taken prisoner. Oh! why such haste? why
did she not wait for my assistance? But, thank
God! I am come, and in time to succor her.'

Without a moment's delay, he spurred into the
midst of the helpless crowd, trampling them down
under his horse's hoofs. His lance had been broken
before Pinabello's castle, but he grasped his sword
and swinging it round cut right and left at the
citizens, who fled shrieking before him, leaving
many of their number on the ground with maimed
limbs and broken skulls. As a flight of birds
feeding on the margin of some shining pool skim
happily along, intent upon their sport, until the
rapacious falcon darts suddenly upon them, and
seizing one and wounding another, scatters them
in single flight, each thinking but of himself and
caring not what becomes of his mate; so in like

manner when the stout Ruggiero set upon the
people thus suddenly, they fled on all sides from
before him. None could resist him, for his sharp
sword cut through their steel caps as if the hard
metal were thin laths. The enchanter Falerina
had forged this famous blade to defend the garden
of Orgagna against Orlando. What wonders could
not such a weapon perform in the hands of such
a warrior, whose strength must not be judged of
by that of our modern heroes? more worthy was it
to be compared with that of the Artic bear, or the
African lion! And if Ruggiero ever displayed
valor and daring, surely it was now, when fighting, as he thought, for the life of his fair mistress.

In the mean time, the compassionate lady who
had procured for him Ruggiero's assistance, loosed
the cords which bound the youth, and armed him,
as best she could, with sword and breastplate.
When, thus armed, he had revenged himself somewhat on those who were preparing for him so cruel
a death, he joined Ruggiero, and the pair left the
town, just as the wheels of the sun's golden chariot
sank below the western waves. When the young
man found himself safe beyond the walls, with
courteous gesture and gentle words, he tendered
infinite thanks to Ruggiero, who had thus risked
his life in behalf of one all unknown to him, and
begged to learn the name of him to whom he was
so much indebted.

'I see, indeed,' thought the puzzled Ruggiero,
'the lovely face and form of my Bradamante, but
I do not hear the soft tones of her sweet voice;
nor are these such thanks as she would offer to her
faithful lover. Moreover, how can she so soon
have forgotten my name?'

To learn the truth of the matter he therefore courteously replied:

'I feel sure that I have seen you elsewhere, but though I have thought and thought again, I cannot call to mind where it could have been. I pray you, if you remember, tell me, and give me also the pleasure of hearing who it is I have to-day helped to escape the flames.'

'It may be,' replied the other, 'that you have seen me, but when, and where, I cannot tell; for I have roamed the world, far and wide, in search of adventure. Perhaps, however, you may have met my sister, for she also wears armor and carries a sword by her side. We are twins, and so like each other that our own family do not know us apart. You are not the first, nor the second, who have fallen into this error. For neither our father nor our brothers, not even our mother, can distinguish us. Formerly, indeed, the curly hair, which I wear cut short after man's fashion, and her long tresses plaited and wound round and round her head, made a difference between us; but since she was wounded by a marauding band of Saracens, and was tended by a hermit, who, to dress the wound, cut her hair off short above her ears, nothing remains to distinguish us but our names, hers being Bradamante and mine Ricciardetto, and Rinaldo brother to us both. If you care to listen, I will relate a pleasant adventure which befell me through my likeness to her; pleasant indeed, in the first instance, though it ended in disaster, and brought me into the peril from which you have just rescued me.'

Ruggiero, to whom no strains could be sweeter, no story more grateful, than that in which mention should be made of his dear lady, begged the youth to continue his story, which he did as follows:

'It happened that not long after she had been wounded by those Saracens, my sister was one day wandering about these woods, and growing faint and weary, she dismounted from her horse, and taking off her helmet, threw herself upon the soft grass, and was there found fast asleep by Fiordispina, Princess of Spain, who, accompanied by her court, was hunting in the forest. Fiordispina at first took my sister for some fair and gallant knight, and upon her awakening, she invited her to ride beside her and join the party in the chase. The princess showed her so much kindness that Bradamante told her who she was, and how that, accustomed from childhood to the use of sword and lance, she was now in pursuit of glory, such as might rival the fame of Ippolita and Camilla. The princess was so much interested in Bradamante's account of herself, that when the day drew near its close, she invited her to return to her castle, and there spend some time with her. My sister could not refuse this request, and they together entered that town where, but for your timely aid, the people had cast me into the flames. Here Bradamante reassumed her feminine apparel, and was made much of by the princess and all her court. When the day came for her departure, Fiordispina gave her a beautiful Spanish jennet, with gold-embossed harness, and a mantle richly embroidered by her own fair hand. She accompanied her for some little space on her way, and parted from her with many expressions of tender regret.

'My sister rode so quickly that she reached Montalbano the same evening, and we her brothers, with our mother, ran out joyfully to meet her, for so many days had passed since we had had any tidings of her, that we doubted whether she were dead or alive. When she took off her helmet, we saw, with surprise, that her hair which had once hung in long thick tresses was now cut close to her head, and that she wore about her a gay new mantle. She then told us of her wound, and how the beautiful huntress had found her asleep, and taken her to her castle and had there treated her so kindly.

'The Princess Fiordispina was well known to me, for I had often seen her at Saragossa, and also in France, and had much admired her fair cheeks and bright eyes, though I had never allowed my thoughts to dwell upon her beauty, knowing that hopeless love is after all but a vain and foolish dream. Now, however, hearing so much in her praise, all my old flame was rekindled, and I thought how easy it would be to gain access to the castle and to pay my court to the beautiful princess in the disguise of Bradamante. Should I go? or should I not? Long did I debate the matter, but at last I took my sister's horse, donned her armor, and went my way. When I arrived at the castle the princess received me very graciously, taking me for Bradamante; at first I allowed her to remain under this delusion, but after a time I disclosed to her the truth; and the regard which she had at first shown me for my sister's sake, I now gained for my own. In this safe disguise I often visited the castle, and so prospered in my suit that the princess allowed me to hope that I might some day pay my court to her openly, and ask for her hand. Unfortunately, before she granted me this

10

favor, our secret was, by some mischance, betrayed to the king her father. You, who have just rescued me from death, can have no difficulty in imagining the rest of my story and the sorrow which now fills my heart.'

As Ricciardetto ended this narration, they were ascending by a rough path a steep precipice, on the top of which stood the castle of Agrismonte. Aldigiero of Chiaramonte, brother of Malagigi and Vivian, was governor of this castle; he was a valiant and prudent captain, and he watched with unceasing vigilance over the safety of the fortress in his brother's absence.

He loved his cousin Ricciardetto with brotherly affection, and received him, and for his sake, Ruggiero, with exceeding kindness; but he did not greet them with his usual cheerfulness, for he had received news that morning which had much disturbed him. He met Ricciardetto with these words:

'Cousin, my news is bad. I have to-day heard by a sure messenger, that the wicked Bertolagi of Bayonne, with the offer of a large amount of treasure, has bribed the cruel Lanfusa to deliver up to him your loving cousins Malagigi and Vivian; whom, since Ferrau took prisoner, she has kept confined in her dark dungeons. She is, according to this disgraceful compact, to give them over to-morrow to the Manganzese, at the place where her territory borders with Bayonne, and Bertolagi is to be there in person to pay over the gold. Our Rinaldo is, even now, being informed thereof, for I sent him a message in hot haste, but I much fear he will not arrive in time, the distance being so great. I have not sufficient men to sally forth myself; the will indeed is present, but the power is wanting : and I know not what to do or to say, for should that traitor get hold of them, he will assuredly slay them.'

This terrible news grieved Ricciardetto, and grieving him, it grieved Ruggiero also. Seeing them silent, and without resource, he boldly cried, ' Be of good cheer. I take this enterprise upon myself ; my sword can, if need be, do the work of a thousand, and it shall set your brothers free. I ask neither men nor help, but will do the deed alone. All I desire·is a guide to lead me to the spot where this base bargain is to be struck, and I promise you that you shall hear from hence the cries of those miscreants.'

What he said caused no surprise to one of the listeners, who from what he had seen knew his boast could be made true, but the other paid no heed to him, or only as to one who speaks much of what he knows little ; until Ricciardetto led him aside and told him how Ruggiero had saved him from the flames, adding that he felt sure he could, at fitting time and place, make good all, and more than all, that he had promised. Aldigiero, thereupon, paid him great respect, and at supper, where plenty crowned the board, he treated him with becoming deference; it was then agreed upon, that without waiting for further help, they should set out the next morning to rescue the two brothers.

Heavy sleep soon after closed the eyes of all but Ruggiero, who was kept awake by much and anxious thought. The news that Agramante was so straitly besieged, which he had heard from the courier that morning, weighed heavily upon his heart, and he felt that every hour he delayed in

hastening to the camp would tend to his dishonor.
If, instead of flying to the help of the king, he
were now to accompany his enemies, and then
turn Christian, and be baptized, he knew that such
conduct would be ascribed to cowardice, rather
than to any honest wish of embracing the true faith.
Yet the idea of departing without taking leave of
his dear lady much distressed him. He had hoped
to find her at the town whither they were together
bound to the rescue of Ricciardetto, and he could
not understand how he had missed her; until remembering his promise to go with her to Vallombrosa, he thought perhaps she had gone thither
with the expectation of meeting him, and that she
would be surprised at his absence. It grieved him
to think that she should believe he had wilfully
disobeyed her injunctions, and had gone away without telling her why he did so, and he wished it
were possible to send her a message. After re-
flecting upon these things, he resolved to write and
tell her all that had happened to him. He knew
not how to get the letter safely delivered, but he
trusted by some happy chance to fall in with a messenger; and so impatient was he to carry out this
idea, that jumping out of bed, he called for lights,
pen, ink, and paper, which were immediately
brought to him by the attentive servants, and began
to write.

After the customary complimentary salutations,
he told Bradamante of the demand for his services which had reached him that morning from
the king; who, if he hurried not to his succor,
must lose his life, or fall into the hands of his
enemies. He added that she must herself see that
if he refused to help Agramante in this strait and

peril great blame would attach to him. Yet one
who was destined to be her husband must, above
all others, keep his honor unsullied ; for to one so
pure nothing mean or unworthy might dare ally
itself. If he had, hitherto, striven by noble deeds
to gain an honorable name, and having won it, had
held it dear and endeavored to preserve it un-
stained, how much more precious was it now become to him, since she was to share it. The promise he had given her by word of mouth he now
repeated in writing ; that as soon as this campaign
in his king's service was ended, he would, if his
life were preserved, openly proclaim himself, what
he had long wished to be, a faithful Christian ; and
then proceed to ask her in marriage from her father
and from her brother Rinaldo.

' Let me,' he added, ' but first raise the siege for
my lord, that the vulgar crowd may be silenced,
who might otherwise say in scorn, " Ruggiero, as
long as Agramante was in high estate, abandoned
not his side by day or night ; but now that fortune
favors Charlemagne, his banner floats beside that
of the conqueror." I will only tarry some ten or
twenty days in the Moorish camp, until I have
raised the siege. After that, I will seek some just
and plausible pretext for withdrawing from it altogether. Having done thus much for my fair fame,
I will, henceforth, devote the rest of my life to you.'

In such words as these did Ruggiero express
himself, not content until he had filled all four
sides of his sheet of paper; then he folded and
sealed the letter, putting it into his bosom with
the hope of next day finding some one by whom
to send it to his dear lady. He lay down again
and quickly sank to rest, for kind sleep waved her

wand dipped in the waters of Lethe over his weary
limbs; and he slumbered, until the dawn, with
pink and pearly clouds, scattering her flowers over
the happy world, appeared, and the day came forth
from his golden bower in the shining east.

Aldigiero was first on foot, just as the birds
among the green branches began to welcome the
new-born light. The other two, hearing him astir,
speedily joined him, and all three, equipping themselves in complete armor, set out. Ruggiero had
entreated the two cousins to allow him to go
alone on this enterprise, but they would not listen
to such a proposal and insisted upon accompanying him. When they reached the place where the
shameful bargain was to be completed, they found
it to be a wide plain, exposed to the full rays of
the burning sun, unsheltered by beech-tree or
cypress, laurel or myrtle; only a few low bushes
grew upon the arid and sandy soil, which neither
mattock nor ploughshare had ever turned up.

The three bold warriors drew rein and stopped
as they beheld coming towards them, by a path
which crossed the plain, a knight clad in armor
inlaid with gold, whose device, upon a field vert,
was the rare and beautiful bird which fable tells
us was fated to live a hundred years.

CHAPTER XI.

> Thick clouds of dust afar appeared,
> And trampling steeds were faintly heard,
> Bright lances, above the columns dun
> Glanced momentary to the sun.
>
> SCOTT.

RUGGIERO, with the two cousins, awaited the approach of this knight of haughty aspect, who bore on his shield the bird that, dying at the end of a hundred years, revives from his own ashes. As soon as he saw them he defied them, crying out, 'Is there, perchance, one among you who cares, with either sword or lance, to make trial of our respective merits?'

'Gladly,' replied Aldigiero, 'would I run a tilt with thee; but a more serious encounter, at which if thou tarry here, thou mayst assist, leaves me but scant time to parley, far less to try jousts with thee. Six hundred men-at-arms and more are about to pass by, with whom it will behoove us to try the fortune of war, in order to rescue two of our party, who are now prisoners in their hands.' He went on to relate the cause of their lying in wait, and the knight answered:

'So just is your excuse, that I have nought to say against it; and I am ready to believe you three fearless knights. I did but desire a bout with you to try of what mettle ye might be, but since I see you are bent on other and greater sport, I only pray to be allowed to use this sword in your service, when you shall find that I am not unworthy to fight in your company.'

If any are curious to hear who thus offered to take part in this perilous adventure, know that she (for *he* would here be out of place) was the renowned champion, the lady Marfisa. They accepted her proposal gladly, believing her to be some knight-errant; and Aldigiero soon afterwards pointed out, fluttering in the breeze, a light pennon surrounded by soldiers, who, on their coming nearer, they saw by their Moorish habit to be a great band of Saracens; in their midst they could distinguish the prisoners, bound, and riding upon two small and sorry nags. Marfisa at once exclaimed:

'Since here they come, why not forthwith begin the fray?'

'Because all the guests have not yet arrived,' said Ruggiero. 'Let us go to work warily, and not endanger our success by impatience.'

He was still speaking, when clouds of dust and the glitter of lances in the opposite direction, announced the approach of the Manganzese traitors; who came up, leading mules laden with treasure, cloth of gold and other rich stuffs, for which the two unfortunate brothers were to be exchanged. They heard Bertolagi parleying with the Moorish captain, and at the sight Aldigiero and Ricciardetto could refrain no longer, but putting lance in rest they attacked the knave. One thrust him through the body, the other through the head. Would that all traitors could be so disposed of!

Ruggiero and Marfisa lost no time in setting upon the other troop, and in a trice three fell to each, among them the captain of the Infidels; whereupon a panic seized both bands, which led to their complete destruction; for the Manganzese believed themselves to be betrayed by the Saracens, while the latter imagined they were being assaulted by the Manganzese, and both furiously assailed each other with bows and arrows, swords and lances. Ruggiero and Marfisa struck out on all sides, and helmet and cuirass were but as dry wood to the flames at the touch of their weapons. The other two let the Saracens alone, and only fought against the Manganzese. Ricciardetto's valor was equal to his strength, and his hatred of that vile race made him redouble both; the same passion animated Aldigiero, who, bold as a lion, became a very Hector on seeing the feats of Ruggiero and Marfisa, each of them the flower and paragon of chivalry.

The latter often turned her eyes with wonder on her companions, but chiefly did Ruggiero excite her astonishment. She could have believed him Mars himself come down from the skies, for under the stroke of Balisarda the hardest iron was no better than cardboard. Not less did the mighty feats of the lady attract the admiring glances of Ruggiero; her enemies fell under her blows like brittle ice, and if she thought him Mars, he might, had he known her to be a woman, have called her Bellona.

Routed by the valor of these four bold champions, the Moors fled on one side, the Manganzese on the other, abandoning both their treasure and their prisoners; and lucky was he whose horse was fleet, whilst those on foot had but a poor chance.

Malagigi and Vivian, with happy faces and happier hearts, quickly unloosed their chains, and when all had taken off their helmets, they hastened to tender their respectful thanks to the damsel, whose sex was then betrayed by her wavy golden hair, and by the beauty and delicacy of her features. They begged her to disclose to them a name so worthy of fame, and she, always courteous with her friends, told them who she was, and while they all admired her, she had only eyes and words for Ruggiero, esteeming the others beneath her notice.

The pages, on unloading the mules, in addition to silver vessels, embroidered dresses for ladies, sets of furniture in Flanders work of gold and silver, and other precious things, had found stores of bread, pasties and confections, with flasks of costly wines; they therefore now came to invite the company to partake of a refection which they had spread near a fountain shaded by a lofty mountain from the rays of the noonday sun. This was one of the four famous fountains of France built by Merlin. He had caused to be sculptured on the wall of pure transparent marble, which enclosed it, forms of such divine excellence that they seemed to be alive, and to want but voice to speak. The foremost figure was a youthful knight crowned with imperial laurel, and near him stood three others, all bearing the Golden Lily for their device, while their names were inscribed on their helmets and on the border of their long mantles. These were Charles V., Maximilian of Austria, Francis I., and Henry VIII. of England. They were followed by a lion carrying a shield with like device, and on it was inscribed the number 10.

As Marfisa and the knights considered with admiration this beautiful bass-relief, they wished they could know more of these kings, of whom nought was told but their names ; and Vivian turned to Malagigi, who was standing by, and said :

'Do you tell their story, which I think you know.'

'No author has as yet written their history,' was the answer, 'for those whose effigies you see here have never yet lived upon the earth. Merlin, the great Wizard, in the days of King Arthur of Britain, caused this fountain to be engraved with the story of events yet to come ; and not until seven hundred years from this time will these kings make their age renowned by their glorious achievements. Like the sun, to which all other lights must yield, Francis I. will in royal magnificence outshine them all. In the first year of his reign he will cross the Alps, and, surrounded by the flower of French chivalry, will descend into the rich plains of Lombardy, and there win many famous battles, displaying the prudence and valor of great Cæsar, the good fortune of Alexander, without which the grandest designs end in mist and smoke, and a magnanimity to which I can find no parallel.' Malagigi went on to tell them something of the other kings, and of the great Italian nobles who should distinguish themselves in their days, such as Ippolito d'Este, Ippolito di Medici, and the famous Andrea Doria.

After listening to this history and finishing their repast, they lay down on soft carpets to rest during the noontide heat, while Vivian and Malagigi, for their greater security, kept watch by them in arms. After a time they saw a lady, alone, and unattended, riding rapidly towards them. This was Ippalca, who, after following Rodomonte for some distance, beseeching him and abusing him by turns, and finding neither of any avail, had turned back to seek for Ruggiero in Agrismonte. On the way some one told her that she would find him here with Ricciardetto, and being familiar with the place, she had come straight to the fountain. Like a cautious messenger, she made as if she knew nothing of Ruggiero, but with eyes still red from weeping, directed herself to Ricciardetto, who, recognizing her, rose to meet her and to ask her errand. She replied, sufficiently loud for Ruggiero, who was close by, to hear:

'Obeying your sister's commands, I was leading a valuable charger called Frontino, a great favorite of hers; and was some thirty miles on the road to Marseilles, whither she was to follow me in a few days, and where I was to await her arrival. I was going along without any fear, feeling sure that if I said the steed belonged to Rinaldo's sister, none would dare take him from me; but all my confidence proved vain, for yesterday a vile Moor came up and carried him off, and though I followed him and told him to whom Frontino belonged, I could not induce him to restore him to me. When I found prayers and threats equally unavailing, loading him with curses and reproaches, I left him at a short distance from hence, trying, with no small difficulty, to defend himself and the horse against the attack of a knight, who, I much hope, has already avenged me.'

Ruggiero, scarcely able to contain himself till

she had ended her story, now jumped up and besought Ricciardetto so urgently, in return for the service he had rendered him, to allow him to go alone with the maiden, in search of this noble charger, that he could not refuse his request. After taking leave of the company, he therefore went off with Ippalca, who, as soon as they were out of hearing of the others, told him that she was sent by one upon whose heart his image was deeply graven to give him a message, which she proceeded to deliver, adding that the Moor who had carried off Frontino had said, with great insolence, 'Since I learn that this horse is Ruggiero's I take it with all the more pleasure. If he wishes to recover it tell him —I seek not to conceal it — my name is Rodomonte, whose glory has filled the world with its fame.'

Ruggiero's countenance betrayed the indignation with which he listened to her. Dear as Frontino had always been to him, he was now still dearer as his lady's gift, and longing to regain him, and to take vengeance on Rodomonte for the insult done to himself, he rode rapidly on, guided by the maiden, until their road divided, one path keeping along the plain, the other mounting the hill; but both eventually meeting in the valley where Ippalca had left Rodomonte. The mountain path was steep but short, the other level and easy but considerably longer. Ippalca, hoping the sooner to recover Frontino, led the way up the hill, and Ruggiero trotted after her; but when they reached the valley they found Rodomonte gone, and saw by the fresh traces of horses' hoofs that he had taken the road by the plain, in the direction of the fountain.

Ruggiero, thinking soon to overtake him, bade

Ippalca return to Montalbano, assuring her that she should ere long have good news of Frontino, and drawing the letter from his bosom, he begged her to deliver it to her mistress with many messages of regard and apology. When she had fully committed these to memory, she took leave of him, and turning her palfrey's head in the opposite direction, she arrived at Montalbano that same night; while he galloped after the Saracen, but did not come up with him until he found himself again at Merlin's fountain.

CHAPTER XII.

> Each horseman drew his battle blade,
> And furious every charger neighed
> To join the dreadful revelry.
>
> CAMPBELL.

THE stranger with whom Ippalca had left the King of Algiers fighting was Mandricardo, King of Tartary, who was roaming about in these parts accompanied by Doralice, a lady who had formerly been in love with Rodomonte, but who had lately abandoned him for Mandricardo. When she saw the king descending the hill and coming towards them, she pointed him out to the Tartar, saying :

'See, here is the haughty Rodomonte coming to attack you, for he is very angry at having lost my favor.'

Thereupon Mandricardo rode to meet him, and without wasting many words, the two proud Infidels set upon each other; a furious combat ensued, which must have ended in the death of one or the other, for there were few their equals in the Saracen host for valor and skill in arms, had there not come up one of the couriers sent by King Agramante to recall all wandering captains and knights-errant to his standard, that they might aid him to raise

the siege, in which he was so closely beset by the
Emperor of the Golden Lilies, that unless succor
was speedily afforded him he must surrender.
The courier recognized the combatants by their
coats-of-arms, as well as by the skill with which
they wielded their weapons, and not daring to
interfere between them he told his errand to Doralice, who boldly placed herself between the two,
and said:

'My lords! I command you by the love which
I know you both bear me to put up your swords
and to keep them for a worthier cause. I pray
you hasten to the aid of our camp, which is now
besieged by the Christians and which is in great
danger.'

The messenger thereupon delivered the letter
he had brought for Rodomonte from Agramante,
and the two kings, after some parley, agreed upon
a truce until such time as the siege should be
raised, solemnly swearing upon the lady's fair hand
that until then there should be peace and friendship between them.

The Tartar king was, however, in some difficulty, for his horse had been killed in the fray;
luckily for him he spied Orlando's gallant charger,
Brigliadoro, feeding on the river's bank not far
from them, and he caught and mounted him; it
happened that not long before he had picked up
the good sword Durindana; why the unfortunate
Count had lately abandoned both sword and steed
in these valleys is told in the story of that knight.

The two kings rode on with Doralice until they
came upon the four Christian knights reposing by
the fountain with Marfisa, who had laid aside her
armor, and had attired herself in some of the costly

feminine apparel found among the Manganzese booty. Malagigi and Vivian, who were still on guard, rode to meet the strangers; when Mandricardo, with his usual impetuosity, instantly challenged them, and succeeded in unhorsing both, one after the other. The more prudent African looked on in silence, not choosing to waste time in these chance encounters. Aldigiero, on seeing his brother's discomfiture, vaulted into the saddle, and riding full-tilt at the Pagan, dealt him a thundering blow on the helmet, whereat his own spear shivered into fragments; but the Tartar did not yield one inch, and gave him a thrust in return which pierced through corselet and buckler, and wounded him in the shoulder so severely that after staggering for a few moments in the saddle, he fell senseless to the ground, staining the green grass all around with his blood. Nothing daunted, Ricciardetto next came boldly on, levelling his huge lance so steadily, that one glance sufficed to convince all who saw him that he belonged to the chief among the Paladins of France; and so would the Infidel have learnt to his cost had not Ricciardetto's horse at the first onset slipped and fallen upon him. Mandricardo, seeing no knights were left with whom to tilt, fancied that he had won the joust, and going up to the damsel, he said:

'Fair lady, since none remain to do battle in your behalf, you must, according to the well-known usages of war, yield yourself my prisoner, and join our company.'

But Marfisa lifted up her head and said with a haughty glance:

'You err greatly in this opinion. I might allow

11

you to be in the right, were one of these knights
whom you have overthrown my chosen lord or cav-
ailer; but I trust to myself alone for defence, being no novice in the use of sword and buckler.
Bring hither my armor and my charger,' she cried
to the squire; and throwing off her robe she stood
before him in a close-fitting doublet, upright and
agile as any Mars. She girt on her sword, and
when fully equipped vaulted with a light spring
into the saddle, and wheeled round her horse; and
after making him bound two or three times high
in the air, she levelled her lance at the Saracen,
and began the assault. Just so must Pentesilea
have appeared when she defied the Thessalian
Achilles in the camp before Troy.

Both lances shivered like glass in the fierce encounter, but those who wielded them were not seen
to yield so much as a finger's length. Marfisa
desirous to see if at closer quarters she would meet
with like measure from the proud Infidel, now drew
her sword. The Tartar did the same, and their
strokes fell fast and loud, but with so little effect
on the well-tempered steel and mail, that they might
have gone on fighting all that day and the next
also, had not Rodomonte thrown himself between
them, and reproached his rival with causing so great
delay.

'If you insist upon these combats,' cried he,
'mine has the prior claim, being still unfinished.
But you know well that we agreed upon a truce
until we had given help to our Moorish camp.
Till then all tilts and jousts were to be avoided by
us.'

Then he turned with deference to Marfisa, and
as he pointed to the courier, told her the message

brought from Agramante, and begged her, not only to abandon, or at any rate to defer the present combat, but to accompany them, and afford the Moorish king her assistance, whereby her fame would be more exalted than by such chance encounters, of little moment compared to the great matter they had in hand. Marfisa had long wished to try the mettle of Charlemagne's Paladins, and indeed had come to France from far-off lands, chiefly for the purpose of ascertaining whether the report of their great deeds was true, or a mere idle tale; she therefore gladly agreed to this proposal.

At that moment Ruggiero rode up, and recognizing Frontino, he pointed his lance, and in haughty tones challenged Rodomonte, who that day performed a greater deed than Jove himself ever achieved, for he conquered his own proud spirit, and refused the combat; the first and last time that he was known to do so. He knew Ruggiero, and had often longed to try a tilt with him, but he was now so anxious to hasten to the pressing need of his king, that if Achilles himself had defied him, he would not have hearkened to him. Smothering his wrath, he made excuse, and invited Ruggiero to go with them to the camp, adding, that in so doing he would show himself a faithful cavalier to the king, and that when the siege was raised, they would all have time to decide their private quarrels.

'I consent with a light heart,' said Ruggiero, 'provided you restore me Frontino.' At some future time I will prove your conduct unworthy a man of honor in taking him from a defenceless maiden; but not a moment's truce can I grant you until I have him back.'

.ese were disputing, one refusing to de-
..p the steed, the other demanding instant
..isfaction, Mandricardo interposed with another
grievance. Ruggiero, tracing his descent from the
heroic Hector, carried the arms of Troy, a white
eagle on a field azure, but Mandricardo also bore
for his device the king of birds, and on seeing Ruggiero's shield, he raised his angry protest and challenged him for daring to usurp his coat of arms. As
a spark in dry wood fanned by the breeze, so did
Ruggiero's anger blaze forth :

'You think to daunt me,' he cried, 'because I
am engaged with this knight, but I will soon show
you that I can both take my horse from him and
Hector's shield from you. That white bird, the
ancient cognizance of my race, shall be of evil
omen to you, who usurp what belongs to me
alone.'

'It is you who usurp my crest,' shouted Mandricardo as he drew his sword. Whereupon Ruggiero, never failing in courtesy, dropped his lance
and grasped Balisarda, tightening withal his hold
of his buckler. But Marfisa and Rodomonte threw
themselves between, and begged them to desist,
reminding Mandricardo of his compact. The Tartar king, however, would not listen, but declared
himself ready to fight Ruggiero, Rodomonte, and
the whole world, at once and on the very instant,
and Ruggiero, all unused to such insults, refused
with like indignation to hear of truce or delay.
Marfisa went from one to the other, trying to pacify them, but, as a flood which as fast as it is
dammed up in one quarter finds outlet in another,
so their wrath burst through all bounds, and at last
she exclaimed :

'My lords, I pray you listen to my advice. Either let us all fight out our several quarrels in due order, in which case I claim to finish mine with Mandricardo; or if we are to succor Agramante, let us hasten to Paris at once, and for the present, lay aside all these disputes.'

'With all my heart,' cried Ruggiero, 'provided I have Frontino. He must restore my horse, or leave me here dead on the field.'

'So be it!' said Rodomonte, 'but I call all to witness that if evil befall our king, the fault lies not with me.'

The incensed Ruggiero, paying no heed to this protest, raised his weapon, and rushed upon him like a wild boar out of the forest, and in the confusion the King of Algiers lost hold of the stirrup. Just then, however, the savage Mandricardo shouting out, 'With me is your quarrel, O Ruggiero!' aimed a blow at his helmet, which, had it not been tempered as adamant, must have cut through to the jawbone, and as it was made him bend to the very saddle-bow. Before he had time to rise, the King of Algiers fell upon him, and in the struggle Ruggiero let go both rein and sword-hilt. Balisarda fell from his hand, and his horse carried him off across the plain with Rodomonte after him. Marfisa, indignant that two should set upon one, engaged Mandricardo, and the Christian knights having by this time recovered their overthrow, Ricciardetto threw himself before Rodomonte, and kept him back, while Vivian put a sword into Ruggiero's hand, who again assailed Rodomonte with such fury that he reeled and lay senseless under his blows.

Looking round at that moment, Ruggiero saw

Marfisa in a sorry plight, for in a sudden bolt, her horse had slipped on the soft smooth grass, and now lay on his side unable to rise. He rushed to her rescue, and had Balisarda been in his hand, it would have fared ill with the Tartar king. By this time Rodomonte had recovered himself, and seeing Ricciardetto standing by, and angry at his former interference, he was about to attack him, when a new incident occurred, which, in one instant, changed the whole scene. Doralice's trained palfrey, which had stood perfectly quiet up to this time, now took sudden fright, and after rearing and plunging gave a great leap and galloped off with the terrified damsel, who screamed and shrieked for assistance. The King of Algiers was the first to ride after her, and Mandricardo quickly followed them, leaving Ruggiero raging like any lion, and Marfisa equally furious at this unlooked-for conclusion to their combats. They could not hope to overtake Frontino and Brigliadoro with their steeds, so after some consultation, they determined to follow the two kings to Paris, and there, as soon as the siege was raised, to demand from them satisfaction.

Ruggiero first bade farewell to Vivián and Malagigi and to the wounded Aldigiero, with proffers of his service should they meet again. To Ricciardetto he made more hearty offers of friendship, at all times, and in good or evil fortune, and sent respectful salutations to his sister, without however betraying their secret. Marfisa was so angry and so anxious to reach Paris, that she forgot to take leave of the young knights; but they rode after her and said farewell to her from a distance.

So Ruggiero and Marfisa followed the others on the road to Paris, and we shall next find them all in the Saracen camp, where Charlemagne and his army had much cause to rue their arrival.

CHAPTER XIII.

CHARLEMAGNE IS DEFEATED. DISCORD WORKS MISCHIEF AMONG THE SARACEN CAPTAINS.

> Revenge impatient rose ;
> He threw his blood-stain'd sword in thunder down ;
> And with a withering look,
> The war-denouncing trumpet took,
> And blew a blast so loud and dread,
> Were ne'er prophetic sounds so full of woe.
>
> COLLINS.

RODOMONTE and Mandricardo were joined on the road to Paris by King Gradasso and King Sacripante, who were, as you may remember, among the knights enticed into the enchanted palace of Atlante. When the four kings caught sight of the long rows of white tents in the Christian camp, and the fluttering pennons of the beleaguered Moors beyond, they drew rein, and after some consultation they decided upon at once cutting their way through the enemy and joining Agramante. With loud shouts of 'For Spain and Africa,' the little band dashed in amongst the Christians, with such impetuosity that the rear guard, taken completely by surprise, fell back in great confusion on the main body of the army.

Ruggiero and Marfisa came up soon after this, and seeing the state of affairs they lost no time in following up the assault, upon which a complete panic seized the Christians, who thought that their

Swiss and German mercenaries had mutinied; until the Emperor, roused by the tumult, came out with his lords, and with much difficulty succeeded in re-establishing some degree of order among his troops. Not, however, before our knights, leaving a long line of dead, dying, and wounded in their path, had reached in safety the Moorish camp, and had been received within their entrenchments with acclamations of joy and surprise. Agramante at once decided upon following up this advantage, and marching out at the head of all his army he forthwith attacked the Christians. Kettle-drums, cymbals, clarions and trumpets sounded the call to arms from every quarter, and the broad standards and banners of war were floated to the breeze.

Charlemagne, on his side also, hurriedly assembled his levies and allies, British and German, French and Italian; they were soon spread out in long array, and a furious battle ensued. Unluckily for the Christians, Orlando and Rinaldo were both absent. The unhappy Count was still roaming through the world in his fruitless search for Angelica; while Rinaldo had no sooner led his Scotch and English reinforcements to Paris, and had there helped to win the great battle in which the Saracens were defeated by the Emperor, and shut up within their entrenchments, than, believing them to be together, he had started in quest of Orlando and the fair princess, and was now seeking them in vain through all the abbeys and castles of France.

The Moors fought with dauntless valor, and led by the terrible Rodomonte, the furious Mandricardo, the bold Ruggiero, the famous Gradasso, the valiant Marfisa, and the unrivalled Sacripante, they won the day, and drove Charles and all his host, calling upon 'St. John and St. Denis to the rescue,' back into Paris. Many, unable to press through the throng at the bridge, seeing death before and behind them, and longing in vain for the wings of Icarus, jumped into the Seine and were drowned. Many more were slain, and not a few among the chief paladins of France were taken prisoners. But for the desperate efforts of Charlemagne and his trusted knight Brandimarte, few would have reached the shelter of the walls, within which it was now the turn of the Christians to be besieged, while the Moors spread over France and devastated the country far and wide. Perhaps the cry of the unhappy people reached the ears of their guardian angel St. Michael, and moved him to send the spirit of discord into the camp of the Saracens, with strict injunctions not to depart thence, until the flame of former quarrels had been fanned and fresh animosities stirred up among their chiefs.

However this may be, the day after the battle, the knights all went up together to make their appeal to Agramante. Marfisa was the first to demand instant satisfaction from the Tartar king, refusing to give place to any, or to delay her claim for a day, or even for an hour. Rodomonte was equally urgent in wishing to fight out the quarrel with his rival. Ruggiero insisted upon his prior right to regain by arms his lost steed; and Mandricardo declared that he would not for a moment suffer Ruggiero to usurp the white-winged eagle for his coat of arms, and was so frantic with rage that he protested he was ready to fight all three at once, rather than give way to any of the others.

Agramante did his utmost to reconcile their differences, but, seeing it was of no avail, he at last commanded them to draw lots for the order of their combats, and thus commit the decision to the will of the fickle goddess. The King of Algiers and Mandricardo came out first; Mandricardo and Ruggiero second; Ruggiero and Rodomonte third; and last of all Marfisa and Mandricardo. The lady was greatly mortified at this result; Ruggiero was not much better pleased, for he knew that the strength of his antagonist would be so far expended in the first combat that not much would be left for his satisfaction.

A little way out of Paris there lies a dale, surrounded on all sides by a low bank, which gives it somewhat the aspect of an amphitheatre. A castle which had once stood there had been destroyed by fire in the late wars, and was now a ruin, just such a one as that which may be seen to this day by any one who goes from Parma to Borgo. In this place the lists were set up. A square space was measured out and enclosed by low rails, with a wide entrance at each end; opposite to these openings two pavilions were placed outside the palisades; the one at the west end was set apart for the King of Algiers, who had chosen Ferrau and Sacripante to act as his squires on this great occasion, and to assist him in buckling on his armor and his huge shield, on which was emblazoned a serpent, the device of his house. Gradasso and Falsiron did like service for the King of Tartary in the pavilion opposite the east gateway. Lofty scaffoldings were erected on either side, in which were seated the most distinguished spectators; among them the kings of Africa and Spain, with their chief captains and nobles; the Queen of Castile, with the princesses and noble dames of Arragon, Seville, and Granada; and King Stordilano, with his daughter Doralice, magnificently dressed in a particolored robe of crimson and green. All the available space outside was occupied by an immense throng of people; and the man considered himself fortunate who could secure some vantage ground of bank or tree, from which to look on at the expected sight.

One of Agramante's heralds had gone round the lists, setting forth the laws of the tournament, and forbidding the spectators to take part therein, either by word or gesture, and the crowd were beginning to show signs of impatience at the non-appearance of the combatants, when the sound of voices in angry dispute drew all eyes to Mandricardo's tent.

Gradasso had just finished arming the King of Tartary, and was about to gird him with Durindana, the famous sword which had belonged to Orlando, when looking down he saw the quarterings of Alcmonte inscribed on the pommel, and recognized it as his own, the same which the young Count had taken from him long ago near a fountain in Aspromonte. He examined it, and felt sure that it was the very sword with which he had done such great deeds when he first came from the East, and when with it he had helped to conquer the kingdom of Castile; but how it was that he now found it in the hands of Mandricardo he could not divine. He first asked him whether he had taken it by force or by stratagem, but when Mandricardo began to explain, he would not let him finish his story, interrupting him with:

'Think not that I will allow you, or any one else, to keep this sword. Go, seek yourself another; for know, that whether you took it from Orlando, or picked it up on the road, you took what did not belong to you; it is mine; I will defend it with my life, and in these very lists am I ready to maintain my right to it. You must follow the old custom of fighting for your arms before you use them, and must win this sword from me in battle ere you draw it against Rodomonte.'

'No sweeter sounds can reach my ear,' replied the Tartar haughtily, 'than a challenge to the combat; but Rodomonte must first consent to the delay.'

Here, however, Ruggiero interfered, and said he would allow no change to be made in the order of battle already agreed upon.

'For,' said he, 'if Gradasso is right, you may not wear the white eagle until you have won it from me. But on this I do not insist, as I have consented that my turn should come after that of the King of Algiers. If, however, you in any way disturb this arrangement, I will upset it altogether, and insist upon fighting for my device at once.'

'If you were each of you a Mars,' cried Mandricardo, irritated beyond measure, 'neither of you should deprive me of my good sword or of my noble cognizance.'

Thereupon he lifted his closed fist and gave Gradasso such a blow on the right arm, that he dropped Durindana. Flushing crimson at this public insult, and bent on vengeance, the king drew back to unsheathe his scimitar, while the Tartar, turning to Ruggiero, said:

'Come on, O Ruggiero, and Rodomonte as well.

Let who will attack me, African or Spaniard, I defy you all, and will turn my back to none;' and swinging the sword of Alcmonte round his head, he held up his shield with a proud and scornful mien.

'Leave him to me!' cried Gradasso; 'I will soon cure him of this madness.'

'No, by Heaven!' shouted Ruggiero, 'this is my quarrel, and I will not give it up to you. Stand back!'

'Out of my way!' cried the other, and a strange *mêlée* began among the three, when the bystanders interfered, and the appearance of the kings of Africa and Spain, who came up to inquire into the cause of the uproar, awed them into respectful silence. While they were trying to appease this tumult, sounds of contention arose from the other pavilion. The King of Circassia having, with the assistance of Ferrau, arrayed Rodomonte in complete armor, had led him to where Frontino stood pawing the ground and chafing his gilded bit with impatience. Sacripante, before holding the stirrup ready, satisfied himself, as was his duty, that the steed was well shod and bridled, and in every respect properly caparisoned. While he was carefully examining him, admiring his perfect proportions and strong and active frame, it suddenly struck him that this was none other than his own horse Frontalatte, upon whose back he had fought so many battles, and who was so much prized by him that when he lost him he vowed for many a day to go afoot. Brunello had stolen the charger from him before Albracca, on the same day that he had carried off the ring from Angelica and the sword from Marfisa; and on returning to Africa he had given him to Ruggiero, who had changed his name to Frontino.

When he had made quite sure that he was not mistaken, the Circassian turned to the King of Algiers, and said :

'I must tell you, my lord, that this is my horse which was stolen from me before Albracca. I could bring many witnesses to the truth of this, but since they are far away, if any dare deny it, I am here armed, ready to prove my words with my sword. Nevertheless, for the sake of the good fellowship which for the last few days there has been between us, and also because I see your need of the steed, I am willing to lend him to you for to-day ; on condition however that you acknowledge the loan, otherwise you shall not have him without fighting for him.'

Rodomonte, than whom none prouder ever bore arms, and who, I verily believe, surpassed in strength and courage all the fabled heroes of antiquity, replied :

'If any but you, Sacripante, had dared to speak to me in this wise, he should have found to his cost that he had better have been born dumb. But for the sake of the friendly companionship which, as you say, has lately existed between us, I content myself with advising you to put off this attempt to deprive me of my charger until you see the issue of the combat between me and the Tartar, and that, I trust, shall be such as to induce you to say, " I pray thee, keep the steed."'

'Thy very courtesy is insult,' answered the indignant Circassian ; 'and I now tell thee plainly I forbid thee to mount my horse, and doubt not but that I will defend him as long as I hold a sword in my hand.'

From words they soon came to deeds, their fury blazing up like fire among straw. Rodomonte was armed *cap-à-pie*, while Sacripante wore neither mail nor buckler, yet the skill and agility with which he wielded his weapon enabled him to defend himself against all the power and strength of the King of Algiers. As swiftly as a windmill his sword turned in parrying the blows of his adversary, until Ferrau and some others threw themselves between them, and divided them. Agramante, in the mean time, having heard the sounds of tumult from the other tent, had bidden Marsilio keep peace there, and had hurried up to see after this new quarrel, and at sight of their king the two combatants bridled their fury, and respectfully stood aside.

Agramante, with grave and quiet dignity, asked the cause of all this contention, and when it was explained to him, he tried, but without success, to reconcile them; for the one refused to do aught but lend his charger, the other, proud as ever, protested that nothing should induce him to receive as a favor what he could take by force. The king asked the Circassian how he knew that the horse was his, and where it had been stolen from him; and as he narrated the circumstances of the theft, his cheek crimsoning with shame at the recollection, Marfisa, who was standing by, changed countenance, for she remembered losing her sword at the same time, and she as well as the bold Sacripante now recognized the fleet courser which had flown from her on that day as if on the wings of the wind. The courtiers who were present looked significantly at Brunello, whom they had often heard boast of these clever feats, and when Marfisa

learnt who he was, and moreover, that instead of
ordering him to be hung up with a halter round
his neck, according to his deserts, his sovereign had
bestowed upon him the kingdom of Tangiers, her
old anger at the wrong done her blazed forth with
fresh fury, and she determined not to lose a moment
in taking her revenge upon the miscreant.

She bade her squire bring her helmet, for with
this exception she was fully equipped; indeed, I
have heard that not more than ten times in her
life had she been seen without her cuirass since she
first buckled it on. She then strode straight up to
the tribune where Brunello was seated and seizing
him as some falcon clutches a wretched chicken in
its talons, she dragged him before the king, he all the
time crying and begging for mercy so loudly that
his shrill screams, which were heard above all the
noise and tumult of the camp, caused the people to
run together to see what was the matter. Marfisa
then, in haughty tones, thus addressed Agramante:

'I demand, O King, to take possession of this
rogue, thy vassal, in order that with mine own
hands I may hang him up by the neck, for having,
on the self-same day that he took from this knight
his horse, stolen from me my sword. If any here
present dare say me wrong, let him stand forth;
for in thy presence will I maintain that he lies,
and that I am in my right. But as I would not
be accused of causing delay, or of interfering with
the combats already arranged among these more
worthy champions, I will grant him three days'
respite, at the end of which, unless any appear in
his defence, I will regale the birds of the air with
his carcass, and hang it on the tower I see yonder,
by the edge of that wood.'

So saying, she lifted the unhappy wretch by the hair of his head, slung him on her horse's neck before her, and without waiting for reply rode in the direction of the tower to which she had pointed. Agramante stood in mute amazement, so dismayed at all this turmoil that he did not know which way to turn. His first thought was to ride after her and rescue Brunello; for though he had long ceased to regard him with any special good-will, he deemed that he himself would be personally insulted and dishonored were he to permit one of his courtiers to be thus carried off before his very eyes. But King Sobrino, one of his most trusted allies and counsellors, dissuaded him from doing so, saying that such an enterprise would ill beseem his high rank, and would carry more risk with it than it was worth; adding that Brunello so richly deserved his fate, that if the lifting of an eyelid could save him, he, for one, would not have him do even that much in his behalf, but would advise him to let justice take her course.

The king was nothing loth to follow this prudent counsel, for he felt he had a more difficult and important matter before him in trying to settle the disputes of the five knights, who were all so clamorously intent upon first taking the field.

He began by calling upon the kings of Algiers and Tartary, in the name of loyalty and friendship, to give up their claims upon the lady who was the cause of strife between them. Finding them, however, deaf to his remonstrances, and obstinate in insisting upon their rights, he declared that the lady should be arbiter, and herself decide which of the two should be her chosen consort. To this they agreed, and solemnly swore to abide by her decision, each confident that he was to be the accepted suitor.

Rodomonte had loved Doralice long before Mandricardo, and was believed by all who had seen him wear her colors in so many tournaments, jousts, and battles to be certain of success. But Mandricardo had perhaps more sure tokens of the lady's favor, for when the two stood before her, she cast down her eyes and said she loved the Tartar best. If great was the astonishment of all, far greater was that of Rodomonte. At first he remonstrated, until reminded by the king of his oath, when he yielded; but rebuked by his lord, and scorned by his love, he determined to remain no longer in the Moorish camp, and followed by only two of his squires, he made his way through the crowd, and departed, a prey to anger and bitter mortification. So does some infuriated bull, when defeated by his rival, leave the herd and wander alone by the edge of the wood or in the meadows beside the stream, filling the air with his loud and angry bellowing.

Ruggiero was on the point of following Rodomonte to reclaim Frontino, when, remembering his appointed combat with Mandricardo, he turned into the lists, comforting himself with the hope of being soon free to go in pursuit of his well-loved steed.

Discord, and Pride her chosen confederate, had indeed reason to congratulate themselves and to rejoice over the result of their day's work in the camp of the victorious Saracens.

CHAPTER XIV.

THE COMBAT BETWEEN RUGGIERO AND MANDRICARDO.

He dropped the lance, he dropped the reins;
He fell as falls the dead.
MACAULAY.

WHEN King Agramante found that he could not persuade Ruggiero and Gradasso to allow Mandricardo to bear the white-winged eagle of Troy or to wear the sword of Orlando, he said at last :

'Let us waste no more words, but again commit the decision to Fortune : on this condition, however, that he who comes out first shall fight the quarrel of both ; winning or losing for himself, he wins or loses for the other also. Your valor and skill in arms are known by all to be equal, and I feel sure that, upon whichever the lot may fall, he will do his utmost to win the day ; should he fail, Fortune must bear the blame.'

Upon the knights consenting to this proposal, their names were written upon two slips of parchment, and tossed into an urn ; a child was told to put in his hand, and to the bitter mortification of Gradasso and to the extreme delight of Ruggiero, he drew out the name of the latter. The two spent the rest of the day together, Gradasso giving

Ruggiero the benefit of his experience in the use
of arms, and helping him to test and to examine
his weapons and armor.

The people were so eager to witness the combat
that many spent the night on the ground, and
long before day every single place was occupied.
The foolish crowd thought of nothing but the excitement and interest of the moment ; but Sobrino
and Marsilio and the wiser among the Saracen
leaders foresaw how great would be the injury to
their cause, whichever fell, and blamed Agramante
for allowing the combat to go on, warning him
that either of these knights could do more for him
in contending with Charlemagne than ten thousand
of the common herd.

On the other side, neither the prayers nor the
tears of the lovely Doralice were wanting to induce
the Tartar king to withdraw his challenge.

'Alas!' cried she, 'how little has it availed me
that your quarrel with Rodomonte ended without
bloodshed ; for how can I ever hope for happiness
or peace of mind if, on the slightest provocation,
you are to be always ready to don cuirass and helmet ? How short-lived has been my joy, and how
foolish my pride in the thought that so great a king,
so renowned a knight, was willing to risk his life
for my sake, since I find that for so poor a trifle he
is ready to incur like peril. It is not love for me,
but the mere pleasure of fighting for fighting's
sake, that moves you. How does it concern you
what device Ruggiero bears upon his shield ? I can
see neither harm nor advantage to you in his wearing or in his abandoning this crest ; but in the battle
upon which you are entering, how little can you gain,
how much may you lose. So much that my heart

sinks at the very thought. Ah! if, indeed, it be so, that you prize a painted bird more than your own life, yet have pity on mine, for think not that I will survive you.'

With these and many more such-like entreaties she tried to shake his resolve, but he, kissing the tears from her sweet face, told her to dry her eyes and to have no fear; for that he felt himself more than a match for his adversary, and that he was sure of victory.

She was still remonstrating, and he was still trying to comfort her, when at the dawn of the next day Ruggiero, fully equipped, presented himself before the barriers and blew his horn. No sooner did the Tartar king hear the notes of battle than he called for his arms, and looked so proud and so defiant that even Doralice had need to hold her peace. He then mounted the great Count's charger and rode into the lists, where the kings and princes and their courtiers were soon assembled.

When the squires had clasped their glittering helmets, and put the lances into their hands, the trumpet gave the signal, and the two knights spurred on to the attack with such force that the earth shook beneath their horses' hoofs, and their spears shivered into a thousand pieces. Nothing daunted, they unsheathed their swords, and returning to the assault aimed straight at each other's vizors, for like good knights and true, they disdained to dismount their adversary by wounding his charger; such being deemed contrary to the laws of noble tourney, where to slay an adversary's horse was considered a disgraceful proceeding. I leave you to imagine how Durindana and Balisarda were wielded by such hands. The blows rained like hail upon the doubly lined vizors; but the skill of the defence was not less than the fury of the attack. Mandricardo got the first advantage, in which our good Ruggiero was nearly killed; for one of these heavy strokes cut open his shield, and piercing through the cuirass beneath, entered the tender flesh. The blood of all ran cold at the terrible sight, for by far the greater number of the spectators favored Ruggiero. I think his guardian angel must have interposed to save him, for he recovered himself as quick as lightning, and struck Mandricardo's helmet with the point of his sword with such force that the latter, completely stunned, let drop his bridle and reeled in his saddle, while Brigliadoro, not much pleased with his new master, galloped wildly round the lists.

A wounded lion never raged more furiously than the Tartar when he regained his senses. Turning Brigliadoro with one great bound on Ruggiero, he stood up in the stirrups, and raising his sword aimed at his helmet. Had he straightway reached it, he must have cloven it to the very chin. But Ruggiero was too quick for him, and striking him below his uplifted arm, he cut through the mail and drew back Balisarda crimsoned with blood. Although, however, Durindana's stroke thus lost some of its force, it made Ruggiero stoop to the very saddle-bow and close his eyes with pain, and had not the steel of his morion been so strong yet worse might have happened to him. As it was he was able to pursue his advantage and to wound his adversary again in the right side. Mandricardo, beside himself with rage, now prepared for a supreme effort, and throwing away his shield, he grasped his sword with both hands.

'Ah,' cried Ruggiero, 'you show indeed how unworthy you are to bear that famous crest, since now you cast it from you, and but a little while ago you cut it in twain. Never again shall you claim it.'

Alas! it was now his turn to feel the sharp edge of Durindana, which pierced his vizor, and then fortunately glancing aside from his face, fell upon his breast-plate and cutting through the fine linked mail as if it were wax, wounded him in the ribs. The swords of both were now stained with blood, and the lookers-on differed as to which had the advantage. Such doubts, however, were soon set at rest by Ruggiero, who, aiming full at the place left exposed by the abandoned shield, pierced through the cuirass, and buried his blade in the heart of Mandricardo, who had to give up the white-winged eagle, the famous sword, and what was still more precious to him, sweet life itself.

He did not however die without in some measure revenging himself, for as he let go Durindana, it fell upon Ruggiero's helmet, and penetrating steel morion and headpiece, entered two fingers' breadth into his skull. Stunned and senseless, he fell first to the ground, and as the blood gushed from his wounds, all thought that Mandricardo was the victor; so much so that Doralice folded her hands, and thanked Heaven that the combat had ended according to her wishes. She had scarcely done so when Mandricardo fell so heavily from his horse that it was seen that he was dead, and the other only wounded; and sorrow and joy quickly changed sides.

How shall I describe the congratulations of the princes and captains, above all the favors and caresses which the king lavished upon Ruggiero: for not one of his knights did he value half so highly. Nor did the noble ladies of the court fail to join heartily in these expressions of pleasure and good-will. The king's chief physician, who had been sent for, soon arrived, and assured them that none of his wounds were mortal, and such great affection did the king bear him that he caused him to be carried to his own tent, that he might be near him day and night. Durindana was given to Gradasso, while Mandricardo's shield and armor and all his weapons were hung up over the bed of Ruggiero, who begged the king to accept the gallant charger Brigliadoro, well knowing how much he would prize him.

We must now return to that noble lady who sat at home in Montalbano, weeping and sighing in vain for the arrival of her knight. Ippalca had told her all that had happened, and had given her Ruggiero's letter and his many messages; but Bradamante had so fully expected to see him that when she took his letter, her face clouded all over with disappointment, and her eyes filled with tears. Yet she kissed it over and over again, and read it at least a dozen times, as often asking for all he had said to be repeated to her, her tears falling fast as she listened. Ippalca somewhat comforted her by reminding her of his promise to come again within fifteen or twenty days, saying she felt sure that he would be true to her, and keep his word. With these assurances, and with hope the never-failing companion of all true lovers, she was fain to content herself and to wait for the wished-for day, taking care never to absent herself from Montalbano for even an hour.

We know how impossible it was for poor Ruggiero to keep his promise. The suffering caused by his wounds increased so much that he lay for more than a month on his bed hovering between life and death. Days and weeks went by, but no tidings reached Bradamante. Ricciardetto, indeed, came and related to her the story of his deliverance, with that of Malagigi and Vivian, but with so much mention of Marfisa, of her great valor and exceeding beauty, that it only served to increase her anxiety. Though Bradamante joined in her praises, she felt anything but satisfaction at hearing that Ruggiero had gone to Paris in her company, and was secretly distracted with fear lest he should forget her when in the constant society of so beautiful a lady.

While the unhappy damsel was thus waiting and weeping all in vain, Rinaldo, the most illustrious of her brothers, one day arrived at the castle, accompanied only by his page. After that fruitless quest, of which I have told you, he was on his way to Paris, when the news reached him that Vivian and Malagigi were about to be given up to the Manganzese. He at once had hastened to Agrismonte, and there, hearing of their safety and that the brothers and cousins had all gone together to Montalbano, a longing seized him to see them and also to embrace his dear mother; so he determined to join them. After spending some happy days among them, he departed, taking with him Ricciardo, Ricciardetto, Alardo, and Guicciardo, the eldest son of the house, and also his cousins Malagigi and Vivian. Bradamante excused herself from accompanying them, saying that she was sick, as indeed she was, with hope deferred and bitter disappointment.

CHAPTER XV.

For those that fly may fight again,
Which he can never do that's slain.
HUDIBRAS.

RINALDO therefore took leave of his lady mother and of Bradamante, and with his brothers and cousins set out for Paris at the head of seven hundred men-at-arms : a gallant little band, chosen from among the bravest and the sturdiest of his vassals, who were at all times looked upon as among the best soldiers in France, and who were so devoted to their lord that although Rinaldo was not accounted rich, either in money or estates, he made himself so beloved by his kind and pleasing manners, and was so generous in sharing with them what little he had, that not one of this valiant company could ever be induced, by offers of gold however lavish, to desert his service for that of another. These men-at-arms, except for some very pressing necessity, had never been moved from Montalbano till now, when knowing Charlemagne's sore need of help, Rinaldo, leaving only a slender guard at the castle, led them with him to Paris. On the evening of their second day's march they met a knight in black armor, with shield and coat of mail crossed by a white band. Ricciardetto rode in front, and

being challenged by the stranger to try a bout with
him, wheeled round his horse and rode at him full
tilt, while the others halted to look on and see how
the joust would go.   In a few minutes Ricciardetto
was overthrown, and laid on the ground two lances'
length from his horse.   Alardo immediately spurred
on to avenge him, but met with a like fate; falling
stunned and bruised to the earth, after his shield
had been split in two.   Guicciardo next put his
lance in rest, though Rinaldo cried out:

'Hold! stop! mine must be the third combat.'
But before he could finish buckling on his helmet
he saw Guicciardo stretched beside the other two.
Ricciardo, Malagigi, and Vivian then pressed forward; but Rinaldo rode up fully equipped, and said:

'We must hasten on to Paris;' adding to himself, for he was not so uncivil as to speak it aloud:
'There is no saying when we should reach it were
I to wait until you had all, one after the other,
been worsted in this tourney.'

The two knights turned their horses round, in
order to gain a fair field for the encounter, and
then rode at each other with such speed that their
lances were shattered in the shock, and their
horses forced back upon their very haunches; and
although Baiardo recovered himself so quickly that
he was scarcely hindered in his course, the other
charger fell over and broke his back.   The knight
leapt from his saddle, and in one instant stood ready
on his feet, and as Rinaldo turned said to him:

'Sir, the good charger of which you have deprived me was so dear to me that much should I
fail in my duty were I to suffer him to die all
unavenged.   So come on! do your best; for truly
now, this must be no feigned battle between us.'

'If you only wish to fight because your horse is dead,' replied Rinaldo, 'trouble not yourself; I will provide you with one, which shall not, I assure you, be less worthy.'

'You are but dull-witted,' answered the stranger, 'if you imagine that all my care is for my horse. But, since you cannot or will not understand my meaning, I will explain it more at large. I wish to see whether you are as good with the sword as with the lance, and whether you are at that game also my equal. Dismount or not, as it may please you; I am ready to give you every advantage, so anxious am I to cross swords with you; only do not let yours remain any longer by your side.'

Rinaldo did not keep him in suspense, but said: 'I promise you, you shall have what you desire; and that there may be no suspicion of undue advantage being taken of you, these my companions shall ride forward, and I will overtake them.'

He accordingly bade them do so, keeping with him only one groom to hold his horse. The stranger much commended the courtesy of the gallant Paladin, who dismounted and threw Baiardo's bridle to his squire, and as soon as his banners were out of sight held up his shield, and grasping his trusty sword, defied the knight to battle.

Then there began a passage at arms such as surprised even the knights themselves, for neither expected to meet with such stout resistance, or to find themselves so equally matched. Though they were moved by no angry feelings, but only by the passion for glory, and did not so much attempt to wound as to disarm one another and to parry each other's strokes, yet their blows resounded fast and loud, and made steel plate and linked mail fly asunder.

This fierce assault had lasted an hour and a half, the sun had sunk below the waves, and night's dusky veil was fast spreading over the heavens, when Rinaldo, finding his unknown adversary not only stand firm against his attack, but give him enough to do to defend himself, began to wish that he could with untarnished honor put an end to the fight. The reflections of the stranger were of a like nature; for though he did not know that his opponent was the Lord of Montalbano, yet he felt sure that he was some knight of great renown and skill in arms; accordingly he also would gladly, could it be without disgrace, retire from so perilous an engagement, more especially as the increasing darkness made attack and defence alike hazardous. Rinaldo at length proposed a truce until daylight should reappear, and hospitably invited the knight to accompany him to his tent, where he promised him good entertainment for the night; at the same time offering him his squire's horse, a fine animal handsomely caparisoned, assuring him that he was well trained for all service. The stranger cordially accepted this kind proposal, and while they were riding together towards the encampment, Rinaldo in conversation, by chance named himself, when the knight exclaimed with much emotion:

'O my lord! what ill luck has led me to fight with you, whom I have so long and so highly esteemed and honored? For know that I am Guidone Selvaggio, descended from the noble Amone, father of your renowned house. I was born and brought up by my mother, the Lady Constance, on the farther shore of the Euxine Sea. The desire to see you and my kinsfolk has led me hither, and now it has come about that there, where

I wished to show most respect, I have shown least.
Ignorance must be my excuse and must plead for
my pardon.'

After many compliments had passed between
them, Rinaldo said : ' You need not trouble yourself with apologies for challenging us ; you could
truly have given no surer pledge of your being a
branch of our ancient stem than the valor of which
we have had proof. Had you shown a gentler
and more peaceful bearing we might have scarce
believed you ; for the lion does not come from the
doe, nor the eagle or the falcon from the dove.'

Thus conversing as they rode together, they
reached the tents, and Rinaldo presented Guidone
to his friends as a brother they had often wished
to see ; they all pressed round him with cordial
expressions of welcome, and exclaimed to each
other at his likeness to their father. Gladly would
he have been received by them at any time, but
more especially so now when the help of his good
sword would be so serviceable to them.

The next morning, as soon as the sun's bright
rays had risen over the ocean, the little band, accompanied by their new-found brother, continued
their march. They went on all that day and all
the next, until they halted on the banks of the
Seine, within ten miles of the beleaguered walls of
Paris. Here they fell in with the two brothers Grifone and Aquilante, whom Guidone knew, having
parted from them but lately. He said to Rinaldo :

' Here are two knights who have few equal to
them in battle. Could we gain their help for
Charles's cause we need stand in little fear of the
Saracens.' Rinaldo, however, had already recognized them by their richly embossed and orna-

mented armor, the more easily as Grifone always rode equipped in white, and his brother in black. Having affectionately saluted and embraced them, he turned to welcome Sansonetto, who came up a little after the other two, and whose great reputation was well known to him.

The whole party then held council together, and decided upon deferring the assault until the third or fourth watch of the night, when sleep should have poured on all her Lethean stream. Rinaldo rested his troop in the shelter of the wood for the rest of the day; and when the sun left the world to darkness, and the Bear, the Scorpion, the Goat, and all the starry constellations which had lain hidden under his greater light, adorned the heavens, he roused the sleeping camp, and silently and with stealthy steps they advanced to the attack. They found Agramante's sentinels fast asleep, and falling upon and killing them at their posts, without having been either heard or seen, they came all unawares upon the vanguard of the Moorish army, and routed them completely, for the panic-stricken Saracens, taken entirely by surprise, could make no stand against such warriors. Rinaldo, in order to inspire greater terror, ordered the horns and trumpets to be blown, and gave out his battle-cry as, in advance of all, he spurred on Baiardo, who vaulted the barriers, overthrew the horsemen, and trampled down the foot-soldiers in his fiery course. At the dreaded sound of, 'For Rinaldo and Montalbano,' the bravest among the Pagans trembled, and not waiting to encounter his too well-known sword, fled in dismay. Guidone, close behind him, performed almost equal prodigies of valor; and friends, brothers, and cousins, with all who followed the banner of Chiaramonte, acquitted themselves as brave men and true.

Charlemagne and his paladins, who had in the mean time been advised of Rinaldo's arrival, and of his intended midnight raid upon the Saracens, now marched out to his aid and attacked their rear. Agramante lay sleeping in his tent, when one of his knights ran in and awoke him, telling him that unless he prepared for instant flight he would be taken prisoner with all his army. He was hastily buckling on his cuirass, when Marsilio and the prudent Sobrino hurried in with the same report, saying that Rinaldo was rapidly making his way through the host, and that if he awaited the arrival of that fierce Paladin, they would all be killed or taken captive. They advised him, therefore, to retire, with what troops he could collect, upon Arles or Narbonne, both good strongholds, in which he might maintain himself, and gain time to restore and to recruit his shattered forces: and so hope at some future time to turn round upon Charles, and defeating him, to avenge himself for this unexpected reverse.

Hard and bitter as was this counsel, Agramante followed it; and by hasty marches through lanes and by-ways, retreated with twenty thousand Moors and Spaniards to Arles, thus escaping from the net which Rinaldo had spread for him.

The king did not forget the wounded and still enfeebled Ruggiero, but had him placed on a smooth-paced palfrey and led beside him, and as soon as they were out of reach of danger he was carried on board a bark and safely and commodiously conveyed by river to Arles. To this place the fugitives, who to the number of some hundred thousand were scattered over the hills and valleys of France, were ordered to repair, as that town, being situated on the river not far from the sea coast opposite Africa and close to Spain, was in every respect well adapted for the collecting of supplies and provisions, and for recruiting the broken army of Agramante.

Marsilio wrote mandates for fresh levies of horse and foot throughout Spain, and ordered every available vessel in Barcelona to be equipped for service. Agramante held daily councils of war, and sparing himself neither expense nor fatigue, exacted heavy contributions from all his African cities and provinces. He sent also to Rodomonte, offering to bestow upon him his own cousin in marriage, with the rich kingdom of Oran as her dower, if he would return to his standard; but that haughty knight refused all such proposals. Marfisa acted very differently, for she no sooner heard of the king's defeat, and of his having fallen back upon Arles with the scanty remains of his forces, than, waiting for no summons, she hastened to offer him the aid both of her sword and her possessions. She had kept the wretched Brunello for ten days in mortal terror of his life, but then, seeing that none had stirred a finger in his behalf, and not caring to stain her proud hands with such base blood, she released him, and taking him with her to Arles, she gave him as a free gift to his master, to whom truly he had done no wrong. I leave you to imagine the delight of the king at recovering her help. Anxious to show his sense of her generosity, he did what he knew would gratify her, and ordered Brunello to be hung in some remote and savage place, where the knave's vile carcass was left to feed the vultures and the crows. The justice of Heaven perhaps ordained that Ruggiero, who might have taken pity upon him, still lay helpless in his tent, and before he heard of it the deed was done.

CHAPTER XVI.

'The day to night,' she made her moan,
'The day to night, the night to morn,
And day and night I'm left alone,
To live forgotten, and love forlorn.'

TENNYSON.

ALL this time Bradamante was watching for the
promised return of Ruggiero; counting the
days as they went by with such impatience that
she sometimes fancied that the horses of the Sun
had fallen lame, or that possibly the wheels of his
chariot were broken! The days, she thought, were
surely longer than the one prolonged of old through
the faith of the great Hebrew captain; the nights
passed so slowly that she often envied the bears,
the dormice, and the moles; and would have been
glad to sleep on without making or hearing any
sound, until Ruggiero's voice should rouse her from
her heavy slumbers. So far, however, from this
being the case, she could scarcely close her eyes
for an hour at a time, but lay tossing from side to
side in weary wakefulness. She would rise and
open her casement to see if Aurora had begun to
scatter the white lilies and blushing roses of dawn
before the path of Tithonus; and yet scarcely was

the sun risen when she longed to see the skies again spangled with the shining stars.

Some four or five days before the twenty had expired, from hour to hour she awaited with joyful expectation the messenger who should announce to her: 'See! Ruggiero comes!' She often mounted to a high turret, from whence she could overlook the thick woods and smiling plain, and see part of the road which led to Paris. If in the dim distance she saw the glitter of arms, or anything that bore the appearance of a knight, she would believe it was her longed-for Ruggiero, and smiles would light up her lovely eyes. Did she see some peaceful wayfarer, 'Surely,' she thought, 'it is his messenger,' and she would take hope. Sometimes, thinking to meet him, she would put on her armor and go down the steep hill into the plain; not finding him, she would fancy that he had reached Montalbano by some other road, and would hasten back to the castle, urged by the same vain expectation which had moved her to leave it; for neither here nor there was he to be found. So the wished-for day went by, and two, three, and many more after it; until neither seeing her lover, nor hearing any news of him, she began to lament herself in such fashion as might have moved to pity the snaky-haired Furies in the shades below.

'Ah!' she cried, 'why seek I one who so persistently flies from me? Why love one who scorns me? Why implore one who does not even deign to answer me? That proud knight knows I love him, but that he may not be moved by my sorrow he hides himself from me. Ah, Love! either I beseech thee bring him back to me, or restore to me my peace of mind. Alas! when wert thou

known to heed either prayers or tears? Yet whom
have I to blame but my foolish self; I soared so
high that I could only burn my wings, and fall
from the heaven, in which I had no power to
remain. For could I fail to be attracted by such
dignity, such wise discourse, such great and noble
qualities? And over and above the beguiling of
mine own phantasy, was I not urged to yield
myself to this love by those who appeared to me
all-worthy of confidence? Did not Melissa en-
courage me? Did not Merlin promise me great
and lasting happiness? Alas! they must have
envied me my sweet and happy repose, that they
so deluded me with these false hopes. Ah! where
can I turn for help — for having once bestowed my
affection upon Ruggiero, I can never again withdraw it.'

Yet her faith in Ruggiero did not quite abandon
her, but again and again recalled to her recollection
the words of Ruggiero's message, and bid her, in
spite of her better reason, still look for his return.
She sustained herself, therefore, as best she could
with this faint hope, until nearly a month had
passed after the twenty days were over, when she
heard news which extinguished even that last spark
and left her utterly comfortless. She was on the
road to Paris she so often took, when she fell in
with a Gascon knight who had come straight from
the Saracen camp, where he had been kept a prisoner since the great battle before Paris. She
accosted him and asked him many questions, and
at length came to the subject next her heart, and
spoke of Ruggiero. The knight who had become
familiar with Agramante's court, gave her a full
account of the duel with Mandricardo; adding,

that Ruggiero had been so severely wounded that he had lain for more than a month at death's very door. And had his story ended here, it would have been well ; but he went on to say that there was a lady in the camp named Marfisa, as valiant and well-skilled in arms as she was young and beautiful ; and that she loved Ruggiero, and he her ; they were rarely seen apart, and it was believed that they had plighted their troth to each other, and that, as soon as Ruggiero's wounds were healed, their public wedding would take place. An event, he said, which would cause great joy among all the infidel kings and princes, who highly valued the noble qualities and great valor of both, and knew how worthy they were of each other.

The Gascon believed what he said to be the truth, and not without reason, for it was the common report in the Moorish camp. The many signs of good fellowship between the two had given rise to it when they first arrived in company to lend aid to Agramante ; and it had been confirmed by Marfisa having, unsolicited, returned to the camp, and having paid many visits to Ruggiero while he languished in his tent, often spending with him the greater part of the day, and tending him during his long and weary convalescence. Her haughty disposition, which was well known, made people remark this the more, for having hitherto treated every one with disdain as beneath her notice, to Ruggiero alone had she shown herself kind and gentle.

This Gascon's story caused such grief to Bradamante, that, without uttering a single word, she turned her horse's head, and overwhelmed with jealousy, anger, and despair, made her way back to the castle.

Ah! how calm and happy all loving hearts might be, suffered they not the cruel pangs of jealousy to destroy their peace; the pain of absence is soon forgotten in the joy of reunion, and love, even when unrequited, carries with it its own reward, for hope never quite forsakes the faithful heart; but for this subtle poison there is no remedy; here, neither science nor magic can afford help or comfort. Bradamante threw herself all armed as she was upon her bed, and buried her face in the pillow, trying to suffocate her cries and moans, lest they should betray her secret.

'Ah, Ruggiero!' she sobbed, 'why, surpassing all other knights in beauty and valor, in gentleness and courtesy, could you not add to such great gifts constancy and perfect truth, to which all other virtues yield in excellence? Ah! how easy was it for you to deceive me, a poor simple maiden, who so trusted you, that at your word she could have believed the sun itself to be dark and cold.'

Long she in such wise bewailed and lamented her hard fate; at length she roused herself, and perceiving that she was fully armed, a braver spirit awoke within her, which seemed to address her thus:

'O lady! are lamentations such as these worthy of your illustrious lineage? Were it not better to go to the camp, where you may meet death with glory and haply by the sword of Ruggiero?' 'Ah!' she thought, 'how welcome would it then be. If only I might first take vengeance upon this Marfisa, whose wicked arts have beguiled me of Ruggiero's love, and destroyed my happiness and my life.'

These seemed more worthy thoughts to the

damsel; she therefore forthwith caused a motto, signifying despair and a wish for death, to be inscribed on her armor, and proceeded to choose a surcoat of the color of a faded leaf, embroidered with ramages of the melancholy cypress; a habit which suited excellently well with her doleful humor. She also took her cousin Astolfo's charger and his famous golden lance. You remember when and why he gave it to her, and that none were able to withstand its slightest touch; but when she now took it, she was all unconscious of its marvellous power.

Alone, unattended by page or squire, she descended the height of Montalbano, and took the most direct road to Paris; for the news that Rinaldo and Charlemagne had raised the siege, and obliged the Saracens to retreat, had not yet reached her. She had turned her back upon the mountains, in which the Dordogne takes its rise, and had left the districts of Montferrat and Clermont, when there passed her, riding along the same road, a fair lady, with a golden shield hanging from her saddle-bow, accompanied by three knights, and with a long file of attendant squires and ladies in her train. Bradamante inquired of one who passed close by her who the lady might be, and received the following reply:

'This princess is a messenger sent by the queen of the island called by some Iceland, by others, the Lost Island, because little is known of those distant seas. She has made a long voyage across the Arctic Ocean, to bring to the king of the Franks that golden shield which you may have observed; on condition that he gives it to the most worthy of his knights, upon whom the Queen intends to bestow her hand. Believing herself, as she well may, to be the most beautiful lady in the whole world, she desires to find a knight as much above all others in virtue and valor; and imagines that only at the famous court of Charlemagne can such an one be found. Those who escort the Princess are the three kings of Norway, Sweden, and Finland, countries not far distant from that island. Suitors for the Queen's hand, they have done many and doughty deeds in her honor; but she declares that she sets no high value upon such, performed in those remote regions; but that if, after having measured themselves with the lords of his court, Charlemagne, whom she reveres as the wisest monarch upon earth, should consider either one of them deserving of the golden shield, him will she gladly take for lord and spouse, and will promise to pay him wifely duty and obedience.'

When the squire had finished his tale, he spurred on his horse and quickly rejoined his companions. Bradamante did not care to gallop after him, but continued her journey more at leisure, pondering over his story, and fearing lest the golden shield should excite discord and contention among his paladins, were Charlemagne to consent to declare who among them was best entitled to receive it. Her thoughts, however, soon reverted to Ruggiero and Marfisa, and became so engaged therewith that she paid no heed to the road she was taking, nor considered whether it would lead her to any commodious hostelry in which to pass the night.

As a bark unfastened from its moorings by the wind or some other accident, pilotless and rudderless floats away down the stream, so the love-lorn maiden, letting her bridle fall from her hand,

suffered Rabican to carry her whithersoever he
would. At last, roused from her sad musings by
a chill damp blast of wind, she raised her eyes and
perceived that the sun was about to sink below
the horizon, and that a wet dreary night was fast
closing around her ; so she shook her rein, and riding up to a shepherd whom she saw leading his
flock home from pasture, asked him if he could
point out to her some lodging, however poor, where
she might take shelter for the night from the coming storm.

'I know of none within five or six leagues of this,'
answered the shepherd, 'unless it be the Tower
of Tristan, and few succeed in finding entertainment there. If the guest chamber be vacant, those
who first alight there, be they one or many, are
indeed received with welcome, but on condition
that they hold themselves ready to defend their
lodging against all new comers. Should no more
guests arrive, they rest in peace : otherwise, they
must get up and again don their armor and go out
to battle against the intruders, and if vanquished,
they must give place to these, and pass the rest
of the night outside. In like manner, if a fair lady
enter, it is on the understanding that should one
more beautiful arrive, she must yield her place and
depart.'

The damsel asked the way to the tower where
this strange custom prevailed, and the good shepherd not only told her, but pointed it out on a
height some way off. She urged on Rabican and
trotted along the rough and muddy by-way ; not
so fast, however, but that a dark night had set in
before she reached the tower. Finding the gate
closed, she asked for admittance, and received

answer from the porter that the hall was already occupied by a party of knights and ladies, who had alighted there some short time before, and who were now seated round the fire waiting for the serving up of their supper.

'Not for them shall the cook have prepared it,' said the lady, 'unless indeed it is already eaten. Go! tell them, I know the custom of the place, and await them here, ready to fulfil it.'

When the unwelcome message was brought to the company comfortably seated before the chimney in the great hall, three knights slowly and reluctantly got up, and having put on their armor, prepared to issue forth into the cold and stormy night to where Bradamante awaited them. These were the three northern kings who had accompanied the Iceland princess and her retinue; for, having made greater haste than Bradamante, they had arrived at the tower some hours earlier. Just then the clouds parted and the moon shone forth for a brief space, enabling her to recognize them, as also those within to see from casements and corridors what occurred.

'Few may be your superiors in arms,' said the lady gleefully to herself, as the gate swung open, and she saw them cross the drawbridge, 'but of those few I mean to be one, for I have no intention of passing this rainy night outside, wet and fasting.'

She turned her horse and charged them, and with Astolfo's wonderful lance, she first touched the King of Sweden's helmet and sent him reeling to the ground, and in a trice the other two had followed his example, and lay their full length in the wet mud beside him.

As she passed through the gateway she was
made to swear her readiness to sally forth and fight
any other knights who might arrive; and the baron
of the castle, who had witnessed her valiant conduct, came out and welcomed her with every mark
of respect and deference. So also did the Iceland
princess, for rising from her seat and advancing
towards her with a gracious smile and courteous
salutation, she took her hand and led her to the
fire, and then as Bradamante, laying aside her
armor, took off her helmet, a gold net with which
she confined her hair came off with it, and the long
soft tresses falling about her shoulders betrayed her
to all, a maiden as lovely in face as bold in arms.

As on the stage the curtain rises and displays
some Elysian scene sparkling with a thousand
lights, or as the sun's bright disk shines forth clear
from the surrounding clouds, so like some angel of
Paradise appeared the damsel's radiant countenance
as she raised her vizor and let fall her golden hair,
which since it had been cut by the hermit had had
time to grow, though scarcely to its original length.
The baron recognized her, for he had often seen
her, and he redoubled his respectful attentions;
but while they were sitting in cheerful conversation round the fire waiting for supper, it suddenly
occurred to him that it was contrary to the rule of
the castle that two such beautiful ladies should be
lodged there together; and he therefore felt himself obliged, though with great regret, to call upon
two ancient retainers and some ladies of his house
to decide to which should fall the palm. Often
they looked, and much they debated; at last they
agreed that the daughter of Duke Amone surpassed the Iceland princess as much in beauty.

as she excelled the kings, her companions, in valor.

'Madam,' said the baron, 'since it is decided that this lady's beauty, all ungraced as it is by dress or ornaments, exceeds yours, I must now call upon you to obey the custom which bids you depart from Tristan's Tower.'

On hearing this hard sentence, the poor princess turned very pale, and her bright pretty face clouded all over at the thought of the cold storm of wind and rain which she would have to face outside. But the kind Bradamante took pity upon her, and said to the Baron, with a smile:

'I cannot allow that your reasoning holds good, or that it is of much account whether I, or this lady, be considered the most beautiful, since it was not by my beauty, but by my valor, that I made good my claim to this night's entertainment. For supposing that my beauty had been considered inferior to hers, would it then have been just to deprive me of the shelter I have so fairly won; and which, believe me, I will not either for this lady, or for myself, give up, without another recourse to arms?'

Perhaps the baron was convinced by her arguments, perhaps by her threatened alternative; at any rate, he declared himself satisfied, and willing to abide by her decision.

As a flower refreshed by a shower lifts its drooping head, the princess raised her glad face at Bradamante's bold words, and they sat down to enjoy the supper, which was fortunately not disturbed by any further arrival of errant knight or dame. Bradamante, however, was too sorrowful and too sick at heart to care for such delights, and soon rose up from the table, and when the princess followed her example, the baron beckoned to an attendant and ordering him to fetch some lighted tapers, he offered to show and to explain to his guests the curious and beautiful pictures which adorned the walls of his hall.

CHAPTER XVII.

BRADAMANTE'S DREAM. SHE SENDS FRONTINO
TO RUGGIERO.

Dreaming she knew it was a dream,
She felt he was and was not there.
TENNYSON.

APOLLODORUS, Zeuxis, and the yet greater
Apelles, whose fame, thanks to history,
will last as long as the world, or, at any rate, as
long as men can read and write; and those who
have lived nearer to our own times — Leonardo,
Mantegna, Bellini, and he who, whether in sculp-
ture or in painting, was equally divine, Michael,
well named Angelo, with Titian, as great an honor
to his native Cadore as Raphael to Urbino and Se-
bastiano to Venice; all these great painters have
done things worthy of wonder and admiration; but
the paintings with which this hall was adorned
were still more admirable and surprising, for they
portrayed the story of events yet to come: an art
now, alas! lost to the world.

As the baron of Tristan's Tower led the ladies
round the walls, he said:

'You must know that of the battles here depicted some few have taken place, but the greater
number are still unfought. They relate to the
wars which, with varying success, will be waged
for many centuries to come by the French beyond

the Alps. Merlin the wizard was sent here to paint their history, when and wherefore I will now proceed to tell you.

'When Fieramonte, King of the Franks, crossed the Rhine with his army and conquered Gaul, he, seeing that the power of the great Roman Empire was daily decreasing, invited Arthur of Britain to join him in a descent upon Italy. But Arthur, who never undertook any great enterprise without consulting Merlin, was dissuaded therefrom by the wizard, and learnt from him and warned Fiera-monte of the many disasters which would befall his people should he enter the beautiful land which the sea and the Alps bound and the Apennines divide. Merlin showed him how that the armies of almost all who should succeed him on the throne of France would there be destroyed by the sword, or devastated by famine and pestilence. Short-lived success after long struggle, little gain, and infinite harm would they carry back from Italy, where the lily shall never be allowed to take root. Fieramonte gave heed to the wizard, and turned his sword elsewhere, and it is believed that at his request Merlin portrayed on these walls the story of these wars to come; in order that his suc-cessors might also take warning, and learn that as all who undertake the defence of Italy against her enemies shall gain to themselves glory and renown, so all who descend into those plains to enslave that people and make themselves lords of that country shall find beyond those mountains an open grave.'

The Baron showed them where the long story began, and pointed out Sigisbert, who had scarcely reached the banks of the Ticino when he was

14

driven back, routed and discomfited : Clovis, who passed the Alps with more than a hundred thousand men, whom he left dead on the fields of Lombardy : Childibert, whose army fell a prey to heat and pestilence, so that not more than one in ten returned to France : Louis of Burgundy, who, being taken prisoner, swore to leave the Italians in peace, but breaking his word and again falling into their hands, was deprived of both his eyes, and sent home blind as a mole.

Time would fail me were I to repeat the whole long story ; how Charles succeeded Charles, and Louis Louis, until he pointed to the wars in which Francis I., the Emperor of Germany, and the King of Spain took part, and the Pope, who sometimes sided with one, and sometimes with the other ; and to the famous field of Pavia, where the noblest of French chivalry were slain, and where Francis was seen standing at bay against the host of the enemy, and when his horse had been killed under him, defending himself on foot, until, overpowered by numbers, he was forced to yield himself prisoner, and was sent to Spain.

The great deeds of the Viscontis, the Dorias, and many other Italian nobles, who fought bravely in defence of their country, were not forgotten ; and so interested were the ladies in this history that they turned back again and again to look at these wonderful pictures, and to read and re-read the names which were inscribed below them in letters of gold. After spending some time in talking over all he had told them, the Baron bade them good night, and left them to repose.

But long after all were asleep Bradamante lay awake, tossing upon her uneasy couch, and not until daylight appeared could she close her weary eyes. Then she dreamt that she saw Ruggiero and that he said to her :

' Why ? O my Bradamante ! do you thus torment yourself ? Why do you believe that which cannot be true ? For trust me you shall behold the rivers run up hill ere you see my heart turn to aught but you ; for before I cease to love you I must cease to love the light of mine own eyes. If I have so long delayed fufilling my promise it is because other wounds than those of love have detained me.'

But the dream vanished, and with it Ruggiero's beloved form, and the maiden's tears flowed anew.

' Alas !' said she, ' what seemed so sweet was but a vain dream, and the bitter reality is only too true. Kind sleep promised me peace, but with the sad awakening all my pain returns. If sleep can give me such joy, and the awakening such pain, would I might sleep on, never to awake !'

The sun had risen bright and dispersed all the clouds of the preceding night when Bradamante arose and put on her armor, and having thanked the Baron for his hospitality, set out to continue her journey. The princess had left the tower some-what earlier with her retinue, and had rejoined the three kings. She rallied them gently upon the wretched night they must have passed, exposed to the wind and rain, and to add to their discomfiture, she mischievously informed them that their mighty bravery had been overcome by the courage of a maiden warrior. Overwhelmed with shame and confusion, they entreated Bradamante, when she came up, to allow them to try another assault with her ; but she declined, saying that she had no time to waste, and saluting them in passing, she hurried on.

That evening she reached a castle, where she found good refreshments and comfortable lodgings; but she was too perturbed in mind to enjoy either, for she was there told that Agramante had been defeated by Rinaldo, and had retreated towards Arles with Charlemagne in pursuit. Feeling sure that the Saracen king had carried Ruggiero with him, she rose at early dawn, and took the road to Provence. After riding for some hours she came upon a fair young lady, apparently in great distress, for she was weeping bitterly, and Bradamante, meeting another damsel who seemed to be as unhappy as herself, could not but pity her; so she greeted her kindly and asked her the reason of such grief.

The lady looked up, and seeing, as she imagined, a gallant young knight, told her that some way further on, Rodomonte, King of Algiers, had taken possession of a bridge on the road, where he not only barred the passage to all who travelled that way, but had taken many prisoners; among them her own true knight, over whom the narrow bridge and the deep stream afforded this king an advantage which his valor alone would not have given him.

'If,' she added, 'you are as bold and as charitable as your countenance leads me to hope, for Heaven's sake do vengeance for me upon this pagan, who has taken from me my own dear lord, and made me so miserable and so forlorn. Or, at least, advise me in what land I may find one strong and valiant enough to overcome him, in spite of his bridge and his river. In thus helping me, not only will you act the part of a noble cavalier and

true knight, but you will do it on behalf of the
most faithful of all faithful lovers. Of his other
virtues, many and signal though they be, it perhaps
becomes not me to speak.'

The magnanimous Bradamante, to whom anything which promised glory was always welcome,
much more so now, when her life was so little dear
to her, determined to go at once to this bridge; and
thus made answer:

'For what little I am worth, O lovelorn lady!
I gladly offer myself for this difficult and perilous
enterprise. The more willingly because you tell
me of your lover that which I warn you can be
said of few, if of any. For by my troth I swear
that in love I believed all men were liars.' She
finished speaking with a sigh which came from the
bottom of her heart, and after a pause added:

'Come let us go!'

The next day they arrived at the river and the
terrible bridge. A sentinel, who was placed on purpose to give warning of the approach of strangers,
blew the signal on his horn, and as was his wont,
the pagan king, ready armed, appeared before the
bridge, demanding the surrender of their arms and
horses, and threatening death and destruction to
all who should dare to attempt to cross it. It does
not belong to this story to tell how Rodomonte
came into possession of this formidable post.

'Let us first,' said Bradamante, 'come to some
agreement in this matter. For learn, O proud
Pagan, that I am here to avenge the injuries done
to this and to many other fair ladies. If I am
defeated in this combat, I do not refuse to yield
myself your prisoner; but if, as I hope and believe,
I get the better of you, I shall not only take your

horse and armor, but I shall insist upon your releasing all your prisoners.'

'Your bargain sounds fair enough,' replied Rodomonte, 'but I cannot at once give you up my prisoners as they are not in this country, for I have sent them all over to my kingdom in Africa. This much, however, on my word of honor I promise, that if you succeed in unhorsing me they shall be set free in as short a time as a messenger can carry over the order. As for yourself, if you become my captive, I shall desire nothing from you but your love; for by your golden hair and your fair face I have already recognized you.'

The lady smiled bitterly with anger and scorn, and without vouchsafing a word in reply, wheeled round her horse and put the golden lance in rest against the arrogant Moor. It did not fail her, but sent him reeling across the narrow bridge, leaving her so little room to pass that if Rabican had not been so agile and so dexterous that he could almost have found footing on the edge of a sword, she would not have succeeded in crossing it. Turning to the prostrate pagan she said, mockingly,

'Now, have you learnt which must yield himself captive?'

Rodomonte, petrified with astonishment, could not and would not reply, but getting up from the ground mute and crestfallen, staggered back a few paces, then taking off his shield and helmet, with all his armor, he threw them against the rock, and after commanding his squire to go and see to the carrying out of the order for the release of his prisoners, he departed alone and on foot, and for a long time no more was heard of him, except that he was living in some dark and gloomy cavern.

Bradamante hung up his arms as a trophy on the rock above the bridge, and inscribed below how she had won them, and how she had freed the passage to all who came that way. She then asked the lady, whose downcast face was still wet with tears, in what direction she wished to turn her steps.

'My road,' said she, 'leads me to the Saracen camp at Arles, where I hope to find a ship and safe escort to the opposite coast, for I shall never rest until I have rejoined my dear lord and spouse.'

'I will gladly,' said Bradamante, 'accompany you part of the way, until we come in sight of Arles; there I will beg of you to find out that Ruggiero, of the court of Agramante, whose fame has reached all lands, and to give him this charger, which I have but now taken from the haughty infidel. I also pray you to repeat to him, word for word, this message : " A knight, who is about to charge you publicly with having broken your plighted word, has bid me give you this steed that you may be prepared to meet him, and desires you don steel and mail, and come out to do him battle." Say to him this and no more, and if he asks my name, tell him you know it not.'

'I cannot weary in your service,' answered the lady; ' for willingly would I spend my life in helping one who has done so much for me.'

Bradamante thanked her, and placed Frontino's bridle in her hand. The wandering ladies travelled together along the banks of the Rhone until they came within sight of Arles, and heard the roll of the not very distant sea. Bradamante stopped before the outer barrier in the suburbs, but the lady crossed the drawbridge, and going through

the barbican gate, asked a passer-by to guide her
to the inn where Ruggiero lodged. There she
alighted, and gave him his gallant steed and the
damsel's message, and then, in haste to carry out
her own errand, she went her way without waiting
for reply; leaving him in great perplexity, for he
could not divine who it was who thus challenged
him, sending him so welcome a gift and at the
same time so insolent a message. In vain he
puzzled himself with trying to conjecture who
could possibly accuse him of broken faith, for the
name of Bradamante would have been the very
last to occur to him. He fancied it must be Rodomonte, though why he should send him such a
message he could not conceive; but with no one
else in the wide world, so far as he knew, had he
any quarrel.

Meanwhile the Lady of Montalbano was im-
patiently standing at the gate, blowing a note of
defiance on her horn. Agramante and Marsilio
were told that a knight stood without sounding a
challenge to single combat; and young Serpentino
della Stella sprang forward and asked leave to don
mail and steel, and to silence this arrogant champion. Agramante having consented, the people
rushed in crowds to the ramparts, and the kings
with all their court followed to see the expected
sight. Serpentino rode forth from the gate in embroidered surcoat and gilded armor; but both were
soiled in the dust at the first onslaught, and the
lady, catching hold of the bridle of his flying steed,
brought it to him, saying: 'Mount, and ask your
lord to send me a better adversary.'

The king marvelled at the gracious act, crying
aloud:

'He is his prisoner, by all the laws of chivalry. How comes it then that he lets him go free ? '

Grandonio di Volterna, one of the proudest grandees of Spain, next went forth breathing threats of vengeance.

'Think not,' he cried, 'that thy courtesy will avail thee aught ; for when I have vanquished thee I mean to carry thee prisoner to my king, if I do not rather leave thee dead on the field.'

'Thine insolence,' she replied, 'shall not prevent my counselling thee to turn back before thy bones ache in contact with the hard ground. Go, tell thy lord that I came not to ask for battle with such as thee.'

These biting words moved the Spaniard to fury, and making no answer he wheeled his charger round, and rode straight at her. No sooner, however, did the magic spear touch his shield than he tumbled over headlong, and lay with his feet in the air. The generous Bradamante held his horse for him likewise, saying :

'Did I not warn thee 'twere better to do my embassage than indulge thy foolish love of fighting ? Go, bid thy king choose me an opponent more worthy of my arms ; for I care not to weary myself in doing battle with such as thee.'

While the lookers-on from the battlements were exhausting themselves in conjectures as to who this doughty champion might be — one guessing Rinaldo, and another Orlando, Ferrau offered himself for the third joust.

'Not,' said he, 'that I have any hope of success ; but that these knights may take comfort in their overthrow by seeing the like fate befall me.'

He carefully examined the temper of his steel

and the joints of his harness, and proceeded to choose the very best and surest charger in his stalls. He then rode out to meet the lady with a courteous salutation, which she returned as she asked his name. He told it, for it was not his custom to conceal it.

'I do not refuse to fight with you,' she replied; 'though another would have pleased me better.'

'And who?' asked Ferrau.

'Ruggiero,' was her answer. As she murmured the name with difficulty, her beautiful face blushed red as a rose, and after a while, she added:

'The fame of his glorious deeds has brought me here, with the one desire of meeting him in single combat.'

'If it fares no better with me than with others,' said Ferrau, 'that noble knight, with whom thou dost so much wish to joust, shall revenge my fall.'

The lady had raised her vizor while speaking to him, and as he looked at her he thought to himself, 'Surely this is some angel from Paradise.'

They turned and took the field, and it happened to Ferrau as to his friends, and again Bradamante held his horse for him, saying: 'Return, and forget not the words thou didst even now say.'

Ferrau, overwhelmed with mortification, went back to the court and told Ruggiero, who had just come up, and was standing near the king, that the knight desired to do battle with him, and Ruggiero, little thinking from whom it came, rejoiced at the challenge, and called for his armor.

CHAPTER XVIII.

I could not love thee, Dear, so much,
Loved I not honor more.
LOVELACE.

WHILE Ruggiero was buckling on his mail the
king and his courtiers discussed who this
warrior, who wielded his lance so excellently well,
might be; and asked Ferrau if he had recognized
him.

'I am quite sure,' was his answer, 'that he is
none of those whom you have mentioned. I saw
his features for a moment, and it struck me that
he might be Rinaldo's youngest brother; but I do
not believe Ricciardetto could acquit himself in
this fashion, and therefore I imagine it must be his
sister Bradamante, who, as I have heard, is very
like him. Report says that she equals Rinaldo in
valor; but to me it seems that she is mightier
than her brother, or than even her cousin Orlando.'

At the sound of the dear and familiar name
Ruggiero flushed crimson, his heart beat and his
hand trembled, so that he could scarcely buckle
on his armor. His blood ran cold with fear lest
the love that she once bore him were all spent, and
he knew not what to do, whether to go out to meet
her or not. Marfisa rode up at that moment, ready

armed — it was rare indeed to find her otherwise — and, determined that Ruggiero should not deprive her of the glory of a conquest of which she already made sure, she put spurs to her horse and galloped through the gate, bearing aloft on her helmet her proud crest, signifying that, like the phœnix, she esteemed herself without a rival.

With a throbbing heart Bradamante stood expecting the appearance of Ruggiero, but when she saw the unknown device, she asked the stranger's name, and on hearing that name, which of all others she had learned to hate and to dread, she, maddened with rage, turned her horse, and urging him to his full speed, aimed her spear straight at Marfisa's heart ; but scarcely did it touch her breast-plate when it sent her headlong to the ground. Furious and amazed at this unwonted downfall, the lady sprang to her feet, and drew her sword, upon which her no less haughty antagonist said :

'How is this ? know you not that you are my prisoner ? The indulgence I have shown to others, you, O Marfisa ! must not expect. The report I hear of your arrogance and villany make you too unworthy of it.'

Marfisa at this insult trembled from head to foot. Speechless with indignation, she struck wildly at Rabican, and would have killed him had he not leaped aside, and thus given Bradamante time to touch her again with the lance and overthrow her.

In the mean time the report of the wonderful feats of the unknown champion had reached the Christian camp, which was not more than a mile or two distant, and some of Charlemagne's paladins had come to look on at the joust. Agramante saw them from the ramparts, and wishing to be

prepared for any unforeseen accident, he ordered
several of his captains to arm and to take their
stand before the walls. Among them was Ruggiero, who, when first Marfisa had so hastily gone
forth to attack his dear lady, had trembled for the
safety of the latter, and was now as much filled with
anxiety, as with astonishment, at the unlooked-for
result. Both the damsels were dear to him, though
in very different degrees : for the one he felt ardent
love ; for the other calm friendship. Whilst he
was longing to part them, but knew not on what
pretext to interfere, his companions rushed to the
help of Marfisa, and the Christian knights to that
of Bradamante. A general *mêlée* followed, during
which Bradamante, looking around in search of
Ruggiero, caught sight of the familiar silver eagle
on its azure shield, and spurred towards him,
crying :

'Defend thyself, O Ruggiero ! and boast no
more of thy conquest over a simple maiden's heart.'

Ruggiero, who would have recognized the tones
of her beloved voice among a thousand, thought
that she alluded to his promise of return, and was
about to excuse himself ; when with closed vizor
she rode straight at him, and he perforce was obliged
to steady himself in the saddle and to couch his
lance ; yet he held it in such wise that it glanced
aside. She also, struck with sudden remorse, allowed hers to swerve, and they rode past without
touching each other. Bradamante turned to fly,
but Ruggiero intercepted her, saying :

'I shall die if I may not speak with you. Alas !
what have I done that you should thus fly from
me ? For Heaven's sake hear me !'

As soft breezes from southern seas dissolve the

ice-bound torrents, so these few words touched the heart of Bradamante, and all her anger disappeared like melting snow. She could not speak, but signing to him to follow, she led the way apart from the crowd to a little dell, in the midst of which stood a lofty tomb of white marble, overshadowed by a grove of cypresses. An inscription told who lay below, but neither Bradamante nor Ruggiero had leisure or inclination to read it; for Marfisa, who, on seeing them leave the field, had mounted her horse and followed them, reached the grove almost at the same moment, intent upon taking vengeance on Bradamante. How unwelcome her appearance was to both I leave to all true lovers to imagine, but to Bradamante it seemed a confirmation of all her suspicions; and crying out:

'Ah, faithless Ruggiero! now indeed you leave me no doubt of your perfidy. Now let me die, but not unavenged!'

She struck and overthrew Marfisa with the golden lance, and then casting it away, she leapt from her horse, and prepared with uplifted sword to cut off her head; but Marfisa was upon her feet in an instant and had already unsheathed her weapon. A fierce combat began, which must have ended in the death of one, if not of both, had not Ruggiero thrown himself between them. Finding them deaf to all his entreaties to desist, he disarmed them by force, and carrying away their swords laid them down at the foot of a cypress some little distance off. This interruption so enraged Marfisa, that, running after him, and regaining possession of her sword, she turned it against him, crying out:

'O caitiff knight! thus to transgress the laws of

chivalry and to interfere in fair combat ; my hand
shall punish thy audacity.'

It was useless for Ruggiero to try to pacify her
or to make her hear reason, so that at last, losing
all patience, he drew his sword from the scab-
bard — a welcome sight to Bradamante, who had
also picked up her sword, and now stood leaning
on it and gazing with happy eyes at Ruggiero, who
seemed to her the very god of war, and Marfisa to
be a Fury let loose from hell. Ruggiero, using only
the flat of his sword, spared Marfisa as far as he
could ; but she had no such compunction, and dealt
him a blow which so disabled his left arm that
he could scarcely hold up his shield. At length
thoroughly roused, his eyes flashed like lightning,
and he lifted his sword, taking so sure an aim
that, had it fallen it would have fared ill with the
lady ; but it struck against the cypress underneath
which they were standing, and at that very moment
an earthquake shook the plain, and a terrible voice
came forth from the tomb, which startled them with
these words :

'Hold, O Ruggiero ! refrain, my Marfisa ! Let
there not be strife between you ! Listen to my
words, for they are true, and learn that you are
brother and sister, children of the same parents
and born in the same hour ; therefore I beseech
you not to lift up your hands against each other.
Galaciella was your mother, whose cruel brothers
first murdered your father Ruggiero, and then placing her alone in a frail bark, abandoned her to the
mercy of the waves. A kind Providence watched
over her and guided the little skiff in safety to the
shores of Africa, and there she landed and soon
after died ; but her blessed spirit did not ascend to

heaven before she had given birth to two helpless infants. I, happening to pass that way, saw them; and after burying your mother as honorably as I could on those desert sands, I wrapt you, my children, two tender babes, in my cloak, and carried you to my dwelling on Mount Carena. There I brought you up with loving care, until one day, when I was absent, a band of Arabs passing by seized you, my Marfisa, and carried you away. Have you no recollection of it? Your more swift-footed brother escaped them, and when I returned I vowed to take more diligent care of my remaining treasure, and you, Ruggiero, can testify if your guardian Atlante kept his promise. The mysteries of science, the secrets of magic, were all exhausted by me in your service, until, finding my efforts to keep you out of danger frustrated, I pined away and died. I foresaw, however, that you and Marfisa would one day visit this spot, and I ordered my body to be laid in this tomb, and obtained permission to linger here until I had disclosed to you the secret of your birth. Long has my spirit wandered around these groves, waiting for the wished-for day. Now, having fulfilled my mission, I must leave the pleasant light and depart to the land of shades. Farewell!'

The voice ceased, and for some moments the three stood in silent wonder. Then Marfisa joyfully recognized Ruggiero, and he her. They kissed each other, and recalling to one another the events of their childhood, one said, 'I did this;' the other, 'You said that,' or 'We did so and so;' thus convincing themselves of the truth of what the voice had told them.

Ruggiero then confided to his sister how dear Bradamante was to him, and related, in touching

words, all she had done for his sake, nor ceased
until he had succeeded in banishing all thought of
discord from their hearts ; in token of which they
lovingly embraced each other. Afterwards, Marfisa
asked her brother to tell her about their family,
and how their father had been killed, and who
were the brothers who had treated their mother so
cruelly.

Ruggiero began by saying that they were descended from one of the sons of Hector, who, after
leaving Troy and wandering over many seas, had
landed in Sicily and founded Messina. In after
times, some of the family migrated to Rome, and
more than one emperor belonged to their illustrious
line. 'From one of these,' said he, 'was descended
our father Ruggiero, who married the daughter of
Agobante, King Agramante's uncle. He was afterwards betrayed by Agobante into the hands of his
wicked sons, who murdered him, and as you have
heard, abandoned and thought to murder our
mother, their sister.'

Marfisa listened with attention up to these
words, and smiled proudly when he told her of
their distinguished ancestry ; but when she heard
of the treason of the uncle and cousins of Agramante, she interrupted him, saying:

'O my brother ! surely you should have avenged
our father's murder ! How comes it that you live
in friendship with Agramante, and have taken service with the kinsman of those traitors ? This stain
upon your honor must be wiped out. I vow to
God (and none other will I henceforth know but
He whom my father worshipped, Christ the Lord,)
that I will never lay aside this armor until I have
revenged the death of my father. It grieves me

15

deeply that you should be fighting under Agramante, or any other Moorish captain; far rather would I see you sword in hand against them.'

At these words, how joyously Bradamante lifted her lovely face and entreated Ruggiero to follow his sister's counsel, and to come over to Charles, who would heartily welcome him for the sake of his father, whom he had loved and honored, and whom he was still wont to call his 'peerless knight.'

But Ruggiero gently refused, saying that he could not act thus quite yet. Perhaps had he known earlier all he now knew, he might have done differently; but Agramante had been his loving lord, had buckled on him his first sword, and he could not now turn traitor to one who had been to him so kind a master. Yet, as he had before promised, so he now again promised, to take the first opportunity of quitting with honor the service of the Moorish king for that of Charles.

Thus it was finally settled, for Ruggiero stood firm against all their remonstrances.

'Have no fear,' whispered Marfisa to Bradamante; 'I will take care that such an opportunity shall not long be wanting.'

Ruggiero then bid them farewell, and turned his horse in the direction of the Moorish camp.

CHAPTER XIX.

Now by the lips of those ye love, fair gentlemen of France,
Charge for the golden lilies, —upon them with the lance.
MACAULAY.

PERHAPS it may seem to you that Ruggiero
would have done better had he accompanied
Bradamante and his sister, and had he not a second time abandoned his lady-love for the sake of
his king. But I think, if you consider the matter
more carefully, you will see that he was right in
obeying the call of honor and gratitude, and that if
Bradamante had insisted upon his remaining with
her, she would have shown little love and less
sense; for to all loyal hearts honor should be dearer
than life itself. Ruggiero might hope to return to
Bradamante, but his good name once lost could
never have been regained.

Marfisa and Bradamante, who soon became great
friends, rode together to the Christian camp, where
Charlemagne had assembled the largest army he
had yet mustered, hoping to complete his victory
over the Moors, and to deliver France at last from
this long and tedious war. Bradamante's arrival
caused great rejoicing. People came running out
to meet her, and she had to bend her head in salutation now to one side, now to the other. First

Rinaldo, then Ricciardetto with her other brothers and relations hastened to welcome her with shouts of joy; and when she told them that her companion was Marfisa, whose fame was known from distant Cathay to the further coasts of Spain, the news spread like wildfire, and caused great excitement. Captains and soldiers, nobles and squires, all rushed out and thronged to gaze at the lovely pair.

They besought and soon obtained an audience of the Emperor, and Marfisa for the first time bent her proud knee and did homage to the great son of Pepin, for he alone among princes appeared to her worthy of such deference. Charles received her very courteously, advancing to the door of his tent to meet her, and leading her to a seat by his side above all the nobles of his court. Marfisa then addressed him, and in a clear voice said:

'Great and glorious monarch, who hast caused thy fair banner of the Cross to be reverenced from the Indian Seas to the Atlantic Ocean, by the fair-haired Scythians and by the dusky Ethiopians, I confess that envy of thy great fame and hatred of thy creed moved me to come hither from the far East to do battle against thee. Not content with having crimsoned the plains with Christian blood, I was meditating further designs against thee, when by a strange accident I learnt that my father, the bold Ruggiero of Pisa, was thy kinsman and servant. I therefore determined that as he was thy subject I would be so also, and I vowed to transfer the enmity I had hitherto borne thee to Agramante and to his guilty house, the descendants of my father's and mother's base murderers.'

She added that she wished to be baptized, and

that she intended henceforth to fight for the Cross
of Christ, which she had hitherto persecuted. The
Emperor replied very graciously that he was well
aware of her father's great merit and of the antiquity of her illustrious lineage, and that he would
gladly acknowledge her as his kinswoman and as
his adopted daughter. Thereupon he rose and
kissed her on the forehead, and Rinaldo and his
brothers and many other paladins crowded round
to be introduced to her, while Malagigi, Vivian,
and Ricciardetto begged to recall themselves to her
recollection.

Charlemagne recommended her to the Bishops
of the Church, that they might instruct her in the
Christian faith, and her baptism took place on the
following day with very great pomp and splendor;
Archbishop Turpin performing the ceremony, in
the presence of the Emperor.

We must now return to Arles, where there was
trouble and dismay among the Saracens; for a ship
had crossed from Africa bringing bad tidings to
Agramante. His lieutenants sent him word that
the King of Nubia had made a descent upon his
kingdom with 80,000 men, and was ravaging the
country in every direction; therefore, they urgently
begged for aid and instructions. The king saw
himself in a great strait; for while he was endeavoring to wrest France from the house of Pepin, he
was in danger of losing his own dominions. He
therefore forthwith called a hurried council of war,
and looking sorrowfully round upon his captains,
he began:

'However hard it may be for a commander to
own that he has done wrong, I must confess I
erred in leaving Africa so denuded of troops. And

yet I have but little reason to reproach myself, for who could have imagined that so distant a nation, divided from us by such vast tracts of sandy desert, would have come to attack us. I now ask your counsel, whether at once to depart hence and fly to the defence of our native land, leaving this our present enterprise still unaccomplished; or whether to go on and complete our victory here before we take care for the safety of our African kingdom? And in this matter I pray you to give me honestly your best advice.' He turned to the King of Spain, who sat next him; Marsilio rose and bowed low, then reseating himself, he said that he was inclined to think there was much exaggeration in the accounts that had been sent over. Very likely the Arab tribes had descended from the hills, and were plundering and doing some damage; but that where the despatch mentioned thousands they might safely put down hundreds; for he did not for a moment believe that the Nubians could have come in such numbers across the Great Desert. He felt sure that a few shiploads of men would soon put these marauders to flight; and he therefore urged Agramante to go on vigorously with his attack upon Charlemagne, who, in the continued absence of Orlando, could scarcely hope to offer any successful resistance.

King Sobrino, who plainly saw that in this advice Marsilio was thinking more of his own than of the common good, spoke next and said: He could not but regret that his advice against undertaking this war at all had not been listened to in the first instance, instead of the rash counsels of Mandricardo and Rodomonte. Would that those two kings were here now, above all Rodomonte.

He thought it would be the height of folly to risk
the loss of the king's own dominions for the hope
of conquering those of another, which object they
were, moreover, as far as ever from attaining.
Mandricardo was dead, Rodomonte and Gradasso
were absent, and if Charlemagne had not Orlando
with him, had he not Rinaldo, who was quite as formidable, and Guidone and Sansonetto, and a host
of valiant paladins. Still he could not urge the
king to sue for peace as a suppliant, nor to return
to Africa without making one more effort to end
the war successfully; and he reminded him that in
Ruggiero he possessed a knight worthy to be compared with Orlando or Rinaldo, or with any Christian
knight whatsoever. He therefore advised him to
propose to Charlemagne, that in order to avoid
further bloodshed a champion should be chosen on
either side; and that the fate of both armies should
be decided by single combat between these two;
the vanquished agreeing to do homage and to pay
tribute to the victor.

This counsel so pleased the king that he sent
an embassage that same day with this proposal to
the Emperor, who, confiding in the valor of his
brave Rinaldo, readily agreed to it; much to the
satisfaction of both armies, for all were weary of
the protracted contest and longing for repose.

Rinaldo, gratified at the confidence reposed in
him by Charles, was delighted beyond measure and
felt sure of victory. But Ruggiero, though he also
was flattered at the king's choice, and at being
singled out for such distinction, could not conceal
his secret anxiety; not that he feared a Rinaldo, or
an Orlando, or both united; but he knew that should
he kill the brother, he must for ever give up all hope

of being united to the sister whom he had so long and so faithfully loved. Ruggiero bore his torment in silence, as best he could, but poor Bradamante was quite distracted with grief. 'If Ruggiero were killed,' — but of that she would not suffer herself to think for a moment — and yet if Rinaldo were slain, matters would be no better, for she felt that she would with justice incur the scorn of her friends and people were she then to become the wife of Ruggiero, and that she might not even dare hope ever to see him again.

However, when she was in the lowest depths of despair, a kind friend who had helped her on former occasions, the fairy Melissa, appeared and comforted her by promising to devise some means for putting an end to the combat, the prospect of which was causing her so many tears.

In the mean time it was arranged that the two champions should fight on foot, armed *cap-à-pie*, with spear and poniard, but without swords, for perhaps it was known what an advantage the possession of Balisarda would have given to Ruggiero. The lists were set up on the plain outside the city, and at each end, near the pavilions placed for the use of the two knights, an altar was erected.

On the appointed day the two armies marched out in battle-array, and took up their position on either side of the field. Agramante, splendidly dressed and mounted on a magnificent bay charger, rode beside Ruggiero, whose helmet was carried by King Marsilio riding on his other side. Rinaldo rode between Charlemagne and Ugiero, Prince of Denmark, the latter carrying his helmet.

Two priests then advanced, one holding in his hands the book of the Gospel, the other carrying the Koran, and Charles, standing before the altar at his side of the lists, placed his hand on the Holy Book and solemnly swore that if his champion were vanquished, he would conclude peace and promise, for himself and his successors, to pay the King of Africa a yearly tribute of twenty purses of pure gold. Agramante, standing before the opposite altar, swore on the Koran that were Ruggiero vanquished, he would forthwith recross the sea with all his host, and signing a treaty of peace, would pay a like yearly tribute to the emperor. In the same solemn manner, the two champions swore that if either monarch interposed in any wise, by sign or deed, in the coming combat, they would at once break it off, and forsaking the service of the offender, transfer their allegiance to the other. When these ceremonies were completed, all retired to their respective places.

And now the trumpet gave the signal, and the terrible and momentous conflict began. Ruggiero, pre-occupied with the endeavor to spare Rinaldo and yet defend himself — for he as little wished to take his antagonist's as to lose his own life, and indeed scarcely knew what he wished — seemed to the lookers-on to be getting the worst of the fray, and Agramante's face darkened with wrath and dismay, as he turned to Sobrino and angrily reproached him for the advice he had given.

Melissa was not idle all this time, but had transformed herself into the likeness of the King of Algiers, imitating so exactly his bearing and gestures, as also his shield with the well-known dragon's skin, that all believed it was the mighty Rodomonte himself who stood before the king, and with frowning brow and haughty tone, thus addressed him :

'Sire, it was ill thought of to choose this youth as your champion against you tried and valiant Gaul. Do not suffer this combat to proceed, but invent some pretext for interrupting it and trust to Rodomonte to restore victory to your arms.'

Agramante was so elated at the supposed return of this renowned warrior, that he stayed not to consider the oath he had just made, but without more ado broke the compact and ordered his whole army to advance and forthwith to attack the Christians. A scene of indescribable confusion followed, in which Melissa, rejoicing in the success of her stratagem, disappeared; and Ruggiero and Rinaldo, not knowing how or by whom the convention had been transgressed, withdrew from the field, and promised each other to take no part on either side, until they knew which was in fault.

Victory was not long in declaring itself for the Christians. Agramante's young recruits and raw levies, but lately arrived from Spain and Africa, were no match for Charles' veteran troops, led by such captains as Guidone, Sansonetto, and the knights of the house of Chiaramonte. In vain Agramante strove to arrest his flying squadrons, in vain he asked what had become of Rodomonte and looked round for his allies. Indignant with him for having broken his plighted word, Marsilio and Sobrino had abandoned him to his fate, and had withdrawn into the city.

Before nightfall the king saw his army completely routed, and hastily collecting the scattered remnants of his forces, he fled across the Rhone. Securing his retreat by destroying the bridges behind him, he made his way to Marseilles, the nearest seaport, and after two days' delay, partly to give time for the fugitives to come in, and partly because of the winds being contrary, he embarked with what remained of his army on board his ships and set sail for Africa, while King Marsilio returned to Valencia, and began to repair forts and citadels, in a great fright lest it should now be the turn of Spain to be invaded by Charlemagne.

The slaughter of the Saracens on that memorable day was very great, and the site of the battle on the low ground lying between Arles and the Rhone was long marked by the mounds heaped over the buried Moors.

CHAPTER XX.

The winds
Who take the ruffian billows by the top,
Curling their monstrous heads, and hanging them
With deafening clamor on the slippery shrouds.
SHAKSPEARE.

WHEN Ruggiero saw his king defeated he
sadly took leave of Rinaldo, and buckling
on his trusty sword and mounting his good charger,
for his squire had brought him both, with a heavy
heart he left the fatal field.   All the next day and
the following night he wandered about, doubting
in himself what he ought to do.   He longed to return to Bradamante, yet he loved Agramante, and
he felt that, were he now to abandon him in this
his great strait, his heart would often smite him
for his ingratitude, and at last he made up his
mind to follow the king.

He went first to Arles, hoping to find a boat in
which to drop down the river to Marseilles, but
Agramante had either taken or destroyed all that
were in the place, and he was obliged to go by the
coast road.   When he reached the port he found
the fleet had already sailed, and it was only with
great difficulty and after some delay that he suc-

ceeded in procuring a small vessel in which he
embarked, and ordered the pilot to steer straight
for the coast of Africa.

It was fine when they left the harbor, and they
were soon out of sight of land, for a favoring
breeze filled the flowing sails, and they promised
themselves a quick and pleasant passage. But
these hopes were doomed to disappointment; for
at nightfall the wind suddenly veered, and after
blowing for some time right in their teeth, increasing rapidly in violence, it became a regular hurri-
cane, blowing by turns from all points of the
compass. The pilot pointed and shouted in vain,
his voice was lost in the howling of the storm, and
the pale and terrified steersman lost all control
over the helm from the violence of the gale.
Dark and darker grew the night as the rain began
to pour down in torrents; the wind whistled
shrilly in the torn shrouds, the lightning flashed
through the black clouds, and the deafening peals
of thunder mingled with the roar of the waves.
The sailors did what they could; some ran to help
the man at the helm, some to pull in the sails and
to fasten the ropes, some to ply the oars, others to
bale out the water which poured over the sides of
the ship, but all their efforts to make progress
against the storm were unavailing. Their mast
fell with a great crash, their oars were carried
away by the heavy seas, and at last their prow
broke away and left the whole of one side of the ship
exposed, so that the waters rushed in. The little
vessel seemed about to be engulfed in the foaming
billows, but she righted herself gallantly and struggled on against the blast. All that night they
were tossed by the tempest; at one moment lifted

up to the clouds by some huge wave, the next carried down to the very depths, they seemed about to be hidden for ever in the mass of raging waters.

When morning broke they saw before them a bare rock, towards which the storm was fast driving them to certain destruction. The terror-stricken pilot made one more effort to turn the helm and steer off, but the rudder broke under his hand, and all hope of saving the ship was lost. The sailors lowered the cutter, and Ruggiero seeing the captain and his crew about to abandon the vessel, hastily prepared to follow them, but found the little boat so heavily laden that he paused, and as he did so a wave struck it, and it went down with all on board. Some few rose again to the surface, and for a while struggled in the water, imploring the mercy of Heaven with loud shrieks and cries, but one by one they sank, and Ruggiero was left alone.

He was fortunately a good swimmer; so, seeing that the distance from the rock was not very great, he cast himself into the sea and swam towards it. When he felt himself in the water the thought of his baptism struck him with remorse, as he recollected all the promises about it, yet unfulfilled, he had made his dear lady. It seemed to his smitten conscience as if God were punishing him for his delays, and with deep contrition he vowed that, were he permitted to reach the shore, he would straightway become a true and faithful Christian, and would never again wield his sword in defence of any Moor whatsoever, but would return to France and do homage to Charlemagne. Nor would he any longer defer his union with

Bradamante, but would try to obtain her hand from her father as soon as possible.

No sooner had he made these good resolves than it seemed to him as if he were better able to struggle against the waves, and at length, after much toil, his feet touched the sands, and he clambered up on the bare and slippery rock. Here, safe from the perils of the sea, a new fear assailed him lest in solitary exile on this barren spot he should be left to perish with hunger. However, with a brave heart, determined to bear patiently whatever God had in store for him, he trod the hard rock with a firm step, and began to mount the steep cliff. He had not gone above a hundred steps or so when he saw descending the hill towards him an old man of grave and venerable aspect; he was in the dress of a hermit, and his frame was bent with the weight of years. When he came near he said:

'Ah, my son! you thought to cross the sea and to join the Pagan host, and you forgot that God's hand could reach you even here.'

Then he told Ruggiero that his arrival and God's purpose concerning him had been disclosed to him in a vision the night before; and he went on to reproach him with having so long delayed to place himself under Christ's gentle yoke; but then proceeded to comfort him by saying that the Lord never sent away those who truly turned to Him, and related for his encouragement the Gospel story of the 'Laborers in the Vineyard,' who all received their hire. Kindly and earnestly did the holy hermit instruct him in the true faith as they slowly mounted the hill towards his dwelling — a cell hollowed out of the rock, above which there stood a beautiful little chapel. A grove of myrtles, laurels, and juniper bushes, interspersed with tall and fruit-bearing palms, and watered by a murmuring stream of fresh water which gushed out of the rocks above, covered the hill-side down to the very edge of the sea.

The holy friar was now nearly eighty, and for more than forty years had lived here in peace and health, content with the water of the fountain and such fruits and herbs as his grove afforded him. His fire was soon lit, and as soon as Ruggiero had dried himself and his drenched garments he thankfully partook of the fruits and pulse which the kind hermit set before him.

The evening was passed in further instruction in Christian doctrine, and the next day he was baptized in the clear waters of the fountain by the holy friar ; who blessed him and prayed for him that, free from sin and pure from temptation, he might pass safely through this mortal toil which we call life, and ever keep his eyes turned to the path which leads to heaven.

Ruggiero had spent some time with the good old man, when they one day saw a galley approach the rock and anchor below the grove. A boat was lowered, and two knights, carrying, with their sailors' help, a third, whom they carefully laid down on cushions, entered into it, and put off for the shore. The hermit went down to meet them as they landed, and they told him that they had heard of his great sanctity and of his renown as a skilful leech, and therefore they had brought their friend, who had been grievously wounded in battle, and seemed to them nigh unto death, beseeching him to do what he could to restore him.

The hermit kindly told them to carry their companion up to his cell, where so efficacious were his prayers and his remedies that in a short time the wounded knight sat up and spoke cheerfully to his friends. The knights expressed their gratitude to the hermit, and proposed to stay a day or two with him, that he might complete their friend's cure. They sent their servants with orders to bring up from the galley good store of provisions; the hermit's board was soon spread with bread and wine, game, ham, and various meats, and the good old man was, after much persuasion, induced to partake with them of the unwonted feast.

As they sat down one of the knights looked fixedly at Ruggiero, and after a moment they both jumped up and joyfully recognized each other. For this was Rinaldo, and his companions were his cousin, the famous Orlando, and his friend, the wounded Oliviero, who were only too glad to make the acquaintance of Ruggiero, for they already knew him well by name as among the bravest of the brave. When they heard that he had become a Christian, they all three got up and shook him by the hand, cordially embracing and welcoming him as now indeed a brother in arms; Rinaldo doing so the most heartily, knowing how much gratitude his house owed him for the sake of Ricciardetto and Malagigi and Vivian.

How often are truer friendships formed in the humble abodes of the poor and lowly than in the palaces of the rich and great! So was it in the hermit's cell, where these young knights became such fast friends, that had they been of one blood they could not have loved each other more sincerely. Many a time had Rinaldo wished to thank

Ruggiero for his good offices to his brother and cousins, but as long as they were in hostile camps it had been impossible for him to do so. Now, however, he was profuse in his thanks, and the hermit hinted that he had an easy and acceptable way of showing the sincerity of his gratitude, by consenting to become nearly related to Ruggiero, in bestowing upon him his sister's hand in marriage. Orlando and Oliviero joined in and said that there could not be a better arrangement, and that they were sure Duke Amone would welcome so distinguished a son-in-law. Rinaldo felt such high esteem for Ruggiero that he was nothing loth to consent, and the result was that he and Orlando promised that Bradamante should be Ruggiero's wife. They stayed that night and part of the following day on the rock, when their pilot urging them to take advantage of a favorable wind, they were obliged, much to their regret, to take leave of the kind hermit, who stood on the shore and blessed them as they all four stepped into the boat and rowed off to the galley.

There, to Ruggiero's great joy and surprise, Orlando presented him with Frontino and his precious sword Balisarda. After the captain and his crew had been drowned, and Ruggiero had swum ashore, their vessel had not, as he had expected, struck upon the rocks, for the wind had suddenly veered and driven her out to sea again, and not long after she was cast ashore on the African coast near Biserta, where Orlando happened to be. He therefore took possession of her, and, together with everything on board, of the sword and charger, which he knew by report to belong to Ruggiero.

The sails were quickly unfurled to the fresh breeze, the mariners bent on their oars, and under fair clear skies it was not long before they entered the harbor, and landed at Marseilles.

CHAPTER XXI.

> For ever, Fortune, wilt thou prove
> An unrelenting foe to Love,
> And when we meet a mutual heart,
> Come in between and bid us part?
> THOMSON.

ORLANDO sent word to Charlemagne that he
was bringing him Ruggiero, converted to the
true faith; which news so pleased the Emperor
that when the knights arrived before the gates of
Paris he came out to meet them with a long train
of lords and ladies, among these Bradamante and
Marfisa; the latter affectionately kissed her brother,
but the other lady remained modestly in the back-
ground. Orlando and Rinaldo presented Ruggiero
to the Emperor, as the worthy son of Ruggiero of
Risa, who, they said, rivalled his father in virtue
and in valor, and of this, they added, the Christians
had often had in battle more proof than they might
have desired. Ruggiero respectfully alighted, and
the Emperor received him very graciously, and bade
him remount his horse and ride by his side, omit-
ting to show him no token of the favor and high
esteem in which he held him.

The next day Rinaldo told his father that he had
promised Bradamante's hand to Ruggiero, and that

Orlando and Oliviero had agreed with him that no more worthy alliance could be made for her, both with regard to ancient lineage and stainless honor. But Amone was extremely angry with his son for daring to dispose of his sister in marriage without consulting him, and said he considered Ruggiero a very bad match, for he possessed neither principality nor dukedom, nor anything in the world that he could call his own; for his part he thought neither nobility nor virtue of much use without riches.

Indeed Amone had very different designs for his daughter; for Constantine, Emperor of Greece, had lately sent to ask her hand for his son, Prince Leo, the heir to his vast empire, who had heard such reports of her exceeding beauty and virtue that he had fallen in love with her. Amone had replied that he could not conclude so important an affair without consulting Rinaldo, but that he felt sure that his son would be only too delighted to welcome so exalted an alliance. Beatrice was now even more angry with Rinaldo than Amone, and loudly declared that Bradamante should never be Ruggiero's wife; for she had set her heart upon seeing her Empress of the East. Rinaldo, however, was firm, and said nothing should ever induce him to break his word to Ruggiero.

Beatrice, little understanding her noble-minded daughter, fancied that she must be of the same way of thinking as herself, and urged her to refuse Ruggiero openly and boldly, and to tell Rinaldo that she would rather die than become the wife of so poor a knight. Bradamante was silent, for she did not dare to contradict her mother, whom she held in great respect and never dreamt of disobeying; therefore venturing neither to give nor to withhold her assent, she only sighed without answering. But when she was alone she wrung her hands and burst into tears, lamenting her hard fate after this fashion : —

'Alas! what can I do? Can I treat my mother with so little consideration as to set up my will against hers? or do anything so unmaidenly as to take a husband without her consent? Yet shall respect for my mother make me abandon thee, O my Ruggiero! and turn to other hopes and to another's love? Ah! how can I give up Ruggiero, just as with so much trouble and difficulty I have persuaded him to declare himself a Christian? How can I forsake him for another? That at least I will not do, for I would rather die than marry any one else, and I must trust to Orlando and to my brother to help me.'

While the lady was thus tormenting herself, Ruggiero was in no less distress, for Amone's intentions, though not openly proclaimed, were no secret. Much did he lament that Fortune, so lavish of her favors to many utterly unworthy of them, had bestowed upon him neither lands nor money. Nature, indeed, had been generous, and had endowed him with every grace of person and with still more precious gifts of mind. None could rival him in good looks, in valor or in generosity. But the vulgar herd — and I except none, neither emperor nor king, for sceptres and crowns give not this true wisdom, though the grace of God bestows it on a few — sees nothing in the world so worthy of admiration as wealth; neither beauty nor courage, neither virtue nor wisdom; while in this matter of marriage

are rank and riches more considered than in any
other.

'If Amone,' said Ruggiero, 'is bent upon this
alliance, let him at least not conclude it so hastily,
but grant me a year's delay. This would give me
time to conquer that Grecian Empire. Had I
possession of that crown none could think me unworthy to be Amone's son-in-law. But if, regard-
less of Orlando's and Rinaldo's promise, he gives
his daughter at once to this prince, what can I do?
Must I quietly submit to lose her? By Heavens
no! I will rather destroy this Leo and his father who
have disturbed all my happiness. Helen did not
cost more to Troy than shall my lady to this imperial pair. But it may be, my love, that you will
prefer this Greek to your poor Ruggiero, and will
rather espouse an emperor's son than a simple
knight. Yet can I believe that royal pomp and
dignity will tempt the noble mind, the true heart,
of my Bradamante, and that they will be more
prized by her than her plighted word? Will she
forget all the tender vows she made me?'

These words were overheard and carried to
Bradamante, who grieved almost as much over his
sorrow as over her own, and sent him word by a
trusted handmaid that he need not distress himself with the fear that she would prove faithless.
She reminded him that she had already given him
proofs of her constancy, and promised that she
would be until death faithful and true. Like the
rock which the winds and the waves beat against
in vain, like the marble which may be broken, but
once graven can never take another form, so steadfast and immovable to all the shocks of Fate and
Fortune would she remain true to him. Riches

and rank might dazzle others, but could not efface his image graven, not on wax, but on her constant heart.

Perhaps it would have been wiser had she contented herself with these assurances of unalterable affection; but Bradamante was so perplexed with doubts as to what she had best do, that she one day presented herself before Charles and said:

'Sire! if I have at any time done you good service, I beseech you to hear me, and to promise, on your royal word, to grant my petition, which I assure you, you shall yourself acknowledge to be just and right.'

'You deserve, dear lady,' replied the Emperor, 'that I should give you whatever you may ask, even if it be a province of my empire.'

'What I desire of your highness,' said the damsel, 'is, not to permit my hand to be given in marriage to any one who has not first proved himself my superior in single combat.'

The Emperor smiled as he replied, that her request was worthy of her, and told her to be content, for it should be as she wished.

This came to the ears of Amone and Beatrice, who, seeing thereby that she favored Ruggiero's suit, were greatly incensed against their daughter, and furtively carried her off to Rocca Forte, a fortress on the sea-shore between Perpignan and Carcassonne which Charlemagne had lately given to Amone. They kept her here a prisoner, intending some day to send her to the East, and to oblige her, whether she would or no, to marry Leo. The damsel, who was as humble as she was courageous, would have remained dutifully under her parents' control, even had they not kept her so closely

watched; but at the same time she was fully resolved to bear imprisonment or any hardship, even
death itself, rather than give up Ruggiero.

Rinaldo was furious when he found out the trick
his father had played him, in putting Bradamante
out of his reach; but Amone paid no regard to his
anger, and protested that he had a right to dispose
of his daughter as he thought best.

As for poor Ruggiero, he was in greater trouble
than before. He saw that unless he could get rid
of Leo, Bradamante would become that prince's
wife and be lost to him for ever. So without saying a word to any one, he determined to set out for
the East, to fight with Leo, and if possible to conquer Constantine's empire and make it his own.
He ordered Frontino to be saddled, and donned
his armor: assuming, however, a new surcoat, crest
and shield, for on this occasion he did not wish to
carry his well-known ensign, the white eagle on its
azure ground, but chose a milk-white unicorn on
a field crimson. He took with him his faithful
squire, and straitly charged him on no account
whatsoever to divulge his name; and thus accompanied, he started on his long journey.

After crossing the Meuse and the Rhine, he kept
along the right bank of the Iser, and passing through
Austria and Hungary, he arrived at Belgrade. At
the point where the Save joins the Danube, and
with it turns in larger flood towards the Black Sea,
he saw the tents of a great army spread out under
the Imperial standard, and heard that Constantine
was there with his son commanding in person, and
intent upon recovering possession of that city,
which the Bulgarians had lately taken from him.
Their army, covering the heights around the town,

was fronting him on the bank of the river which separated the two hosts.

When Ruggiero first caught sight of them a hot skirmish was going on, for the Greeks were attempting to throw a bridge over the Save, and the Bulgarians had marched down to resist them. The Greeks, however, were four to one, and had already succeeded in placing several boats in line, ready for the bridge. Earlier in the day Leo had marched out in an opposite direction, and making a long *détour* had thrown a bridge over the river higher up, and having crossed it with a body of 20,000 men, he now appeared on the left bank and attacked the rear of the Bulgarians, taking them completely by surprise. As soon as the emperor saw this, he hurried on the completing of the bridge with great vigor, and passed over it with all his army. The brave king of Bulgaria did all he could to defend his position, but he was overpowered by numbers, and refusing to yield himself Leo's prisoner, he was thrust through by many darts and slain. His troops stood firm until their king fell, when finding themselves without a leader, they turned and fled.

Ruggiero saw their discomfiture and determined to help them. He put spurs to Frontino who, fleet as the wind, soon overtook the fugitives who were hurrying to the shelter of the mountains. Arresting their flight, Ruggiero made them turn and face their pursuers; riding so proudly at their head, that he might have moved Mars or Jove himself to envy. His first encounter was with a knight, whose crimson surcoat was richly embroidered with blades and golden ears of millet; he was the son of Constantine's sister and scarcely less dear to the

Emperor than his own. The knight's shield and
cuirass shivered like glass at the touch of Ruggiero's lance, which pierced him through and came
out between his shoulders. Leaving him dead on
the field, Ruggiero grasped Balisarda, and attacked
the company which he had been leading, cutting
off the head of one, the arm of another, killing many
and wounding more, till they fell back before him,
quite unable to withstand the fury of his onslaught.
Upon this, the whole face of the battle changed; and
with restored confidence the Bulgarians vigorously
followed up their advantage, and in their turn pursued the Greeks, who fled in great disorder.

Leo, from a commanding eminence, looked on
at the utter rout of his so lately victorious army,
and in spite of his grief and disappointment, could
not but remark and admire the behavior of the
knight, whose unexpected appearance had so completely turned the fortune of the day. He knew
from his shield and its device, and from the fashion of his gilded and embossed armor, that the
stranger did not belong to the enemy, and he was
half inclined to think him one of the angel host
sent down to punish the Greeks for their many
sins. But whereas many would have entertained
a bitter enmity against him, he, being a magnanimous and high-minded adversary, conceived a wonderful admiration and affection for him, and would
have seen six of his own men slain, or have lost a
part of his empire, rather than that any harm
should happen to so worthy a knight.

Very different was it with Ruggiero, who hunted
far and wide for his rival, hoping to dispatch him
in battle, and to have done with him for ever. But
Leo, like a prudent general, wishing to save what

remained of his army, ordered the retreat to be sounded, and retired by the way he had come, sending word to his father to entreat him to re-cross the river as quickly as possible. Many of the fugitive Greeks fell into the hands of the Bulgarians, and many more were slain and drowned as they jostled each other in crowding over the narrow bridge.

When the battle was over and their victory complete, the Bulgarian chiefs hastened to express their gratitude to the brave Knight of the White Unicorn, acknowledging that without his aid they had been conquered and utterly undone. Some bowed low, some embraced him, others kissed his hands or his feet, all vied with each other in doing him reverence; while at the same time they besought him to become their king and captain.

Ruggiero replied that he was willing to become their general or their king, as it might please them; but on that day he would touch neither crown nor sceptre — not even enter Belgrade; for he must pursue Leo and, if possible, overtake him before he recrossed the river. He could not rest until he had come up with him, for he had travelled so many weary miles with the sole object of challenging him to combat.

Thus saying, he left the assembly, and without waiting to summon his squire, he followed in the track of the fugitive prince. Leo, however, had retreated, or rather fled, in such hot haste that he had reached the river in time to cross it without molestation, and to destroy his bridges behind him.

Ruggiero rode till the sun's last rays had disappeared, and then went on by the pale light of the moon ; for he could discover neither castle nor hamlet to afford him shelter. He journeyed till the dawn of the next day showed him a town on the left hand, where he proposed to himself to spend the day, and to rest his worn-out and jaded steed. The governor of the place was a vassal and friend of Constantine's, but as it was not fortified Ruggiero passed in without question, and found such comfortable entertainment that he was quite satisfied to remain there.

That evening there alighted at the inn a Roumanian captain who had been in the battle, and so near a spectator of the prodigies of valor performed by the Knight of the Unicorn, that he could not even now speak thereof without trembling. As soon as he saw Ruggiero's shield, he recognized the dreaded device which had brought such disaster upon the Grecian arms, and he hurried off at once to ask an audience of the governor in order that he might give him the important intelligence ; the result of which you shall hear in the next chapter.

CHAPTER XXII.

FRESH TROUBLES GATHER ROUND RUGGIERO AND BRADAMANTE.

I've seen the smiling of Fortune beguiling,
  I've felt all its favors, and found its decay ;
O ! fickle Fortune, why this cruel sporting,
  O ! why thus perplex us, poor sons of a day ?
                   Song.

THE higher unlucky mortals climb on Fortune's changing wheel, the more complete and sudden is sure to be their fall, and this poor Ruggiero soon found. He was so elated with his easy victory over Constantine and Leo, that confiding in his good fortune and great valor, he made no doubt of being able to complete their destruction, and to take possession of their dominions. The fickle goddess, however, soon convinced him how little she was to be trusted.

The Roumanian captain told the governor that the unknown warrior who had routed Constantine's army was in the town alone and unattended ; and advised him to take him prisoner, and thereby ensure success to the emperor, who would soon reimpose his yoke upon the Bulgarians were their new commander out of the way. Ungiardo had heard from the fugitives who had taken refuge in his city of the marvellous deeds of the stranger-knight, and he expressed as much pleasure as surprise that, unpursued and of his own accord, he should have come into the net.

He waited until the unsuspecting Ruggiero was fast asleep in his bed; then he sent a company of soldiers, who, surrounding the house, took him prisoner and bound him fast; and the next morning he despatched a courier post haste to carry the good news to Constantine. The Emperor had fallen back with all his army from the banks of the Save, and had retreated during the night to Bellina, a city belonging to his brother-in-law. He was busily engaged in entrenching himself and repairing the fortifications of the citadel, for fear the Bulgarians, under their victorious leader, should pursue their advantage and attack him, when Ungiardo's welcome message reached him.

He was so overjoyed that he could scarcely believe it, and Leo was no less delighted; for, besides reconquering Belgrade, he hoped to gain the friendship of this illustrious knight, and to prevail upon him to join his standard. With such a friend and such a comrade, he felt he need no longer envy Charlemagne the possession of an Orlando or a Rinaldo.

Far different were the hopes and wishes of Theodora, the emperor's sister and mother of the knight with the millet-worked vest whom Ruggiero had slain. She threw herself in an agony of tears at the feet of Constantine, declaring that she would never rise until he delivered this prisoner into her hands, in order that she might wreak vengeance upon him for the death of her beloved son. So long and so urgently did she plead, that though he tried to lift her up, and did what he could to pacify her, it was in vain, and he at last granted her petition. He ordered the prisoner to be brought and given up to her; and to make a long story short, the next morning the Knight of the Unicorn was conveyed to Bellina, and delivered into the hands of the relentless Theodora.

The cruel queen thought a speedy execution too mild a punishment; so she thrust him, bound hand and foot with heavy chains, into a deep dungeon where no ray of light ever penetrated; and putting him under the guard of one of her creatures as hard-hearted as herself, she ordered him to be fed upon a mere pittance of bread and water.

Oh! had the beautiful and brave Bradamante, and the noble-minded Marfisa, known of their Ruggiero's sufferings, how quickly would they have flown to deliver him!

It was about this time that in accordance with his promise to Bradamante, Charlemagne caused a proclamation to be made by sound of trumpet throughout every part of his dominions, so that it was soon known all over the world, declaring that whoever wished to obtain Duke Amone's daughter for his wife must be prepared to contend with her in battle from dawn till sunset, when, if he were still unconquered, the lady would yield herself vanquished, and consent to espouse him. It was, moreover, added, that she left the choice of weapons to her opponent.

Amone, seeing he could not resist the Emperor's will, was obliged therefore to carry his daughter back to Paris; and Beatrice, however angry and indignant, could not, for the honor of her house, but provide her with rich and handsome dresses of various colors and fashions, fit for her to appear in at that gay court. But when Bradamante arrived and found Ruggiero no longer there, it seemed to her to have lost all its splendor and the attraction it once possessed for her. Like one who has known some gay garden in April or May, when adorned with bright and many-colored flowers, and revisiting it again in the short dark days of winter finds it deserted and untrimmed, even so changed the damsel found the court, now that it wanted the sunshine of her lover's presence. She dared not ask about him for fear of exciting suspicion, and all she heard was that he had one day departed, no one knew whither.

She tormented herself by fancying that, in despair of obtaining her parents' consent to their union, he had gone away, determined to banish her image from his heart, and perhaps to seek in some distant land another love who might teach him to forget her. Yet the next moment her imagination would paint him as constant as ever, and she would reproach herself for these unworthy doubts of his fidelity. It was as if one voice should accuse and one should defend him, and by turns she would listen to each, and say to herself:

' Could I but behold again the light of his bright presence, all my foolish fears would fly away, and happy hope would take their place. Ah! return my love, and teach hope to banish fear.' And then she would take her lute, and sing some such plaintive ditty as the following:

As when the sun's departing ray
Sends darkness to the world, and night
Brings shadows in her train which fright
The tim'rous soul, till joyous day
Returns, and fears and shades depart.
So thou, my love, return to me,
Bring light and peace and joy with thee,
And hope to my despairing heart.

17

As when sweet summer flies away,
And winter's shortening days close round,
And snow and frost hold fast the ground,
And days are dark and skies are gray ;
When spring returns dark days depart.
So thou, my love, return to me,
Bring light and warmth and joy with thee,
And life to this poor wintry heart.

As when night's veil doth hide the day,
Each little spark shows red and bright,
Till dimmed by morning's clearer light,
And quenched in sunshine's purer ray,
So fears arise and hopes depart,
Yet thou, my love, come back to me,
Bring faith and hope and peace with thee,
And trust to this poor doubting heart.

How much more bitter would have been her sad
lament had she known that her lover lay in a
miserable dungeon, condemned to a cruel death!

Fortunately a kind Providence ordered that the
fate in store for Ruggiero should come to the ears
of the magnanimous Leo, who soon set about de-
vising some means for rescuing the noble warrior
he so much admired from such an ignoble fate.
With infinite difficulty he succeeded in inducing
the keeper of the prison to allow him to visit
Ruggiero. Taking with him a strong and trustworthy attendant, he came one night to the tower,
and with great secrecy was guided by the gaoler
to the dungeon where Ruggiero was confined.
The man, having opened the door and allowed
them to pass through, turned to relock it, when, all
unawares, the two set upon him, and after they
had gagged him, left him there bound and helpless.
They then lifted the trapdoor, and Leo catching
hold of a cord hung there for the purpose, slid
himself down, and by the light of a torch which he

held in his hand, saw Ruggiero bound hand and foot, stretched full length upon an iron grating not more than a few feet above the level of the water which flowed beneath. Had he been left in this terrible place much longer he must have died.

Leo bent over him, and in accents of great compassion, said :

'Sir knight! the signal proofs I have seen of your valor and heroism have so much attached me to you, that braving my father's anger, and with great peril to myself, I have come to release you from these irons. For I am Leo, the son of that Greek Emperor who, for the great aid you lent his enemies, holds you in mortal hatred.'

While hastening to unfasten his chains, he added more words of sympathy and consolation, and Ruggiero thanked him, saying :

'My lord! I owe you infinite gratitude, and the life which you now restore shall ever be at your service, to take, or to use, as it may please you.'

Leo then carried him to his own house, where he persuaded him to remain for some days in close concealment, until he could procure his arms and charger, which were still in the possession of Ungiardo. Ruggiero was so much beyond measure astonished at the generous kindness of Leo, that all the jealousy and hatred he had once nourished against him vanished, and he felt nothing but intense love and gratitude towards him. He thought of little else, by night or day, but how to contrive some means of proving this gratitude, and it seemed to him that if he could brave a thousand deaths in his behalf it would be little in comparison with what the prince had done for him.

Just at this time came the news of Charlemagne's

proclamation, at which Leo's cheek grew pale, for he was modest enough to know that he was no match in arms for the renowned Bradamante. But an expedient occurred to him, which seemed to promise a sure way out of his difficulty.

He sent for Ruggiero, and opening his heart to him, proposed to accept Bradamante's challenge if Ruggiero would fight the lady in his stead, and in disguise win her, not, alas! for himself, but for Leo. The eloquence of the Greek prince might have done much, but the obligation he was under did far more, to persuade Ruggiero, and after a moment's hesitation, with a smile on his face but despair in his heart, he promised to do what the prince wished. No word of complaint passed his lips, but he was firmly resolved to seek an honorable death, as soon as he had acquitted himself of his debt to Leo, to whom he felt he was about to sacrifice far more than life. At one time he thought of feigning himself to be less strong than the damsel, and of offering his defenceless breast to her sword, for death at her hands would be sweet; but he saw this would not be fair to Leo, and he determined to dare all and lose all rather than break his word.

Thereupon Leo set out for France with a goodly escort, provided for him by Constantine, and accompanied by Ruggiero, to whom Frontino and his armor had been restored. They travelled together day after day, until they reached Paris. Leo did not enter the city, but pitched his tents outside, and sent an embassage to Charlemagne to declare the object of his journey. The Emperor paid him a gracious visit and treated him with great distinction; and when the preliminaries of the combat had been arranged, a day was appointed and the lists set up outside the lofty walls of the town.

The night before the fatal day Ruggiero passed in such agony as a man condemned to death might feel on the eve of his execution. In order that he might run less risk of discovery, he had chosen to fight in complete armor, without his spear, and on foot. Not indeed that he feared the famous golden lance, for its magic power was unknown to all, to Bradamante, and even to Astolfo, and both thought that they owed to their own prowess its wonderful effects. But Ruggiero knew that, should he go forth to the joust on Frontino, he would at once be recognized, for too often had the lady caressed him in Montalbano not to know him again.

He wore Leo's surcoat and bore his shield with its device — a two-headed eagle on a crimson field, and with Leo's sword in his hand, for he had discarded Balisarda's too deadly blade, he entered the lists at the first dawn of day; so like the prince in form and dress and stature that all supposed him to be the Leo who lay in safe concealment within his inner tent. The damsel did not keep him waiting, but at the first call of the trumpet she grasped her sword and began the assault.

Like some lofty tower to the angry winds, like some firm rock to the tempestuous ocean, Ruggiero stood, unmoved and steadfast, against all the hard blows which the lady rained down upon him, aiming now at his shield, now at his helmet, anon at his breastplate; with a sound like the pattering of hail upon the roof, she made the sparks fly from the polished steel, but not once did the hard plate yield or the stout-linked mail give way. So skil-

ful was Ruggiero in the art of fencing, so swiftly
he parried each stroke, so unerringly he turned
aside each thrust, that long before the day was
done the damsel heartily wished the battle were
over.

The sun was fast sinking in the western sky,
when she made her final and desperate effort, and
renewed her attack with redoubled fury; but all in
vain, for when the bright orb of day sank below
the horizon the knight stood firm.

Charlemagne and his court beheld with admiration the skill which could so well defend itself, and
the marvellous courtesy which so carefully avoided
inflicting any hurt upon the lady, and they said to
each other:

'This Leo is indeed worthy to match with our
fair warrior.'

And so accordingly Charlemagne decreed. The
knight, however, without waiting to claim Bradamante, vaulted upon a charger which his groom
held ready, and rode straight to Leo's tent. The
prince threw his arms round his neck and embraced him, declaring that nothing could ever repay the service he had done him. No, not were he
to take the crown from his own head and place it
upon his. Ruggiero's heart was torn with such
cruel anguish that he could not trust himself to
reply, but in silence handing to the prince his
shield, he took up his own, and pleading great
fatigue and want of repose, he bid him 'Good night,'
and went away to his tent.

Then he hastily changed his armor, and saddled
Frontino; and at dead of night, unheard and unseen, he set out quite alone, to go he knew not
whither and cared not where, if only it could be to

find a speedy death. Over hill and dale Frontino carried him all that night, absorbed in grief, tormented by the thought that he had only himself to blame for this finishing stroke to his misfortunes, and filled with remorse for the sorrow he knew it would cause Bradamante.

'Would I had died in Theodora's prison,' he said; 'then at least Bradamante would have pitied me. Now, when she learns that I have loved Leo more than herself, and by my own act have given her to him, what can she do but hate and despise me?'

When the sun rose he found himself in a gloomy forest, a wild and savage place, where he thought he would as fain lie down and die as anywhere else. He dismounted, and taking off Frontino's bridle, let him go free, saying as he did so:

'O! my Frontino! If I could reward thee after thy deservings, thou shouldst not need to envy that steed of olden time who flew to heaven and took his place among the stars. Far more favored wert thou than any steed of ancient days, for wert thou not petted and caressed by her soft hands? Wert thou not dear to my own sweet lady? Alas! why do I call her mine? mine no longer, since I have given her to another.'

All this time poor Bradamante was in Paris, almost as frantic with disappointment and despair as Ruggiero himself.

'How came it,' thought she, 'that, when the whole world had heard of her challenge, Ruggiero alone was in ignorance of it? How was it that this Leo, who had never performed an illustrious deed in his life, had now been able to withstand her? Should she fall at the Emperor's feet and confess her mistake, braving the laughter of her relatives and of the whole court for changing her mind? Yet were not all women changeable, and would she not rather be called variable as the wind and lighter than a leaf, than prove inconstant to her lover?'

While she was in this terrible perplexity Marfisa came to her help; for that haughty lady went the next morning to Charlemagne and said that 'Bradamante having betrothed herself to Ruggiero, she would not, in her brother's absence, permit her to break her troth and marry Leo.'

The Emperor was extremely surprised. He sent immediately for Bradamante, and asked her if this was true. She dared not answer either 'Yes' or 'No,' but her blushing cheek and downcast eyes betrayed her secret.

Orlando and Rinaldo were delighted at this new turn to the affair, hoping that after all Ruggiero would not lose his Bradamante; but her obstinate old father was very indignant, and said he was sure that this was some plot of their contrivance, and that, if any betrothal had taken place, it must have been before Ruggiero was baptized, in which case it was not binding. The court became hotly excited over the matter, some taking one side and some another, though by far the greater number were for Ruggiero, who was an universal favorite. Charlemagne listened to all, but gave no opinion either way, only saying that for the present the marriage with Leo must be put off. Thereupon the proud Marfisa said:

'Had my brother been here, I am sure he would have challenged Leo, and therefore I will now do so in his stead.'

Charlemagne sent her message to Leo, and he confiding in Ruggiero's ability and willingness to help him as before, accepted her challenge. When he heard of Ruggiero's absence he supposed that he had merely ridden out into the country for pleasure, but when he found that he did not, as he had expected, return, he repented of his rashness, and when day after day went by and no Knight of the White Unicorn appeared, he took fright lest some accident should have happened, and sent couriers in every direction to seek for him, in castle and city, through town and country; at last, mounting his horse, he himself set out in search of him.

CHAPTER XXIII.

BRADAMANTE IS RESTORED TO HER RUGGIERO.

Happy, happy pair !
None but the brave deserve the fair.
DRYDEN.

LEO had gone a long way in search of his friend, when he met a lady, who, riding up to him, said :

'If your disposition, gentle sir, is as noble as your countenance, and if your courtesy and kindness conform to the same, you will not refuse your aid to the foremost knight of this our time, who, if succor is not speedily afforded him, will soon pass away in death. The bravest knight who ever wore sword at his side or buckler on his arm, the handsomest and noblest of whom this or any age can boast lies, not far from here, at the point of death : his only fault a deed of too exalted generosity. Do you, my lord, hasten to his help.'

It at once struck Leo that the knight of whom the lady spoke could be none other than he of the White Unicorn ; and without delay, he put spurs to his horse and followed the fairy Melissa, for it was indeed that kind friend, who led him straight to Ruggiero.

They found him stretched on the ground all armed as when he left the camp, his head resting on his shield, and so exhausted that he could not raise himself without assistance, for he had remained there for three days without food or shelter. He lay quite still, murmuring words of anguish and despair, but not conscious enough to be aware of the presence of Leo and Melissa. The former knelt down by him and heard sufficient to understand that an unhappy love had brought him to this sad plight, but who was the object of such passion he could not imagine, for he had never heard a lady's name pass Ruggiero's lips. The prince gently raised his head and looking into his face, spoke to him and kissed him with the tenderness of a brother; till at last Ruggiero looked up as if he recognized him, and Leo in the gentlest and most loving words he could command, said :

'Do not refuse to confide to me the cause of your sorrow. Believe me few misfortunes are so great but that some means may be found to escape from them : and while there is life there is hope. It grieves me that you should have hidden yourself from me, for surely I deserved to be looked upon by you as a friend, and you might have known that I would gladly have given you all that I possessed. My very life was at your service. Ah ! tell me your sorrow, and let us consult together and see if nothing can be done to remove it.'

He added so many tender and affectionate entreaties that Ruggiero could resist no longer, and he tried to speak, but not until after two or three vain attempts did the words come with tolerable distinctness.

'My lord, when you hear who I am, you will agree that it is best for us both that I should die. I am that Ruggiero whom you have as good cause to hate as he has to envy you. Some months ago I left France in order to seek you out and fully resolved not to rest until I had slain you in battle; for I was aware that Bradamante's father favored your suit and that he intended to bestow her hand upon you. Man proposes and God disposes. You know the accident which turned my hatred towards you into the truest and most devoted attachment. Unaware that I was Ruggiero, you asked me to win the lady for you. It was as if you had asked for my heart itself, for the very soul out of my body, but you can bear witness that for your sake I sacrificed my own wishes. Bradamante is now yours. Be happy with her. Your happiness is dearer to me than mine own, and let me die in peace, for life would be only torture without her; nor could she be at ease as your wife whilst I lived; too many and too solemn are the vows that have passed between us.'

Leo was so overcome with astonishment when he heard who Ruggiero was, that for some minutes he stood as motionless as a statue. Such generosity seemed to him to surpass all he had ever heard of. It so touched him that he felt almost as sorry for his friend's distress as Ruggiero himself. Moved by this feeling of pity and somewhat perhaps by the desire to prove himself worthy of his high descent, and not to be outdone by any man in generosity, he said:

'If, O Ruggiero! on that first day when the sight of your heroism attracted me, I had known you to be Ruggiero, I should not the less have admired you. Had I known it when I drew you out of the dungeon, I should not the less have delivered you. Nor the less should I have loved you, and have been willing to do that which I am now about to do for you. Yet then I owed you nothing. But now when you have sacrificed everything for me, shall I not give up something for you? What therefore you have resigned for me I now give back to you. You are more worthy of her than I am. For though I wooed her with hearty admiration, yet, believe me, her loss will not break my heart nor cost me my life. It grieves me far more to think that you had so little confidence in my friendship, that you preferred to die rather than to trust me with the story of your love.'

Ruggiero tried to remonstrate, but it was of no use and he gave in.

'Ah! my lord!' said he, 'I refuse no longer; but how can I ever repay your kindness? Twice have you brought me back to life.'

The prudent Melissa had not forgotten to bring store of cordials and food, of which Ruggiero partook; and Frontino having trotted up when he heard the sound of horses' feet, Leo's grooms caught him; Ruggiero was lifted into the saddle, for he was too weak to mount alone, and they led him slowly to an abbey about half a league off, where they remained with him for three days, until he was sufficiently restored to undertake the journey to Paris. He entered the city with great secrecy, after dark, unseen by any; and the next morning he and Leo presented themselves before Charlemagne.

Ruggiero, in helmet and closed vizor, wore the armor and shield with its two-headed golden eagle, in which he had fought with Bradamante. Leo was unarmed, apparelled in rich vesture befitting his royal rank, and escorted by all his gentlemen and attendants. **Taking** Ruggiero, upon whom all eyes were fixed, **by the** hand, he bowed low and thus addressed Charlemagne :

'Sire, I present to you the good knight who for the whole of one live-long day stood in the lists against Bradamante. If I understand your decree aright, he has thereby won her hand; which I, therefore, now claim for him. None can be more worthy to obtain it ; for none can compare with him in valor, still less in constancy and love. Should any say him "Nay," he is here ready to make good his right in arms.'

Charlemagne and all his court were struck dumb with amazement at these words. They had never seen or heard of this unknown knight, and they all believed Leo to have been victorious in the combat. But Marfisa, who could scarcely restrain herself till the prince had finished, pushed through the throng of courtiers, and said :

'Since Ruggiero is not here to fight for his claim to this lady, I, his sister, take that duty upon myself, and hereby defy to single combat any who dare dispute Ruggiero's right to Bradamante's hand.'

So haughty was her speech, so prompt her action, that the prince thought it best to put an end to the scene. He raised Ruggiero's helmet and turned to Marfisa.

'Behold, lady !' said 'he, 'the knight ready to give account for himself.'

Marfisa gave one look, and then ran and threw her arms about his neck. Then the Emperor embraced him, and Orlando, Rinaldo, — one knight after another crowded round to welcome and to congratulate him. The prince related to them the

whole story from beginning to end in such touching and well-chosen words that many were moved
to tears. Even Amone was induced to go up to
Ruggiero, and begging him to forgive his former
opposition, he asked to be accepted as his father-
in-law.

Bradamante was sitting weeping alone in her
chamber when the joyful tidings were brought to
her, and so overcome was she with happiness that
the color forsook her cheek, and for a moment they
thought she was about to faint with joy.

It happened that the Bulgarians had heard that
the Knight of the White Unicorn had accompanied
Leo to France, and they sent an embassage after
him, which had reached Paris the night before.
This was now introduced, and the ambassadors
declared that in a solemn assembly their people
had elected the knight for their king. They besought him not to refuse the throne they offered
him, but to accompany them to Adrianople, and
there be crowned. Ruggiero consulted Leo, who
said that the Bulgarians had always been trouble-
some neighbors, and that he felt sure his father
would be only too pleased to have in Ruggiero a
sure and firm ally on their throne. Ruggiero
therefore accepted their offer; but told the ambassadors that he could not go to Adrianople until
after the expiration of three months. And Beatrice, who had cared so little for the virtue and
valor of Ruggiero when he was a simple knight,
now that he was to be a king, declared herself delighted with her son-in-law.

Charlemagne took upon himself the arrangement and the expense of the wedding festivities;
and had Bradamante been his daughter they could

not have been carried out with greater pomp and magnificence. All our friends were present. Melissa, Leo, and his retinue; Orlando, Rinaldo and his brothers, and Sansonetto; the Bulgarian ambassadors; and many tributary kings and nobles who had come to do homage to Charlemagne, and to congratulate him upon the victorious conclusion of his war with the Moors.

The rejoicings lasted nine days, during which feasts, banquets, dances, and tournaments succeeded one another. The wedding in which Charlemagne had given away the bride — Marfisa had been the bridesmaid, and Leo the groomsman — took place on the last day. After the ceremony had been concluded the Emperor gave a grand banquet, where Ruggiero was seated on his left and Bradamante on his right hand; and he and all his guests drank long health and prosperity to the 'Happy Pair.' A wish in which I hope my young readers will heartily join.

THE END.

University Press : John Wilson & Son, Cambridge.

www.ingramcontent.com/pod-product-compliance
Lightning Source LLC
Chambersburg PA
CBHW031952060726
47497CB00016B/1471